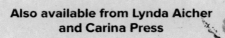

**Also available from Lynda Aicher
and Carina Press**

The Boardroom series

Done Deal (Memo #1)

The Wicked Play series

*Bonds of Trust
Bonds of Need
Bonds of Desire
Bonds of Hope
Bonds of Denial
Bonds of Courage
Shattered Bonds*

The Power Play series

*Game Play
Back in Play
Penalty Play*

And watch for the next books in The Boardroom series,
coming soon from Carina Press!

To the inner battles we all fight. May you have the courage to face each one and find peace at the end.

AFTER HOURS

—

LYNDA AICHER

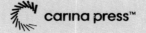

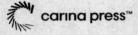
carina press™

ISBN-13: 978-1-335-44805-7

Recycling programs
for this product may
not exist in your area.

After Hours

Copyright © 2018 by Lynda Aicher

www.CarinaPress.com

Printed in U.S.A.

AFTER HOURS

Chapter One

The folder had to be in the boardroom. There was no other place she could've left it.

Avery Fast plowed down the empty stairwell, engrossed in her thoughts as she backtracked her way through her afternoon. She'd already checked the smaller conference room, the break room and Carmen's desk. And that'd been after she'd torn her own desk apart and scanned her boss's.

As the executive assistant to the financial controller at Faulkner Investment Group's San Francisco office, a lot of confidential information flowed through her. Her boss, Gregory Conwell, counted on her to keep the data secured, and she had never let him down in the eighteen months since she'd been in her position.

And she wasn't about to now, either.

Her heels tapped on the stairs, the echo bouncing around the cavernous concrete silo. The single flight wasn't enough to work off her frustration. She brushed her bangs away from her eyes as she swiped her badge through the reader and yanked the heavy fire door open with a grunt.

The Faulkner offices were spread over two floors of a high-rise in downtown San Francisco. A staircase near

the main entrance offered a grander connection than the
fire stairwell she used, but it was also out of her way.
Efficiency was crucial right now.

A clammy sheen had built up on her heated skin the
more her panic deepened. Had someone taken the folder
from her desk? Why? Who? Had she even brought the
folder to the meeting in the boardroom that afternoon?

Doubt twisted with the knot constricting her chest.
She didn't remember doing so, but... The preliminary
quarterly numbers were in it. The ones no one saw until
they were verified, rolled up and strategically manipu-
lated. The raw data wasn't for general consumption, especially the payroll details.

Her stomached roiled at the thought of having to explain what happened. What if someone had found the
folder and shared the information with others? Her job
would be toast—along with her reputation.

Why had she printed them anyway? Oh yeah, Gregory had asked her to. Why couldn't he keep everything
online in the age of digital everything?

The office doors along the darkened hallway were
closed, the lights off behind them, but a dim light shone
from the open door of the conference room. She'd sat on
the far side, near the end of the table during the meeting. Could someone have set the file on the coffee credenza? Or maybe it was still on the table, if she'd even
left it there.

She was out of options. It had to be there.

Her brain stalled about a second after her feet did in
the boardroom doorway. Her mouth fell open. *Oh my...*

The boardroom wasn't empty after all. Nope. Not
even close.

She scrambled to comprehend what she was seeing

while knowing exactly what she watched: sex. Wanton, hedonistic, erotic sex. A woman and *two* guys.

But here? In the office? On the boardroom table?

Heat raced up her back to engulf her chest and neck. Blood roared in her ears, accelerated by her racing heart and the strange desire blasting through her.

She blinked once, twice, but the image remained. Propriety told her to look away. No, she should run away. What was she doing standing there? *Walk the hell away. Now.*

But she didn't move.

The scene was…unbelievable. Unreal. Wrong. And so damn hot.

A single lamp on the credenza provided a soft glow to the room and dulled the edges of the threesome along with their actions. Their reflections were hazy shadows in the large windows along the outside wall. The lights from other buildings and the streets far below provided an open backdrop and little protection from prying eyes.

Like hers.

She should go—before they noticed her. She should.

She searched for moisture in her mouth. Swallowed hard. Slowly wet her dry lips.

What would it feel like to be that woman? The one splayed on the table, naked except for her black stilettos? Her eyes were closed, her red lips parted in a silent sigh, or would that be a cry of pleasure? Her black hair was spread in a messy array across the wood, her wrists bound by two thick cuffs over her head. She was lean yet curvy. Beautiful. And totally lost in what was being done to her.

Her back arched, a soft moan escaping to flow with a sultry lethargy through the room. It swirled around

Avery to drag her deeper into the eroticism. Avery's breath hitched. Her nipples puckered with sharp tingles that raced to her pussy.

The men were feasting on the woman. That was the only way she could describe it. Both of them. At the same time. A guy in a dark suit had his back to Avery, his head buried between the woman's spread legs. Another in a white dress shirt and navy tie was sucking on a nipple while rolling the other between his fingertips. He stretched back, the tip clearly caught between his teeth, and the woman's back arched impossibly more. She squirmed, another purring moan tumbling out before a gasped "Please."

Yes, please. Avery's back bowed in time with the woman's, her nipples aching for the same attention.

It didn't make sense. She'd never enjoyed porn. And she'd certainly never considered going to a live sex show. Yet…

She swallowed. Inhaled. The heavy scent of sex and arousal flooded her, adding another layer of stimulation. She sucked in another long, slow breath. The hedonism flowed through her to dislodge every concept of conservatism or impropriety she held.

A low growl—yes, growl—from one of the men tore through the room. Raw, fierce, exalting. No man had ever made that sound with her.

A soft whimper of want tumbled out before she realized it was there. *Oh, God.* She clamped her mouth shut, fear charging in. Had they heard her?

She took a step back, prepared to flee. Guilt sped in, yet it wasn't enough to make her go. She'd be mortified if they caught her, but what would they do next? Would the men switch places? Would they fuck her? Both of them? At the same time?

Her pussy clenched, lust swarming hot and fast from her core. Her head spun with so many desires she couldn't process them. She shifted her feet and bit her lip to keep quiet.

She'd never had a guy who'd been that devoted to her pleasure. Ever. Let alone two.

The woman gasped, her legs spreading even wider. The man between her legs pumped his arm, a low sucking and squelching sound emanating. Avery's eyes widened on another inhalation. She couldn't actually *see* what he was doing, but she didn't need to.

Her pussy pulsed again. Her nipples tightened even more. They ached to be touched. Her hand inched up before she clenched her fist and forced it back to her side.

The woman on the table turned her head. Her eyes fluttered open as a soft cry bled from her lush lips. She closed her eyes only to reopen them, her focus squarely on Avery.

Oh, shit.

Her panic pounded out a frantic SOS in her head, yet she remained trapped in the moment. A sultry smile curved over the woman's ruby-red lips, her hooded eyes conveying the pleasure the men were giving her. Passion overrode logic along with every ounce of self-preservation Avery had. Heat flashed another wave of want over her chest and burst into an aching demand between her legs.

She gripped the doorjamb, her head swaying with the heady sensations. The eye contact made the whole experience intimate. Like she was supposed to be there.

But she wasn't.

The woman wet her lips in a slow pass that screamed seduction. The movement swiped out at Avery in the tease that it was. And for some damn reason, she wanted to tease her right back. Her tongue pushed at her teeth, but she kept them tightly closed.

This was insane. She'd never been sexually attracted to women. Not really anyway. Not enough to act on it.

But...

What am I thinking?

She jerked her gaze away, determined to leave only to freeze again.

Another man stood in the darkened back corner of the room, arms crossed over his chest, feet spread in a power stance. And his eyes were locked squarely on her.

Her muscles seemed to petrify along with her thoughts. She had no doubt that he'd been watching her the whole time. He didn't move either. Not even a flick of his lips or brow. He simply stared at her. Waiting.

Embarrassment doubled down on the lust blazing through her to set Avery on fire from head to toe. Heat flamed over her cheeks before sinking down her neck—and she still didn't move.

His face was shadowed, but she didn't need the florescent lights to know exactly who he was: Carson Haggert, the chief technology officer for *all* of Faulkner.

And possibly one of the sexiest men she'd ever encountered.

His tie was loosened, suit jacket gone, shirtsleeves turned up to expose his forearms, but he still emanated that all-consuming authority that prickled over her skin whenever he was near. It consumed her now, sucking the truths from her and exposing every lascivious thought running through her mind.

The exposure trembled down her legs, and she locked her knees to stop it from showing. A high whine of unabashed pleasure winged past her in an unnecessary reminder of what she'd walked into. The pace of the sucking sound increased with the woman's panted breaths and soft moans.

"Make her come."

The hard command shot from Carson to crack through the mounting tension. Avery flinched, her lips parting in confusion. His focus was still squarely on her. Did he mean Avery was supposed to make the woman come? Or were the men supposed to make Avery come?

Three short cries were followed by a long, drawn-out note that left no doubt about who was supposed to make whom come. And she wasn't included in the party. At all.

She was the intruder.

The uninvited observer.

The one risking her job by standing there.

That last thought finally got her moving. Mortification set in the second she spun around and fled down the hallway. Her heart pounded in another flight of panic, this one dogged by fear.

The closed office doors sped by, her pace increasing the more reality reemerged. She'd just watched an illicit sex game play out in the boardroom. And she'd been caught doing so.

She threw herself against the crash bar, slammed through the fire door and flew up the stairs as fast as her heels and pencil skirt allowed. Her hand squeaked against the metal railing when she gripped it to turn on the landing. The door slammed shut below, and she flinched, tensing. She shot a quick look back, at once fearing Carson had followed her while hoping he would.

And then what? Would she be fired? Threatened into silence? Harassed?

She yanked on the door handle when she reached her floor only to stumble forward when it didn't open. Of course it was locked. She jerked up, her arm throbbing, and fumbled for her ID badge clipped to her waist. Her hand was shaking when she finally swiped her ID through the card reader.

She dashed to her office, her head swiveling the entire time. Would Carson show up before she could leave? Would he cut her off at the exit? Block her flight of embarrassment?

Force her against the wall and lay a hot demanding kiss on her?

Right. Like that had a chance in hell of happening.

It took more precious seconds for her to grab her purse, lock her drawers with fingers that refused to cooperate and swipe her coat off the rack before she could flee the office entirely. Her pulse rate didn't decrease one iota the entire time.

Not when she peeked around the corner in the hallway or tried to quietly tiptoe down the wooden staircase near the office lobby. Not when she bit her lip and seemed to wait forever for the down arrow to light up on any one of the bank of elevators. Not when the ding of arrival pinged through the silence to signal her freedom.

And not when she caught a glimpse of Carson Haggert staring at her from across the lobby, a knowing smile curling his lips as the elevator doors closed.

She clenched her purse tighter, adrenaline flying through her system to leave her sweaty and chilled at once. Her mind reeled, thoughts scrambling in and out before a single one could take hold.

She wasn't naïve or exactly sheltered, but this stuff didn't happen to her—or anyone she knew. Nothing in her thirty years of life had prepared her for this. Not one thing.

The rapid click of her heels across the marble-tiled lobby echoed through the open atrium to highlight her flight. The security guard studied her, a brow raised in unasked question.

"Night," she managed to croak out over the scratchy dryland that'd overtaken her throat. The chilled dampness hit her in the face the second she shoved through the revolving glass door. She sucked in a deep breath and slipped into her jacket before the foggy air could sink into her bones.

The sidewalk was fairly empty, which made the air seem colder and the shadows deeper. She laughed at herself, yet the quick tap of her heels didn't slow. A glance over her shoulder showed a few people huddled into their coats, chins tucked low against the chill. But no Carson, even though she'd half expected to see him.

Expected or wanted?

God, she *was* being naïve and stupid.

The fluorescent light buzzed under the protective cover of the bus shelter that provided zero protection from the curling wisps of fog. Her silk shirt clung to her back, and a shudder overtook her entire body. Goose bumps broke out on her bare legs despite the erotic warmth that still encased her. She huddled further into her trench coat, but it didn't help.

How had she gotten herself into this mess? If she'd left the boardroom when she'd first realized what she'd walked in on, then she wouldn't be so screwed. No, if she hadn't misplaced the reports in the first place, she wouldn't have returned to the office to hunt for them only to stumble into an illicit ménage à trois.

Images of the steamy threesome combined with the commanding presence of Carson crashed in as the bus pulled up. Another shiver trembled down her, ending with the tight clench of her pussy around the unfulfilled want.

No. No way. There was no way she'd ever be able to do something like that. She shook her head in an attempt to clear the visuals scorched into her memory. It didn't work. Would they be imprinted forever, tormenting her with ideas and longings she'd never dare act on?

She didn't glance at any of the other passengers on the short ride home, instead opting to stare unseeing out the window. What would they think if they knew what she'd seen—done? Would any of them care?

The events of the evening were finally sinking in when she trudged toward her building. A warm yellow glow lit up the window of her little two-bedroom condo. The curtains shifted, and then the shadowed outline of her two cats appeared as they perched on the window ledge to greet her.

There. That was her life.

One that didn't include office sex scandals or orgyfests in the boardroom. Would that be classified as an orgy? Probably not, given there— Stop!

She stomped up the four flights to her condo, determined to put the night behind her. She wouldn't think about any of it. Not tonight. Not tomorrow.

Not ever again.

Right.

And what would happen when she saw Carson Haggert at work?

Chapter Two

"We might have a problem," Carson stated the second he closed the door to Trevor's office. "Hopefully not, but…" He shrugged.

Muted sunlight brightened the room through the floor-to-ceiling windows that lined two sides of the corner office. The extended line of the Bay Bridge was on display before it reached the Oakland skyline in the far distance. The view was stunning and just one of the perks of being the founder's son and president of Faulkner's West Coast office.

Trevor James jerked his head up, eyes narrowing. "What kind of problem?"

A sexy, quietly gorgeous one. Devastating. Seemingly innocent. Definitely curious.

Carson unbuttoned his suit jacket and took a seat in one of the visitor chairs placed before the large executive desk. "The private kind."

Trevor sat back, a brow rising. "Day or evening?"

"Evening."

"Okay." A single nod communicated his understanding. "And you're going to fix it, right?"

A dozen different images sprang into Carson's mind of exactly how he'd like to "fix" this potential problem.

Against the wall or over that boardroom table would work. Or behind her, stroking her as he whispered every naughty command at the couple on the table. But Avery Fast was a company employee. The HR and legal issues associated with that nixed all those solutions.

"Do you want the details?" he asked. The general ones. Not the dirty details running on replay that were causing his dick to stir like a hormone-crazed teen.

Carson propped his ankle on his other knee and studied his friend and boss. They'd become friends at college and had stayed in touch afterward. In this instance, his employment at Faulkner was truly a case of who he knew, but his PhD and years of experience in the tech industry had earned him his position, not his connections.

"Do I need them?" Trevor asked. A few years older than Carson and far worldlier, Trevor was a master at managing at thirty thousand feet. He led decisively and trusted others to do their jobs while somehow controlling the details despite rarely asking for them.

Carson gave another shrug. "Potentially." If Avery decided to go to HR. He'd debated on coming to Trevor at all. But the fallout—if there was one—would land on Trevor even though he hadn't been there last night.

Trevor's low humph was followed with a sardonic smile. "Then keep the details until it's a 'yes.'" He stretched his neck, rubbed at the exposed side in a rare show of stress. This was his friend now, the guy he'd gotten drunk with more times than he could remember. "But give me a summary."

A summary. Of how Avery had bitten her lip to hold in her moan? Or the desire and want that'd blazed in her eyes when she'd discovered him?

"A female employee walked into the boardroom last

night." Carson let that sit for a moment. "One who wasn't invited."

"Shit." Trevor rolled his head on his shoulders before dropping his hand and sitting forward. "You didn't check the office first?"

"Of course, I did." Carson scoffed. "It was empty except for the cleaning guy in the lower offices. And I told him to stay downstairs until I left."

Trevor arched his brow again. He'd had that questioning-doubt look down long before Carson had met him. The gray that now lightened his dark hair along with the dogged maturity slapped on him by time and his position didn't change the effect at all.

"What?" Carson brushed the silent reprimand off. "That's a calculated risk and you know it." The potential of getting caught always heightened the scandalous appeal. He pointed at Trevor. "You taught me that."

"I did." The throaty agreement was full of the dark mischief Trevor kept hidden. His smirk spoke to the many encounters they'd shared since he'd introduced Carson to the Boardroom over three years ago.

The illicit group took controlled risks in the form of sexual acts that rode the edge of societal acceptance. For Carson, being a member allowed him to both push and relieve the stress that came with his position. Plus it was fucking hot. Wrong in a world built on right and often his to control. That power got him off better than any one-night stand or relationship ever had.

Trevor dropped his smile and stood, the businessman back in place. "I trust you'll find a solution that benefits everyone." He came around the desk, buttoning his suit jacket as he did.

Carson nodded as he rose to meet him. "I'll see what

I can do." Maybe Avery would stay quiet. And maybe
he'd be able to forget the passionate shock that'd flushed
her cheeks and peaked her nipples so beautifully beneath
her silk blouse.

Sure thing.

"Keep me informed." Trevor paused. They were about
equal in height, but Trevor had an air about him that
drew attention, and Carson was happy to let him have it.

"Will do," Carson agreed. Hopefully there'd be nothing to report.

The long route back to his office took him past Gregory's office. Avery was at her desk, head down, focused
on her computer screen. He'd always found her beautiful, but he'd kept his attraction to a detached admiration appropriate for the work setting and his position.
Now, that polite distance was shattered, and his brain
wasn't shifting back.

Her golden hair was slicked back into a sleek knot
at the base of her skull, a wisp of bangs softening the
rigid appearance. Her navy blouse rested on the swell
of her breasts, the V-neck high but alluring—at least to
him. Would her nipples show against the silky material? Would they pucker for him like they had last night?

She didn't look up, and he didn't approach. Her brows
were drawn, fingers tapping quickly over the keyboard.
Her intensity vibrated around her from the slight dip of
her brow to her hunched shoulders and the tight pinch of
her lips. Lips he now knew could part in lust and want.

Christ. His stomach clenched over nothing more
than a benign memory. One that was incredibly innocent compared to all he'd seen and orchestrated since
he'd joined the Boardroom.

Avery straightened, back arching in a stretch that

pushed her breasts up. Her head dropped back to display the tempting expanse of her throat. *Fuck*. The soft curse slipped from his lips in adoration and frustration. Did she know he was watching—again?

She flexed her fingers, lowered her chin down and stood. Her gaze lifted, and he stepped around the corner, heading back to his office before she spotted him. His pulse beat a pronounced rhythm on his neck and pumped an inappropriate amount of blood to his dick.

But that was part of the draw, wasn't it? The fact that he shouldn't be turned on at work. That she was technically off-limits. Inappropriate and wrong, just like the Boardroom itself.

"Can you bring me a coffee, Jean?" he asked his assistant as he passed by her desk, his suit jacket buttoned to cover any telling displays he failed to control. "Please. And set up a meeting with Gregory— Never mind. I'll take care of that." He could imagine Avery's panic when she saw the meeting request even though it had nothing to do with last night.

"Certainly," she replied, her smile crinkling the corners of her eyes. Midfifties, whip-smart and able to follow the technical lingo that came with his job, Jean was a treasure he never abused or took for granted. Dealing with just one bad assistant had shown him the value of cherishing the truly good ones.

Her short hair was dyed a dark brown with red highlights woven strategically through the curls. She tugged at the hem of her violet suit jacket as she stood. Maybe it was past habits or simply personal choice, but she always wore a suit despite the office being business-casual. But then again, so did he.

"You have meetings at ten, eleven and two today."

The reminder was unnecessary but appreciated. "Thank you." And he'd be grateful for her ten-minute warning before each one. Programming was still his drug of choice, and he often got lost in it even though his position limited the time he could invest in it.

He shut his door and sat at his computer to scan through the portion of Avery's HR information visible to him. Thirty years old, from the Midwest, a BS degree, employed at Faulkner for eighteen months. He knew the last part, remembering clearly when Gregory had hired her. All fresh-faced and ready to please. That quality was inherent to every competent assistant whether they acknowledged it or not.

And now she'd shoved herself directly into his path when he'd deliberately ignored every enticing thing about her.

He grabbed his personal cell phone after Jean delivered his coffee. This was not a business call. "Gregory," he said when the line picked up. He spun his chair around to stare at the bay view through his floor-to-ceiling windows. "Where are you?"

"In my office." Annoyance lined his tone. "Why?"

"Has your assistant spoken to you today?"

"She speaks to me every day."

Carson rubbed his brow at the sarcasm but managed to bite back his sigh. "About any evening-related activities?"

Gregory's grunt crossed the distance in a sharp bark. "No. Am I to guess that she might in the near future?"

Carson winced. "If she does, let me know."

The Boardroom had had instances in the past that'd threatened their exposure. Ones that'd been quietly handled before any names or events were leaked. This call clearly broached that subject without being specific— and that was his intent.

"Should I be concerned?" Gregory finally asked, his tone now serious. He'd been a Boardroom member before Carson. So had his wife, Tam. They were still members, but their participation had subsided after the birth of their twins, which also increased their personal risk if the Boardroom was ever revealed to the public.

"Not yet." Hopefully not ever. "I'll take care of it." He chuckled to himself at the mafia-style sound of his statement. Like he was going to make Avery "disappear." That'd look good on his résumé.

"Are you the reason she was so flustered this morning?"

She was flustered? Carson laughed aloud this time. "I didn't do a thing." Except watch her. She'd stumbled into the room and stayed all on her own. But it'd become his problem to clean up since Avery worked for Faulkner and they'd been in their boardroom last night. The other participants were strangers to her.

Gregory scoffed. "Right."

Carson didn't bother to defend himself. Instead, he changed the topic over to actual business. He'd give Avery some space, see what move—if any—she made.

Maybe she'd let it go, but he couldn't.

There were things he had to ensure, and he couldn't leave them to chance.

Chapter Three

"Avery," Gregory called from his open door. Her shudder was instant and uncontrolled. "Can you come in here, please?"

Did he sound angry? Disappointed? Disgusted? Anything?

No. Not really.

She grabbed her pen and a notebook out of habit. Her stomach did yet another flip and clench. It hadn't stopped since last night, and no amount of antacids had calmed it. Was this when he fired her?

Over what, though? Her losing the confidential data or walking in on a sexcapade?

Sleep had been nonexistent last night. Her mind had run on a constant loop between the lost folder and the sex scene she'd been caught watching. She'd processed every possible outcome and scenario during that time, and none of them had ended with her job and dignity in place.

Yes, she could go to HR, but Carson was an executive. He held the power. He'd likely deny everything, and what was she going to complain about? The sex? How hot it'd made her feel? How envious she'd been? Or that she'd been caught clearly ogling the show?

Nope. Not going to happen. She nodded to reaffirm her already set decision. She wouldn't say a word. Let it go—that was what her mother was always telling her to do. In this instance, it fit.

Her smile was slight when she entered Gregory's office, her chest so tight she could barely force air through her lungs. "What do you need?" Did her voice sound strained to him?

He looked up, his rugged features showing no sign of annoyance. The wrinkles weren't stacked up on his brow, and that was clearly a smile. "Thanks for printing these out for me." He pointed to the quarterly reports before he flipped the folder shut. "I looked through them at home last night."

He had the reports. He'd had them *all along.*

Avery's blood boiled, hot, steaming. It ran up her chest and tingled in her hands. She contracted her abdomen to trap it inside and took one slow breath. "It would've been nice if you'd left me a note or text saying you'd taken the folder," she said through a strained grin, not bothering to contain the iciness that covered her temper.

"Sorry," Gregory mumbled. "I was in a rush last night. Tam had a meeting, and I needed to pick the twins up from day care."

And Avery had nothing better to do with her evening than to stress over the missing reports, sending her on a wild-goose chase that'd landed her in Carson's sex den. Okay, that almost made her smile for real. Or was that a bubble of hysterical laughter threatening to burst free?

"I've made notes," Gregory went on, completely oblivious or willing to ignore her annoyance. He handed the folder to her over his cluttered desk. "Can you manipulate the reports before four?" His brows rose with the question, but he clearly expected her to say yes.

She took the folder, cursing it silently. "Which is more important? These reports or the payroll updates?" A small measure of satisfaction curled through her at his wince. Yup, both were equally important.

"Payroll and then the reports." His eyes narrowed, his heavy brows dipping low.

Avery met his gaze. She had nothing to back down over. He'd made her life a brief hell and he should be aware of it.

"Is something wrong?" he finally asked. The heavy timbre of his voice matched his stockier frame. In his midforties, Gregory had what would be labeled as a "dad body." Not out of shape, but not gym-fit either.

She debated her answer before giving him the truth. "I looked everywhere for this folder last night." She held it up as evidence. "I even returned to the office when I realized I didn't know where it was." An unnecessary trip that'd landed her in the middle of...Carson's sex den. Her lips quirked.

Those thick brows of his rose a notch. He sat back, head tilted slightly, contemplation chasing away his initial show of surprise. "Again, I'm sorry." The careful articulation of his words screamed of a man tiptoeing around an unstable female. It both irked and placated her. "Your dedication is appreciated."

Her shoulders lowered as her irritation eased. "Thank you." He'd listened and apologized. That was more than some bosses had done in her past. Her smile was genuine this time. "I'll get you the payroll info before lunch." She took a step back, halting when he continued to stare at her. "Is there something else?"

Another kink dug into her stomach the longer the silence grew. She had zero idea how she'd respond if he asked about the sex den. Because he'd only ask if he knew, and if he knew then Carson had told him. Then she'd stress over who else knew and what they were thinking of her. And if they knew how much watching had excited her. How the images kept running through her mind on an erotic loop.

"No," he finally said, sitting forward to move some papers around on his desk. "That's all."

She hightailed it out of his office, closing the door behind her without him asking. The privacy was for her this time. Her skin was heated again, her blouse clinging to her back when she hadn't realized she'd been sweating. Her desk chair gave its familiar squeak as she sat down. A quick look around assured her no one was watching. She ducked down, opened the bottom drawer on her desk and made a quick check of her armpits. Sweat rings were not acceptable at any time, especially in the office.

She jammed her emergency bar of deodorant into her purse and made a quick trip to the restroom. A polite greeting was spared for the woman at the sink before she ducked into the stall.

The starched firmness washed from her shoulders and spine in one big swoop the second the latch clicked its sound of safety. She slumped forward, her hand providing a brace before her forehead hit the door. The coolness of the metal soaked into her palm, and she longed to press her heated cheek to it, the ick-factor be damned.

How would she survive this day?

A slow breath in. Out. Repeated. The bleached latrine smell penetrated her senses and finally motivated her to move.

She'd survive by not thinking of Carson Haggert and his sex den. She smiled, the whimsical humor dampening her stress. It was easier to make fun of what she'd seen than address the longings it'd unlocked within her.

Her movements were mechanical and quick as she applied another coat of deodorant. Hopefully, her lustful hot flashes were done. No—they *were* done. Period.

She was at work and that was what she'd do—work.

The rest of the morning progressed like usual. She took calls, scheduled meetings for Gregory, did her own work. Her lunch break was blessedly normal too. A quick salad from the café down the street with two other admin assistants. She laughed at their jokes and commiserated over their job complaints.

See? Normal.

The sun was out that day, unhindered by fog or clouds, and she sat back to soak up the rays while appreciating the warmth. It sank into her bones to leave a languid flow behind. This was why she'd moved to the Bay Area. Or at least one of the reasons. The Ohio winters were long, cold and claustrophobic at times with a spring that was often slow to emerge.

"I'm going to have to work late tonight to get it done," her friend was saying.

Avery tensed, her attention sailing back to her lunch dates. Her sunglasses shielded her eyes, which had gone wide. "Oh yeah?" she offered, thoughts launching to the boardroom. Did Carson consider that working late? Was that a code to participate in Carson's sex den?

Oh. My. God. Avery suppressed a shudder and bleached the thought from her mind before it took hold.

She would *not* walk around the office wondering who was "working late." That was just…gross.

Her friend sighed, picking at the last of her salad. "Hopefully, not too late." She glanced at her phone. "Not if I get back and focus on work."

The afternoon was winding down when Avery pushed Save on the last of the quarterly report changes. Pride danced a little jig through her at making the four-o'clock request with a few minutes to spare. She pressed Print on the series, the buzzing whirl of her private printer kicking in moments later.

She could do this. Carson and his sex den hadn't crossed her mind once that afternoon. She'd smirked when she'd passed the boardroom, though, the doors closed for a meeting. Did they sanitize the table afterward? Would she ever be able to set anything on it again without wondering if it was clean?

Fortunately, she didn't attend many meetings in there. The one yesterday had been a rarity.

"Good afternoon, Ms. Fast."

Avery whipped around, the reports clutched in her hands. Her heart somehow stalled and raced at once, causing her chest to constrict and her brain to go blank. Carson Haggert stared down at her from the other side of her desk. His smile teasing—right? That little curve matched the glint in his eyes—right?

Was he thinking of last night? Was this when the taunting started? The harassment? Would he do that? How should she respond?

He cleared his throat, the deep rumble caressing her skin. "Is Gregory in his office?" He nodded to the closed door, his brow lifting slightly.

Gregory. Her boss. Of course, he was here to see him. Not her.

She wet her lips, kicking herself for her floundering stupidity. He didn't need more evidence of exactly how much of a dork she was. "Yes," she managed to say, her voice croaking on the single word. Wonderful. She swallowed, set the reports down and stood. "Let me check if he's free."

She kept her back straight, her steps precise as she made the short walk to Gregory's door. She knocked, waited for his call to enter, acutely aware of Carson watching her. A shiver of tingles fluttered down her spine. His presence alone seemed to suck the air from the room, and she struggled to keep her breathing even.

"Yes?"

Gregory's muffled call allowed her to open the door. She popped her head in, a glance confirming he wasn't on the phone. "Dr. Haggert is here to see you." Her voice was clear and even that time. Professional—thankfully.

Gregory stretched back, arms raised over his head before he let them drop. "Send him in."

She turned to Carson, a polite smile hiding the wave of nerves chattering through her stomach. "You can go in." She stepped aside to let him pass.

He nodded, his smile stretching higher on one side. "Thank you."

Damn his voice for being so low and rumbly. He'd always sounded like that, from the first time they'd been introduced. Only now it came across as seductive, with a dark and naughty edge.

She swallowed again to both hide her sigh and to dislodge the lump that'd formed. He passed her on a slow wave of masculine cologne and dominance. She inhaled, the woody musk invading her. Sultry, like his voice. Yet teasing, like his smile.

He stopped before her, the space between them down to inches in the doorway. Her heart raced, palms growing damp to match the clamminess that suddenly coated her nape. She held her smile, though.

With him a good six inches taller than her, she looked past his lips with the distinct dip in the top center, the dark stubble that was starting to frame his mouth, the nose with a defined bump on one side to his blue eyes. Dark blue with a ring of gray on the outer edge. Eyes that seemed to look into her and had witnessed her open display of lust.

"Would it be possible for you to bring me a cup of coffee?"

His request processed at slug-speed in her mind. Coffee? Could she get it? Would he like her to caress his broad chest too? Maybe run her fingers through his hair. Would the blonder strands show brighter in the sunlight? Was it soft? Coarse? Would the shorter sides tickle her palms?

"Ms. Fast?"

She jerked, blinked, heat racing up her neck. "Yes. Of course." She stepped away, cooler air finally racing over her neck. "Would you like cream or sugar?" Her training saved her now. She brushed her bangs away from her brow, waiting politely.

"Cream, please."

And she was not going down the euphemism sinkhole with that. She looked past him to her boss. "Gregory?"

"Yes, please." Her boss came around his desk. "Thank you, Avery."

She nodded and left for the break room before she

made a bigger fool of herself. What was she doing, ogling an executive like a teenager? She knew better than that. She *was* better than that.

Yet she'd just fantasized about running her fingers through Carson's hair, which was actually mild compared to her many thoughts last night. And he'd been completely professional. No lewd looks or innuendos. No hint that he even recognized her from last night.

Maybe he didn't.

And maybe she hadn't stumbled into his sex den. Ha!

Coffee. Just get coffee. Cream in one. Cream and two sugars in the other. Don't spill it. Don't trip or slosh it down her blouse.

Walk slowly. Head up. Smile in place.

Breeze into Gregory's office, hand over the coffees. Avoid eye contact. Retreat before she got caught in Carson's web again. That alluring, magnetic thing that tweaked her nipples, frazzled her mind and set her aflame.

She closed the door behind her as she left Gregory's office, a relieved sigh bursting free when the latch clicked. That couldn't continue. She wouldn't let it.

He wasn't going to chase her out of her job either. She liked it here. Liked her boss and what she did. She'd made a home in San Francisco after taking the risky leap to move out here five years ago. It'd been hard at first, but she'd made friends, figured out the city and fell in love with the area.

She was staying. Both in San Francisco and at Faulkner.

That settled, she focused on her work again, refusing to look up when Gregory's door opened. She kept typing as Carson strode past her desk, every nerve ending acutely aware of him despite her refusal to acknowledge him or her own reaction.

Her skin buzzed with energy and she had no clue what she was typing, but she held her position. A breath swooped in once he'd rounded the corner, his wonderful sex-and-man scent remaining to tease her. Really?

The desire to bang her head on her keyboard was curbed by the open location of her desk.

She deleted the last two lines of gibberish on her screen before grabbing a bottle of peppermint oil spray. She misted the air around her desk and rubbed some on her nape. Another inhalation found only sweetness and candy canes. Nice.

Perfect.

All was good until Gregory walked out of his office, a manila folder in his hand. "Can you run this down to Carson?"

Avery stared at him for a long moment, silently damning the universe before responding. "Of course." What else was she going to say? She extended her hand, smile painted on once again.

"Thank you." He handed the folder over and turned away. "Oh." He looked back. "Thanks for getting the reports adjusted. I'll look at them tonight. At my home."

Heat spread over her cheeks at his over-obvious clarification. "Thank you." She refused to be embarrassed for standing up for herself, no matter how her body responded. He should've told her last night too.

She stared at the damning folder in her hand, hateful curses silently flung at it. *I am not affected by Carson Haggert.* Nope. Just like her embarrassment, she refused to let him befuddle her, despite her physical reaction.

Maybe she could leave it with Jean. It wasn't like

Avery could avoid him for the rest of her career at Faulkner. The office wasn't that big. But there was no requirement for her to hand-deliver the folder either.

She took the main stairwell down to the lower level where the IT department was located. As she understood it, their office handled the software and networking for the entire corporation. With multiple international and US offices, the complexities were far beyond her understanding.

Her heart sank when she saw that Jean's desk was empty. Maybe Carson was gone too. Then she could leave the folder with a note and be gone.

Relief spread into a smile as she ripped a sticky note from the stack on Jean's desk. She grabbed a pen and bent over to scratch out a brief message.

"Ms. Fast."

Avery jerked up, eyes closing. *Shit*. She plastered on a polite smile before she turned to face Carson. "I didn't realize you were in your office." Her racing pulse agreed with the statement. No, she hadn't checked, but she also hadn't expected him to sneak up on her. She crumpled the sticky note in her hand and held out the folder. "Gregory asked me to bring this down to you."

See, she could be completely professional with him. This was work. She was an adult. What he did on his own time wasn't her business—even if she had intimate knowledge of it.

"Would you mind coming into my office for a moment?" He stepped back, all manners and politeness. There was no hint of insistence or reprimand in his tone or his expression, but that didn't ease the apprehension crawling through her.

She lowered her arm, folder still in her grasp. "Can I ask why?"

His smile was a slow curve that spread in taunting increments. Not malicious, but humorous when paired with the light in his eyes. He arched a brow, the action slightly condescending, slightly doubtful. "I think you know."

So it *was* about *that*.

She shook her head. "It's all right." She glanced behind her to assure their relative privacy. "I swear. I know nothing. I won't say a word." To anyone who knew him at least. There was some gossip her best friend had to hear, and this fit clearly within that arena.

His smile disappeared with his quick nod. "That's good to know. But I still need to speak with you. I think we can both agree that here is not the best place." He made a pointed look at the cubicle farm that stretched in an open sea behind her.

Heat rose from her stomach over her chest, and no amount of willpower kept it from creeping up her neck. *Damn it.*

She looked away, lips pursed to hold in the mortification she'd sworn she wouldn't feel. He couldn't do this to her. *He* was the one who should be embarrassed. A quick glance showed that he wasn't. At least not visibly. If anything, he was amused by her reaction. Maybe by the entire humiliating experience. *Dick.*

He stepped up, and she barely stopped her flinch. Anger flashed in then, determination backing it up. She glared at him, uncaring who he was or what his position was. He didn't get to intimidate her.

He dipped and slid the folder from her hand, eyes never leaving hers. They took in everything once again. She was powerless to stop him, so she let every bit of her annoyance show. He clearly wanted to push—or was he testing her?

"You walked in on something very personal," he said, straightening. He tapped the folder against his palm, eyes narrowing. "I'll be at Chester's in North Beach at seven tonight. Meet me there."

Her brows sprang up. "What?"

"I won't discuss private business at work." He made another pointed scan behind her. "Especially here."

Stubbornness alone kept her from looking over her shoulder. Who was watching? Where was Jean? Was anyone staring at them? She had no reason to be talking to Carson for so long.

"I don't believe we have anything personal to discuss," she countered. Pretending was all she had left. Her anger had faded too quickly, and the brief adrenaline hit was leaving its quaking trail behind. She inhaled slowly only to be assaulted by that hypnotizing woody scent of his.

"We do," he countered, the authority tickling her desire. His gaze landed on her lips, and she bit her tongue to keep from licking them. Was that for real? Was he playing her? Did he think she'd fall into his lap just because he was gorgeous? Or powerful? Or... Yeah, he probably did.

And she just might—if he didn't have the leverage to get her fired.

Even then...

No!

"I'll see you tonight...Avery." Her name tumbled off his lips in that low rumble of his, tempting, sexy, provocative.

Her nipples tightened in a sharp spray of tingles that

left her exposed even though she was fully clothed. "And if you don't?" she asked, her voice intentionally flat.

His chuckle was just as low, a dirty rumble that matched his voice. His smile was real and wide. "I think you want to." His shrug held a calculated carelessness to it. "But it's ultimately your choice." He leaned in an inch. Not enough to be inappropriate, but enough for her to catch his scent. Enough to suck the air from between them.

Enough to make her wonder what would happen if he leaned in more.

"However, we *will* have a private discussion—soon." He paused, his point reaffirmed by his hard stare. "I'm offering you a public option." He took a step into his office, turned back. "Thank you for bringing the file down. Tell Gregory I'll get back to him tomorrow."

About what?

Avery stared after him until his door clicked shut, another array of thoughts and doubts frying her mind. Had she just been propositioned or ordered to meet him?

What should she do?

She should tell him to fuck off—over what, though?

He hadn't threatened her or made an unwanted advance. He'd simply spoken the truth. Whether she wanted to admit it or not—whether she *wanted* to or not—they really should talk.

And his offer seemed like her best option.

Chapter Four

Carson glanced around the room from his seat at the end of the bar. The low ceilings and dim lighting provided a cozy atmosphere that was countered by the upbeat music piped through the sound system. The hipster after-work crowd was peppered with middle-aged couples catching dinner, which offered a nice, upscale balance.

His location gave him a direct line of sight to the front door and a good perspective of the entire room. He didn't recognize anyone. Good. He'd picked this place because it was far enough from the office to avoid their after-work crowd without being completely inconvenient.

He checked his watch, took a sip of his scotch. Would Avery show up?

The line of booths along the wall would've given them a more secluded space to talk, but he didn't want this to be intimate. He was potentially fucked enough as it was. He didn't need to add harassment to Avery's list of complaints.

The door swung open. A fading swatch of daylight shot in. He blinked as his smile spread. Avery stood in the entry, scanning the room. Her cheeks were pink, most likely from the chilly breeze that'd kicked up with the setting sun. But she flushed easily, at least around him. It screamed of an innocence begging to be explored.

He stood, nodding to her when she spotted him. A subtle shift went over her from relaxed to guarded. He could almost see her armor slapping into place. She pressed her lips tight, chin lifting, stride determined. Her black trench coat was cinched around her waist, a red bag clutched over her shoulder in a flash of hot color.

She was on a mission, and he was pretty certain it varied from his.

"Avery," he said, greeting her. "I'm glad you came."

She frowned, her brows pulling together beneath her bangs. "I didn't have much choice, did I?"

He pulled the bar stool out for her, taking her coat as she removed it to hang it on the high back. "You always have a choice," he leaned in to tell her, nudging the stool forward.

A light peppermint scent drifted over him to drown out the wet bar smell. He inhaled again, held it. Goodness and Christmas. He hadn't picked the scent up when he'd been at Gregory's office, but it'd been there when she'd come to his. "I believe I clarified that earlier."

Her sigh was long and weighted. She shot him a glare as he took his seat. She set her bag on the ground, then twisted to face him, hands clasped on her lap. Her eyes were narrowed with intent.

Damn, she had spunk.

"Look—"

"Can I get you a drink?" he interrupted. Her mouth snapped shut, eyes darting to his half-full glass, suspicion glaring. "No strings. I promise." He lifted his scotch. "Nothing that is said tonight has strings. Another promise." He took a drink, letting the peaty heat sit on his tongue before he swallowed it.

How would it taste licking it off her neck, her breasts? Would she squirm or purr?

A tense pause stretched while she searched him. He didn't look away. Hell, he had no desire to look away from her stunning eyes. A mix of blue and green that ran closer to blue. Did they change based on her clothing color?

It took more strength than it should have to keep from reaching out to see if her cheeks were warm or chilled. The tinge complemented the shade of her lipstick, a light pink that meshed with her porcelain skin tone.

"And," he went on when she remained silent, "this has nothing to do with work. Not this meeting or anything that is discussed." He signaled for the bartender. "No one will ever know of it—unless you tell them."

Her eyes widened at that. She shifted her focus to the bartender, compressed her lips. "A glass of red wine, please. House is fine."

Carson's relief eased out on a low exhale. Maybe this wouldn't go too badly.

He remained silent until her wine was set before her, then he lifted his glass in a toast. "To a productive conversation."

Her burst of laughter was clipped and sharp, but the remaining smile took the edge from her stiffness. She shook her head, eyes closing briefly. Her shoulders dropped and she clinked her glass against his. The wine was dark against her pink lips when she took a sip. He couldn't take his eyes away from the common act that became sexy with her.

"Okay." Her glass clicked on the wood bar top when

she set it down. "I'm here. I already told you I won't say anything about last night." She winced, looked down. "I'm sorry I walked in on...that. It wasn't intentional. I swear."

"I never thought it was." Her surprise reaction had been proof enough of that. He pulled a folded paper from his inner pocket, smoothed it out. He retrieved a pen next, twisted it open and set them both before her. "I need you to sign this non-disclosure agreement, though."

She stiffened. "Why?" Panicked defensiveness sprang from her tone.

He eyed her and weighed his options. "Because you saw some very intimate things. An act that could ruin many lives if you choose to talk about it."

Her head was shaking before he finished. "I won't. I've told you that how many times now?"

"And I believe you." He did. "But this—" he tapped the paper "—is for the others who were in the room. They don't know you. I need to ensure they're protected."

She sat back, her soft laugh heavy with sarcasm. "And what about me? What if one of them—or you—decide to twist the story and put me in it?"

"They've already signed this." But damn did he love that she'd thought to protect herself as well. "They'll never talk about anything that happened in the Boardroom."

Her eyes widened again, the pupils enlarging this time. Her thoughts were telegraphed to him like they'd been spoken. Images of last night bloomed in his mind, of Avery watching the trio. Of her flushed and wanting, her hand inching toward her breasts.

She cleared her throat, took a sip of her wine. *Fuck*.

He shifted his legs apart to gain more room for his too-interested dick. How could he not respond to her when her desire showed so vividly?

Her voice was husky when she asked, "Does that happen a lot then?" She waved her hand. "The board-room thing?"

She *was* interested—not that she wanted to admit it. He contained the smile that spread within him and tapped the NDA contract again. Too much was at risk if she didn't sign it.

And so much was possible if she did…

Her glare screamed her annoyance before she snatched up the paper and started to read. A sense of unearned pride burst in his chest when she didn't blindly sign the document. That feisty edge of hers was as tempting as the blushing naïvety. Would she melt or fight? Cry out loud or hold it in?

He hid his smile behind his glass this time, empty-ing the contents.

She set the paper down when she was done and then turned her head to look at him. "Is there a catch?" She nodded to the NDA.

"Nope." He motioned for another drink. "It's exactly what it states. Don't speak about anything you saw in the Boardroom to anyone. If you do, you're liable for the financial penalty and open to lawsuits from anyone in the Boardroom." Would she catch that "Boardroom," as documented, meant the private group of men and women who participated in various acts of group sex, often in public spaces?

"And this?" She pointed to the capitalized Boardroom written on the first line as the disclosing party. "What does that mean?"

And she did.

He gave a small shrug, hiding his appreciation for her shrewdness. "Let's just say it's what you walked in on."

"Really?" she asked. "In the boardroom?" He lifted his brow, and she laughed softly. "This is getting more confusing, but fine." She grabbed the pen and signed her name. "There." She set the pen down, sat back. "Documented proof that I won't say a word, but..." Her eyes narrowed. "Where's my proof that *you* won't say anything?"

"And what would I say?"

Her mouth dropped open. "Seriously? You could get me fired!"

He jerked back, scowled. "I wouldn't do that."

"I said the same thing, and *my* word wasn't enough for you." She brushed her bangs away from her eyes in an irritated shove that matched her scowl.

His admiration came out on a low chuckle. She was getting sexier by the moment. He'd assumed there were brains beneath the beauty, but seeing them in action added a deeper, more interesting layer to her. "You're right." He leaned in, that peppermint scent teasing him closer. Would she smell like that everywhere? Would it deepen when she was turned on? Would she taste as fresh? He retrieved the signed contract and placed it, along with the pen, back in his pocket. "I've already signed one of these. The same rules apply. Your privacy is protected under that."

"Really?"

He nodded. "Everything that happens within the boundaries of the Boardroom are protected. That included you the second you entered."

"And what about outside of it?"

He had a whole hell of a lot of ideas of things they could do both within and out of the Boardroom—if only she was receptive. "You'll have to trust me."

"Of course," she mumbled before taking a healthy gulp of wine. "So…" She shot him a side-eyed glance. "Are we done?"

Not if he had his choice. He crossed his arms and rested them on the bar. Her profile was soft, like her. The long line of her neck was exposed, daring him to drop kisses down the side. Did she have any idea how alluring she was?

He caught a guy staring at Avery, his gaze saying exactly what he'd like to do with her. Carson waited for the guy to notice him and smiled when the guy quickly turned away. Yeah, she was his for as long as she sat next to him. "Tell me, Avery." He waited for her to look at him. The hesitation was back in her eyes, a wariness he wanted to displace. "Are you seeing anyone?"

Her brows drew together. "Why?"

That was probably a no then. "Have you ever seen anything like that before?" He watched her eyes go wide, breath grow shallow. So authentic. There'd been no need for him to clarify his question. Her mind was on last night, and she obviously wasn't disgusted. Not even now, after the shock had worn off.

"Umm…" And there was that flush. Light this time. More pink than deep red. "Not like that." She twisted the stem of her wineglass, her focus on her fingers.

"You were shocked."

"Yes."

"But interested too."

Her head whipped around. "No!" The quick denial was automatic and too insistent.

He narrowed his eyes. "I'm not trying to embarrass you, truly."

"Well, you're doing it anyway."

"Are you embarrassed by my questions or your response?" he countered softly.

She stared at him for a long moment before dropping her head back, eyes closing as her defeated laugh teased him over the din of the crowd. Her hands fisted on the bar, a grim smile curling over her lips.

He'd cornered her and had zero regrets about it. She'd liked what she'd seen—he'd bet his job on that. And he wanted to explore that interest with her. But she had to be willing, her own curiosity driving her.

"Why do you care?" she finally asked after taking another hefty drink of her wine.

Because you're beautiful. And that was a shallow answer. The truth went much deeper. The tension drew tight between his shoulder blades, the importance of his response dancing on his awareness.

He could walk away right now. He should. And what would he miss if he did?

"Because I think you *were* interested. I think you found it hot even though your background said you shouldn't." He turned to her when she didn't reject his words. Her lips had parted, want battling with denial in her eyes. "I think a part of you would love to let go like that, but you've never dared to before. Or maybe you've never had the opportunity." He leaned in, tempted to steal a kiss but knowing she'd run if he did. "I think you want to see more. Do more. Try more."

She swallowed, the action snapping at the energy that hummed between them. He had her, if he could just get her to admit to her desire.

To let go.

"You—" She cleared her throat. "You think a lot."

His laugh was lost beneath his breath. "There's nothing wrong with wanting that," he said. "What you saw last night was between consenting adults."

Her tongue snaked out in a slow glide between her lips. He clenched his hand to keep from touching her. A caress down her arm, a possessive stroke along her jaw. She was primed for persuasion, and he wouldn't be that guy. "How does it work?"

Her breathy question tempted him closer. His dick was so damn interested he had zero chance of hiding it if she glanced to his lap. "What, exactly?" he asked, his voice lower and intimate, matching hers.

That alluring blush spread over her cheeks once again, but she didn't look away. "The sex." He lifted a brow, and her flush deepened. She fluttered her hand around in another encompassing motion. "I mean the group thing. How does it get arranged? Do you know everyone and them you? How do you face them afterward?"

His amusement rumbled out when her barrage ended. "Now who's thinking too much?" Her lips pursed in a prim rebuff. "The scenes are about feeling, not thinking." That was part of the draw for him. "A heightened escape that lets you safely explore what most of society scorns."

"Safely?" A doubt wrinkle formed between her brows. "How is that safe?"

"The contracts. The select group of participants. The locations. It's all defined to minimize the risk for everyone."

"Until someone like me walks in," she snarked.

Someone who longed to try it but was too rooted in her conservative boundaries to dare. "But you didn't immediately run away." He waited for her objection but got none. A passionate woman simmered beneath that demure skirt and high neckline, he'd bet his career on it. "Would you like to come with me next time? To watch…again?"

Chapter Five

Go with him? To his sex den?

Oh...holy...

Yes.

No!

And when will I ever get another chance like this?

Want pulsed at Avery's weakening resistance. His offer was so tempting, as was he. All rugged professionalism topped off by the dark secrets she was now privileged to know. His web was working its way around her, drawing her closer. Teasing her, tempting her down paths she'd never considered before. Making her want the taboo when she'd shunned it before.

She crossed her legs to suppress the sexual ache that'd only grown stronger since she'd sat down. God, she wanted him along with what he was offering.

Could I? Really?

She reached for her wine, surprised to find the glass empty. Was that why she was even considering his offer? She could play this cool, right? Not like the floundering innocent she was currently projecting.

"What's the catch?" she asked him, propping her chin on her hand, eyes narrowing in her hunt for a lie or any sign of falseness from Carson. Her thumb stroked over the small mole on the underside of her jaw, the motion absentminded and soothing.

His gaze darted to her thumb, lips compressing slightly. "There is no catch." He motioned to her empty glass. "Can I get you another?"

She stared at the wineglass, thoughts spinning from wants to shoulds. Her head was already woozy, her inhibitions a bit too free. Yet, she wasn't ready to leave. Carson was…interesting. Magnetic. Handsome.

Her body hummed with an awareness that dared her to take a risk.

"Sure," she finally relented. She didn't have to drink it all.

He motioned to the bartender, and Avery didn't take her eyes off Carson. He commanded attention but didn't seek it. He only spoke in meetings when needed, never one to drive the conversation. Always courteous, yet slightly elusive.

And he'd been totally focused on her since she'd walked into the bar, even after she'd signed the contract.

She'd caught more than one woman eyeing him up. He could've had any one of them, but his attention was solely on her. The thrill of that sizzled over her skin and hummed with the sexual current running through her veins.

The bartender set the fresh drink in front of her, and she mumbled her thanks while still studying Carson. What was his game? There had to be a hidden loophole she wasn't seeing.

His brow lifted when he caught her staring at him. "What?"

Her lips quirked for some unknown reason. He was beyond sexy with the light shadow of his beard stubble darkening his jaw. His hair had that end-of-the-day finger-combed look, yet he was still in control, which upped his danger level by about a hundred notches.

"Why would you offer me that?" she asked, jumping back to their conversation.

A half smile lifted the edge of his mouth as a dark heat filled his eyes. "Because I think you'd enjoy it." He turned slightly, his body opening to hers. His leg grazed hers, the silky linen of his slacks caressing her skin. An instant flash of goose bumps raced up her inner thigh. Her pussy clenched, need pulsing.

She sucked in a breath but didn't move. His eyes danced with confident knowledge, and she couldn't condemn him for it. She'd done—was doing—a sucky job of hiding his effect on her.

He shifted toward her, and she found herself mimicking him as he dipped his head to speak into her ear. "The sight of that woman spread on the table, lost in passion, the guys focused solely on her pleasure turned you on," he said, his low words a caress. "You imagined what it'd feel like. You wanted to be her. You were fascinated by the eroticism. The taboo."

She closed her eyes, breaths shortening into small gasps. The visuals sprang to life, her body responding stronger than when she'd stood in the doorway seeing them for herself. Her nipples were throbbing pinpoints of desire linked to her pussy. Her neck tingled with every breathy wisp of heat and the awareness of how close his lips were.

"Let me show you that," he urged. A slow line of heat blew from her shoulder to her ear to ignite another wave of goose bumps down her chest. She tilted her head, giving him better access, the silent action saying so much.

She couldn't stop it, though. Didn't want to. "Let me share it with you. Show you the beauty of watching the passion unfold. It's not just sex, Avery."

The low rumble of her name was intimate, almost possessive. She should object to that—to him. She didn't. No, she wanted more. So much more.

"Then what is it?" she whispered, opening her eyes to find his. Longing and lust stared back at her. Dark yet somehow freeing. His obvious desire made her own okay.

His lips parted, and she couldn't stop herself from imagining them on her skin. Kissing. Sucking. She inhaled, his woody scent layering over her.

"Passion. Connection. Trust," he murmured. "A shared give-and-take with the freedom to let go. No judgments. No stereotypes. No societal inhibitions." He blew another line of warm air up her neck. His eyes were closed when he eased back. Hunger lined his expression even then.

She shivered, her craving simmering outward. Yes. She wanted everything he described. But... She lowered her gaze, swallowed. The prominent outline of his dick was clearly displayed up the crease of his thigh. Oh, God. He did want her.

She pressed her thighs together in a futile attempt to stop her reaction. Her pussy contracted, abdomen clenching. How wet would her panties be when she stood? She was so turned on—and he hadn't touched her. She might combust on the spot if he did.

Heat rushed up her neck for the thousandth time that day. Would she ever stop blushing around him? "I—" She cleared her throat, met his gaze. Could he really want her that badly? For the night, no doubt. And would that be so wrong?

"What?" he asked when she didn't continue. "You what?"

"I don't know if I could," she finally finished, honesty spilling out. "What if I didn't enjoy it?" The porn she'd seen usually ran the too-blatant line for her. Yet last night hadn't been like that.

"Then we leave." He stated it like it was simple. Could it really be?

"And after," she pressed. "What happens then? When we go back to work?"

He looked away, his gaze traveling the bar for a long moment. Some of the heat was gone from his eyes when he turned back, and she realized her question had shattered their bubble.

The cold splash of reality jolted her out of her lust-filled haze. Regret mingled with the practical logic that'd plagued her entire life. That was good, she tried to convince herself. She couldn't get lost in him.

But she so wanted to.

"We work," he answered at last. He sat back, taking a drink from his glass.

That's it? She copied him, her hand a little jittery when she picked up her glass. She held it tighter, darting a glance at Carson. Had he noticed?

Her blood still hummed with the energy he'd set to life. The spell might be broken, but his effect on her remained.

"Work is separated from the Boardroom," he stated. "If you can't keep it that way, then this discussion is done."

Wow. She stared at him. His bluntness erased any no-tion that his interest might run deeper. This wouldn't be a romantic adventure, just a sexual one. Could she do that? Separate the two? Especially when she was so attracted to him? "But I signed the contract," she said, just to dig at his sudden withdrawal. "I can't say anything now."

"True," he conceded. "But words aren't the only thing that can damage." He studied her, thoughts flashing over his expression before she could decipher them. She followed his logic, though. No one was a hundred percent safe, ever. Especially in the world of digital everything and instant social media. One accusation or picture could damage his reputation forever.

"Then why do you do it?" She truly wanted to understand. "Why take the risk when you could easily get a woman?"

His smile was slow and almost predatory. "Why did you stay when you could've turned right around and left?"

She sucked in a breath, trapped. A subtle triumph flashed over his expression, and she had her answer. He did it because he enjoyed it. He wanted to and he could.

But could she? Intentionally?

Probably not.

Some values were too ingrained—at least for her.

She rolled her eyes, head shaking as a defeated puff of laughter shot free. "I don't think it's for me," she told him, sliding from her seat. Her leg grazed his again. Everything in her urged her to climb into his lap and let him carry her away.

But would she be damning herself for a few moments of pleasure?

She snaked her coat from the back of the chair, stepping away before she gave in to impulse.

He stayed seated, expression neutral. She couldn't think about what that meant. She grabbed her bag from the floor and turned to the door.

"The offer's open if you change your mind."

She froze, eyes squeezing shut. Her grip tightened around her bag, want demanding she turn around. That she take the risk—just this once.

She gave a single nod before she strode from the restaurant. Risk had its limits, and she had reached hers. At least, that was what she told herself.

Chapter Six

Two weeks later, Avery was still questioning her decision to walk away from Carson's offer. She trudged up the stairs to her condo, mind stuck at the office. And not because of the work waiting for her there.

Her groan echoed up the stairwell, the frustration smacking back at her. "What am I doing?"

She hitched her bag higher and tried to shove her thoughts back. Way back. Like into forgotten territory. Not that it'd worked, yet.

Her door gave a squeak when she shoved it open. Flip and Flop met her at the door, their tiny cat cries announcing her late arrival for their dinner.

"Sorry," she mumbled, bending to pet them both. She'd rescued the pair right after she'd moved into this place. Flip was a black-and-orange calico who liked to turn in circles, while her sister was a soft golden fluff ball who preferred to lounge in the sun. "I thought Karen would be home to feed you."

"Karen is home," her roommate said from the living room. "But you're out of cat food. Didn't you get my text?"

"Crap," Avery mumbled, straightening. She dug her phone from her purse, and sure enough, there was

Karen's text sent two hours ago. The proof of her distraction stared back at her. "I missed it."

"Do you want me to run to the store?" Karen glanced at her as she went to the kitchen, a dirty plate in her hand. The open floor plan optimized the cramped space, while the sliding glass doors to the small deck let in a large amount of natural light.

"No." Avery hung her coat on the hook by the door and kicked her heels off. Her sigh was loud as relief swarmed her pinched toes. "I'll go. Just let me change." Her heels weren't going back on now that they were off.

Karen cocked her hip and crossed her arms over her chest. She flicked her chin at Avery. "Tell you what. I'll run to the market and get the cat food while you change. Then you can take me to the Uphill for a beer."

Another audible sigh gusted out. "Deal. Thank you." She smiled her appreciation and silently thanked the roommate gods for sending Karen her way. They'd met at Avery's first job in San Francisco and had remained friends after they'd both been laid off from the fizzling start-up.

"Excellent." Karen grabbed her purse. "I'll be back in ten." She snatched the twenty Avery held out as she passed. Her short hair was spiked into a wild array of messy-chic that matched her multi-colored leggings and black oversize dress shirt.

"Get the orange bag," Avery called.

"I know." The faint reply reached her before the door slammed shut.

Avery winced. Her neighbor would undoubtedly complain again. Luck and a friend-of-a-friend connection had given her an in to the building that was otherwise occupied by people far more successful and mostly older than herself. The views, deck and location more than made up for the lack of square-footage and any snobbery pointed her way.

They walked into their local bar thirty minutes later, a welcomed blast of stale beer hitting her. She blinked, eyes adjusting to the dim lighting as she scanned for a seat. A baseball game blared from a TV over the bar. Six other flat-screens scattered around the room all had a game of some sort on. The place was crowded for a Wednesday, but then it usually was.

"Over here." Karen grabbed her arm and dragged her to a booth that was just being vacated. The couple had barely stepped away before Karen slid onto the bench and started to stack their dirty dishes at the edge of the table.

Avery thanked the couple and sat across from her roommate. She was used to Karen's boldness by now, but none of it had syphoned off on Avery.

"The usual?" their waiter asked as he stacked the dishes onto his tray. Henry flashed a grin, a dimple pocketing his cheek. The sugary cuteness was offset by the nose ring, three brow piercings and the tattoo sleeve.

"Yes, please," Karen chimed. "And a basket of tater tots."

"Can I get the chopped salad, too?" Avery asked, like he'd say no.

"Got it." He was gone without a note taken.

Karen's gaze lingered on him as he wound his way through the tables to the kitchen. Avery knew what was coming even before the words were out. "Why are the hot ones gay?"

"They're not," she insisted. There was no way Carson was gay. Possibly bi, but he was definitely hot and into women. Or he'd seemed into her.

And she'd walked away.

Karen whipped her head around, brows winging up. "Oh?" She crossed her arms on the table and leaned in expectantly. "Do tell."

The urge to purge every detail sat on Avery's tongue, but she swallowed it back. She'd signed a contract. Could she explain without being specific? "There are a number of men in my office who are hot," she hedged. "And I'm positive they're not all gay."

Karen sat back, mouth twisting in disappointment. She waved off Avery's answer. "I thought you were finally eyeing up a guy."

"I look all the time." She did. It'd just been a while since she'd done more than that. She'd outgrown the one-night-stand thing after arriving in the Bay Area. The random aspect hadn't felt safe when she had no one to worry about her, and it'd lost its appeal after she'd acquired friends.

"You dumped John over a year ago."

"Yup." It was closer to two, but her friend didn't need the additional ammo.

Confusion wrinkled Karen's brow. "Don't you miss sex?"

"I get it all the time," Henry said, winking at Karen. He set their beers on the table, leaning down. "And it's fantastic."

Karen barked out a laugh, hand slapping the table. Avery could only gape as he retreated, an added cockiness to his walk.

"I need to find a man like that," Karen said. "Minus the gay thing."

"Yeah," she mumbled before taking a long hit of her beer. She closed her eyes and simply enjoyed the cold relief as it slid down her throat. Wine did not compare.

Their food was served, the empty plates removed, their third round half-finished before Avery found a segue into the conversation she shouldn't have but wanted anyway. "Are you still seeing Greg?"

"You mean Craig?" Karen was slumped in the booth, a sleepy smile on her face. Avery nodded. "No. He was cute, but the spark wasn't there."

"You say that a lot."

"Because it's true."

Avery couldn't argue that. She'd stopped dating more than one guy for the same reason. And then there was Carson. Her pulse sped up just thinking about him. She'd tried to avoid him at work, but it seemed like he was always around. In Gregory's office, passing in the hallway or in a meeting. She was instantly aware of him when he was near, even if he was on the other side of the lobby. He didn't approach her or act differently, but she knew more now. About him. About what he did. What he wanted.

And that changed how she viewed him. It wasn't negatively either.

"Have you—" Avery stopped. Took a drink.

"Have I what?"

Just put it out there. "Have you ever had group sex?"

Karen's brows shot up, but that was her only reaction. "Hasn't everyone?" She frowned. "At least once?"

"No!" God. Her naïvety was showing more than normal. "I mean…well, I haven't."

"Why not?"

"Why?"

A wicked grin curled over Karen's lips. "Because it's fun." Her sultry tone insinuated how much she'd enjoyed it.

Wow. Avery looked away, shocked but not. Karen was from Southern California and had arrived in San Fran with few inhibitions and an even freer attitude. She'd broadened Avery's horizons on so many things. From gay and women's rights, to personal choice, to racial inequality. Karen didn't hesitate to talk about her sex life, including how often she masturbated, a topic Avery shut down as TMI. But Karen was the one who'd taken Avery to her first sex store and recommended a vibrator—her first.

Now that, she was damn grateful for.

"Hey." Karen kicked her under the table to get her attention. Avery jerked up, scowling as she tucked her legs back. Karen smiled, chin flicking up. "What's going on?"

Nothing. Everything. Possibly…

Avery dropped her head into her hands, a tortured moan grinding out. "I don't know. I'm so confused and have no idea what to do." The alcohol coupled with the burning need to unload set her tongue free. "I want to do it, but I'm scared of what could happen. He said it's safe and I signed a contract and it should be fine, but what if it isn't? What if it disgusts me? What if it's a trick or awful game and I'm the joke? What—"

"Whoa." Karen jerked one of Avery's hands away, forcing her to look up. Her scowl didn't deter Karen. "Wait a minute. Back up and explain."

Avery pulled back, regret already hitting her. She closed her eyes and tried to control her breathing, which was coming way too fast.

"Avery," Karen coaxed. "What's going on? You're worrying me."

Over nothing. This was nothing. She was making it into something when it shouldn't be.

"So umm," Karen started. "You mentioned a contract. Are we talking BDSM here?"

"What?" Her eyes flew open. "No." Right? He hadn't said anything about that. But... "At least I don't think so. No," she quickly corrected, head shaking with her insistence. "It's not that." The woman's hands had been bound, but that wasn't whips and leather and spankings.

Karen studied her, eyes narrowed. "Then what is it?" She leaned in, an evil glint shining. "Do I need to kick someone's ass?"

Avery's laugh had a dry and pathetic edge to it. She took a sip of beer, the lukewarm brew no longer satisfying. She wasn't a thirty-year-old virgin, for Christ's sake, yet she was acting like it. Why?

Because she was afraid.

To try. To explore. Of her own reaction. Of what others would think of her. Of doing something that most would consider wrong—like her parents.

"No," she finally answered. "No ass-kicking needed—except mine, maybe."

"All right." Karen sat back and rubbed her hands together before flexing her fingers. "Tell me why so I can judge how hard I need to hit."

Avery's laughter was lighter this time, her smile genuine. "Thank you." This was exactly what she needed.

"No problem. Now—" Karen motioned with her hand "—spill."

But how much could she say before it was too much? "So..." She took a deep breath, released it, shoving back her embarrassment. "I've been…" Offered? No. "I have an…" Opportunity? Kind of, but that sounded weird. "If you had a chance to…explore—" *yes, that's it* "—a sexual desire in a safe environment, would you?"

Karen frowned. "Is that a trick question?"

Avery shook her head.

"Hell yes." Karen shot her a look that said exactly how silly she thought the question was. "Why wouldn't you?"

It all came back to fear.

Avery shrugged, unable to meet Karen's knowing gaze. This was exactly how she'd expected Karen to respond, which was probably why it'd taken her so long to bring the topic up.

"Okay. Wait a minute." Her friend leaned in, arms crossed on the table, intent. "Is it legal?" Avery nodded. "And you said it was safe, right?" Another nod. "And you're interested in it?" She had to swallow, her nod slower. "So, what's wrong?"

Carson.

He was so damn…everything. She could get lost in him, but she couldn't. He'd laid out that rule with clarity. He wasn't interested in a relationship outside of the Boardroom. "I don't know if I can do 'just sex.'" The admission sounded hokey even to her. "I mean, I've had one-night stands before, but I've never gone sober, premeditated, into one." This was completely different than a drunken oops.

"And that scares you." Karen didn't leave it as a question.

Of course she got that.

"Argh!" Avery dropped her head to the table, tapping her forehead on it over and over. "I don't know." If she could just own her denial, she wouldn't be this confused.

But she couldn't shake the feeling that she was missing out on something really important. An opportunity she'd never get again—even if she ended up hating it.

But she really didn't believe she'd hate it. That was one of the issues.

She *wanted* to watch again. She *wanted* to feel that rush, experience that passion—with Carson.

Her stomach twisted and flipped at that admission. Her nights had been flooded with images of him behind her, touching her, directing her to watch as he told the couple on the table what to do.

God. She swallowed, her legs clamping together to contain the ache that sprang to life. Her hands fisted, desire urging her to give in. Why was she holding out anyway?

Because the values instilled in her since childhood said it was wrong.

And her parents would never know.

But she would.

"Hey." Karen nudged her leg again. Avery didn't move. "What's the risk involved?"

"Minimal. Or so I've been promised," she said to the table. As long as no one else from Faulkner ever found out. Could she demand that?

"So it's your own issues that are stopping you."

When had her roommate gotten so smart? "Yes."

The realization of how foolish she must look with her head on the table finally had Avery sitting up. A gusted sigh broke free when she saw Karen's smirk. Avery attempted to scowl at her but failed, a smile breaking out instead. *Damn her.*

Karen motioned for the tab when Henry walked by, then shifted that knowing look back to her. Speculation mixed with amusement showed so clearly. Avery was tempted to toss her beer on her, but she only shook her head and glowered.

"It seems," Karen started, "that you either need to get over your hang-ups, or accept them." Avery barely held back a "duh." Karen puffed out a laugh. "Apparently, you needed to hear that from someone besides yourself."

Truth. Damn it. She heaved a sigh and gave up on her sulk. It was pointless anyway.

They split the bill and walked back to their place. The air was chilly, the wind whipping up the hill to spread the salty ocean scent. Karen didn't push her further, and Avery was grateful for that. This was her decision to make even if a part of her wished someone would do it for her.

But she was an adult and she'd resent anyone who did decide for her. That was another problem. Choice was a bitch sometimes.

Her thoughts still spun when she settled into bed, and Carson was in the center of them all. Would she ever get him out of her system? Did she want to?

Not really. And that was the biggest problem.

Chapter Seven

Carson ignored the soft tap on his office door, his focus deep within the code string. If he could just figure out how to—

"Excuse me, Carson."

He jerked up at the soft voice, head whipping around to stare at his open doorway. His heart skipped, hope and lust urging it into a quickened beat. Avery Fast stood there. A rust-colored wrap dress hugged her curves before it flared at her waist. Her hair was pulled back into a low side-ponytail that allowed the blond ends to curl against the floral scarf wrapped around her neck.

A slow smile spread that he didn't try to stop. Her posture was tense, lips compressed, but she didn't look away from him. No, her gaze was direct, almost challenging. Why?

"Yes, Avery?" He kept his voice even.

She glanced back before taking a step into his office. "Do you have a moment?"

A whisper of victory snaked in to tease him. He shut it down and swiveled his chair to give her his full attention. "What can I help you with?"

She came closer, her hands clasped before her. Not submissive really but respectful. Or nervous. She glanced at the visitor chairs before his desk. His suit jacket hung from the back of one of them, but the other was free. She looked back to him, her lips compressing.

She'd avoided him since their meeting three weeks back, and he'd respected that space. Had he created a few reasons to see Gregory? Maybe. But he'd remained professional. She didn't deserve to be harassed, especially by him.

"Is your offer still open?" Her words were low and quick.

His eyes narrowed, head tilting as he processed her question. The lust kicked in a second later. She didn't sit nor break eye contact, but that red tinge was spreading over her cheeks to give him his answer. She *was* referring to their private discussion. He'd almost given up on that.

"Of course," he said, his expression neutral. "Have you changed your mind?"

Her expression gave away nothing. Standing before him, strong and sure, she displayed a strength that made him want her more. "Yes." The single word slipped from her lips on a clipped beat.

He slowly stood, slid his hands into his pockets, but stayed where he was. The risk swept in to jack up his adrenaline. Anyone could walk in, but he knew how to play this. Inference and selective wording would gain him what he wanted. And he wanted to show Avery so much. "Are further negotiations needed?"

"A few."

He glanced behind her. Jean's desk was still empty. "Such as?"

Her chest rose and fell with her deep breath, but she didn't fidget. "No one can know who I am."

"Done." Names were shared at the participant's agreement. "What else?"

"Nothing extreme." Her chin nudged up. "Not—" She clamped her lips tight, flashing a small wince. "I don't think I want to…actively participate at first."

At first? The implications behind those two simple words went straight to his dick. Could she really mean that? "So, something close to the original arrangement?"

"Yes." Relief edged the firm declaration. "Would that be possible?"

"Yes." He'd make it so.

"Thank you." She took another deep breath, her knuckles whitening. Her nerves were contained, but they were definitely there. And she was here in spite of them. Her tongue snaked out, a quick flash of pink as it slid over her lip. "So, um…what's the next step?"

The outer office remained quiet, but he kept his voice low anyway. "I'll need the results of a recent STI test. It's a requirement for everyone." The housekeeping details were annoying yet too important to skip.

Her lip quirked up, a smile hovering. "I ah…" She gave a small shrug. "I got one last week. I can send it to you."

His brows flicked up before an appreciative smile overtook his surprise. She'd planned ahead. For some damn reason, that made her even more desirable. It also confirmed that she really did want this.

"Are you free tomorrow night?" His instincts told him to act quickly.

"Oh." She finally glanced away, her gaze going to the view behind him. He was pretty certain she wasn't actually seeing it. She closed her eyes, opened them. Another wave of determination settled over her when she refocused on him. "Yes."

He moved around his desk, checking their privacy yet again. He handed her a note pad and pen. "I'll need a contact number."

She took the offered items. Her brows lifted in question, but she remained silent. She studied him for a long moment. Her eyes were greener today, the rust of her dress drawing out the softer notes. Another knot of relief untightened in his chest when she finally wrote down her number. It surprised him slightly. He'd never been this invested in a new player.

And he'd never recruited one himself. No, he'd left that to the others.

He'd certainly never brought anyone with him.

He took the items back from her, the patter of victory starting. It could still go very wrong—no, he'd make it work. That was what he did. He figured out what people wanted and gave it to them.

And Avery wanted a show. A long, slow, sensual show that titillated more than displayed.

He ripped off her number, folded it, placed it in his pocket. "I'll be in touch." He kept his hand in his pocket to keep from touching her. The flush was high on her cheek, accentuating the bone structure and drawing his eyes to her lips. Full, but not too much with the same pink stain as before. Was that her favorite color? Did she ever change it?

"That's it?" Her brows rose behind her bangs. "I'm just supposed to wait for your directions?"

"Essentially, yes." He paused to see if that sent her scrambling. There was no exception to it, even if she did. "You have to trust me, or there's no point in moving forward." Which had been one of her issues all along.

The moment stretched. The low hum of the outer office drifted in as a reminder that this wasn't an office topic.

"All right." She gave a decisive snap of her head. "I'll trust you." A sardonic smile twisted her lips, before she frowned. "But don't think that trust is blind. Lose it, and it's gone for good."

His laughter rumbled up in a low appreciation. "I won't." He nodded at Jean as she took a seat at her desk. "You have my word." He raised his voice then. "Thank you for bringing the information over. I'll call Gregory if I have any questions."

Her shoulders snapped back, eyes going wide, but she quickly recovered. "Thank you, Dr. Haggert. I'll let him know." She left, pausing to greet his assistant before she moved from his line of sight.

One inhale brought her scent to him, teasing with promises and possibilities. Sex and innocence mixed with a passion he couldn't wait to expose.

He glanced at the clock, took a quick scan of his calendar. He messaged Trevor through the private Boardroom app he'd developed. Need a coffee?

A reply came back before he could sit. When?

Now. At Marco's.

I'll meet you there in ten.

Carson snatched his suit jacket from the back of the chair and slid his private phone into his pocket as he strode from his office. "I'll be back in thirty," he told his assistant, not waiting for her acknowledgment. He had arrangements to put into place.

Others contacted him when they wanted his form of guidance during a Boardroom scene. He'd never set one up for himself.

And he still wasn't. This was for Avery.

The spring warmth hit him when he stepped onto the busy sidewalk. The midday traffic honked its irritation and merged with the construction noise. He dodged slower pedestrians, mostly tourists with large bags and wandering gazes.

Marco's was a smaller coffee house a few blocks from the Financial District with little signage and zero curb appeal. He absorbed the caffeine hit when he stepped inside, his slow inhale igniting his brain cells by simple anticipation. A glance showed a short line and open tables.

He was sitting at a back table, two cups of coffee waiting when Trevor walked in. His presence got an appreciative glance from the lady by the window and a wave from the barista.

"Haggert," Trevor greeted him, unbuttoning his suit jacket as he sat. "Is it time for details?"

It took a moment for Carson to follow his question. He frowned. "Not bad ones, no."

Trevor took a sip of his coffee, an appreciative smile spreading as he sat back. "Teisha took care of me."

Carson glanced at the barista. Her black dreads were pulled back in a messy knot, her movements decisive as she mastered the expresso machine. She looked up and gave him a cheeky wink. Carson puffed out a laugh, nodding. "She did." He had no fucking clue what kind of coffee Trevor drank, but Teisha had known.

Trevor sat forward, forearms braced on the table. "What's up?"

"The issue I've been monitoring has shifted," Carson said without preamble. "She's in. At least, she wants to try it."

A slow nod was Trevor's response. "You'll manage that, right?"

"Yes." He couldn't wait. "I'll be arranging something for tomorrow night." He'd place the details and request on the app when they were done here. It usually didn't take long for people to jump in and a location to be offered. He'd been impressed when he'd discovered how expansive the network was, encompassing people from the entire Bay Area.

Trevor gave away little, his expression often masking his real thoughts. But Carson knew how to read him, and he wasn't getting the disapproval he'd feared. Trevor only shot him that inquisitive look, a smirk appearing. "I'm thinking I shouldn't participate."

"Fuck, no!" Carson winced. "Not unless you're masked and voiceless."

"Shucks," Trevor mocked, snapping his fingers. "That's not my thing."

Carson flipped him off. "Have you figured out who she is?"

"I saw the NDA."

Of course he knew. Carson had scanned the signed contract into the app before delivering it to Ryan, the Boardroom lawyer. But as the Boardroom founder, Trevor kept a tight hold over every aspect of it. Including the app management, which was Carson's responsibility. "Thoughts?" he asked.

"Be careful. And don't fuck up my office." His tone was joking, but he wasn't.

"I always am," Carson said with a cheesy smile. He let it drop, going serious. "I have no intention of fucking up anything."

"Except her." Trevor raised that brow. "Am I right?"

Images seared him of Avery bent over a desk, dress rumpled around her waist, each long thrust sinking him deep within her heat. Hell. He shifted, spread his legs wider and shut down the image before he embarrassed himself.

Trevor laughed, and Carson flipped him off again. *Ass.*

He still had a lot to discuss with Avery, including contact between them, others and exactly how far she wanted to go. Would she welcome his touch, beg for it? Moan beneath his hands, cry out when he played with her clit?

"Keep me informed," Trevor said, standing. "Thanks for the coffee." He nodded to the barista as he left, an air of authority following him out the door.

Carson sat back, the tension easing from his shoulders. He checked the time and opened the Boardroom app. He set up a thin profile for Avery, pausing as he considered her username. Very few interacted on the app with their real names, but after so many years in the group, he personally knew a majority of the people he played with.

He considered his own username, which had been Driver for years, and typed in Shotgun for Avery. The reference was loose, but people would catch on soon enough—if she remained in the group.

And that would all depend on the scene he arranged for her tomorrow night.

Chapter Eight

Avery tried to breathe, but her chest was locked down, frozen like her. She was really doing this.

She glanced at Carson, his face shadowed in the dim light of the car. He'd picked her up with a gracious smile, held her door for her, asked if she was warm enough. All manners and politeness, like this was a date.

A *normal* date.

But could she truly classify it as a date? It wasn't a hookup in the traditional sense. Should she call it a sex date? In Carson's sex den? A smile snuck out at that. It died quickly, though. The knot in her chest cinched tighter.

"It's going to be fine," Carson said. Her eyes went wide and she openly stared at him now. He shot her a quick smile before returning his focus to the road.

"How do you know?" She didn't have the positive outlook that he did.

"Do you trust me?" he countered.

Did she? Truly? "For tonight."

His lips twitched up before he gave her a side-eyed glance. "Just for the night?"

The sexy rumble of his voice sent a wave of desire through her. She'd been a load of anxiety since she'd left his office yesterday. They'd discussed limits and wants on a short phone call, and now she was going through with them. Excitement mixed with fear to set every cell on hyperawareness. "That's all I promised," she countered. He didn't need to have more power over her than that.

His soft laugh was a gentle roll she couldn't decipher. She clasped her hands in her lap and stared straight ahead. They'd headed south out of the city, and she bit her tongue to keep from asking where they were going. She'd learn soon enough.

The rest of the ride passed in silence, and she wasn't sure if that was good or bad. The tension prickled over her skin, warning her. Exciting her. She was over-aware of him, attuned to each movement.

He pulled into a parking lot, the name on the building unfamiliar to her. They were in the heart of Silicon Valley amid a sea of modern three- and four-story glass buildings. She logged the company name if only to keep her from thinking about what was ahead.

Carson met her at her door, and she took his offered hand as she got out. A soft gasp left her before she could stop it. His touch was firm, nothing unusual, but she felt it clear to her toes. "Thank you," she murmured.

That first touch was amazing. She'd thought about it, had wondered how it would feel, his skin on hers. Heat and masculine strength. She looked up at him, still stunned that he was with her. That they were going to watch others have sex.

That she *wanted* all of it.

Her heels tapped out an echoing announcement as Carson guided her to the building, his hand on her lower back. It seared her through her layers of clothing until she swore the imprint would be branded into her skin. She tried to absorb the strength it gave. He was with her. This was legal. They weren't doing anything wrong.

Her chest knotted tighter when she noticed a man waiting on the other side of the door. Tall, short brown hair, thin, dressed in a black suit and royal blue tie.

Not one of the guys from the first night.

He let them in with a nod. "The others are already here."

The others... Of course there were others. That was the entire point, but hearing it...

Carson kept a hand on her back the entire way up the stairs and down a hall. The building contained the standard cubical farm broken up by walls lined with actual offices and meeting rooms. Gray industrial carpeting, wood accents around the door frames. Normal.

"You can use this room," the man said when he stopped by a small conference room. "Meet us in the boardroom when you're ready." He waited for them to enter, then closed the door. The click snapped into her consciousness with a ring of finality.

This was really happening.

"You can leave your purse and coat in here," Carson said, his voice low.

She nodded but didn't move.

"Hey." He stepped in front of her to cut off her blank stare at the table. His silver tie offset his black suit, the white shirt crisp beneath. She blinked, sucked in a breath when he skimmed the back of his fingers up her jaw. Oh... Her eyes closed, head tilting to follow his touch. The soft stroke came across as reassuring and protective. "Only what you want, remember that."

She nodded, eyes still closed. He'd said she could

leave whenever she wanted, no questions asked. His fingers trailed down her neck, tingles flaring. Her stomach clenched, breath trapped.

"Tell me if you want something different," he said, the words reaching her in a fog.

Different? Now or later?

He cupped the side of her neck and nudged her chin up with his thumb. Her eyes fluttered open, lips parting on a silent gasp. There was no mistaking the heat in his eyes, the want that matched her own. "This night is for you."

She found that hard to believe. "I would hope it was for everyone involved." Her voice was weak, the attempt at a joke falling flat.

His lips kicked up in a small smile. "It should be. But my biggest concern is you." His thumb stroked up and down her jaw, distracting her with the gentleness. He dipped closer, hesitated. He searched her, the blue pushing back the gray in his eyes until it was almost gone. "Your pleasure is my first priority."

Her breaths shortened, anticipation prickling over her. There was nothing except him. His lips so close. His touch so warm and possessive.

He eased back, and she almost whimpered. He took her purse, set it on the table, then undid the belt on her coat. Her brain finally kicked in and she slid her arms out of her jacket, accepting his help. The cooler air hit her bare arms and exposed neck. A chill swept down but did nothing to stop the internal heat.

His only request had been for her to wear her hair up, so she'd accommodated it. She'd almost asked "why?" but had opted to let the mystery stand. Her messy top-knot was loose with wisps framing her face that somehow left her feeling even more exposed.

"This is nice," Carson, dragging a finger over the thin strap of her dress. The simple black sheath was loose yet showed her curves, ending high on her thigh. Held up by spaghetti straps, the deep V-neck plunged low to display the rounded curves of her breasts.

"Thank you." She'd bought it during her lunch hour today. It was sexier than anything she'd worn in years. It skimmed over her skin in a silky fall of sex and tease. The expense was worth the confidence it gave her even if she never wore it again.

He took her hand. "Ready?"

She stared at their clasped hands, savored the connection that flowed from it. *Trust him.* She dragged her gaze up his arm until she reached his eyes. "Yes."

He led her to another room, and a sense of disconnection slipped over her. She was a different person here. Her self-imposed limitations were gone. This could be her one chance to really know—experience—what had only been a fantasy before.

Her pulse raced, heat flushing her skin as a shiver raced beneath. Her hand tightened around Carson's, but she kept moving.

They slipped into the boardroom without a word. The only light came from the glow of a street lamp through the windows that made up the back wall. She scanned the space, noting the standard long wood table, office chairs and generic landscape pictures.

She forgot all of that in the next second.

There was a couple at the end, where the chairs had been moved away. They were kissing heavily, her dark hair shifting over her back with each dip of her head.

She sat on the table, her legs wrapped around the man who stood before her.

Avery's breath stalled along with her feet. Carson turned back, and she dragged her gaze to his. His brow quirked up.

Still her choice.

Her choice to run or to take a risk.

She inclined her head. His small smile chased away her hesitation.

He led her away from the couple, to the far corner, opposite the entry. The man who'd let them into the building stepped from the shadows to close and lock the door.

This is happening.

Carson positioned her in front of him. Her legs trembled, chest so tight each breath was a struggle. His presence soaked down her back to encircle her in safety.

The couple still kissed. Low moans mixed with the soft smacks. Her red bra and thong were stark against her skin, the line of her back graceful.

"Lay her down."

Avery flinched. Carson's voice was commanding if quiet, the husky rumble saturated in sex and authority. Goose bumps broke out on her skin, desire bursting beneath.

"Shhh," he soothed into her ear. He smoothed a hand down her arm, his breath warming her neck. "I've got you."

She had no idea what he meant, but she nodded anyway. *Trust him.* She leaned back, needing him closer. His touch. His confidence. The contact brought a sigh to her lips. He groaned his approval, the sound just for her.

The woman laid down, her eyes closing, back arching. The memory of the other woman flashed in, but they weren't the same. Not the woman or the moment.

This was so much more.

The sexual energy buzzed in the room. It sensitized her skin—or maybe that was Carson's doing. He ran his palms down her sides, back up. His touch was light, almost teasing as it skimmed over her ribs.

"Make her moan," Carson said. "Both of you."

The woman gasped before she bit her lip. Her expression was lust-filled and wanting. The two men spread her legs, caressing her thighs, dragging their fingers up and around her pussy. She whimpered, brows drawing down. They removed her bra, both men stopping to fondle her nipples until they were hard points.

Avery's breath quickened, her heart beating faster. Carson grazed his lips up the side of her neck, leaving a warm trail behind. She inhaled, tilting her head to give him room. A "yes" was on her lips, but she shut them before it came out. She didn't want to break the spell.

Her eyelids dropped lower, thoughts caught between the erotic show before her and the one happening to her. One man was on each side of the woman. They worked in tandem, kissing down her neck to her breasts. Their movements were in sync but neither spoke. They each trailed a hand down a leg before they clamped their mouths over her nipples.

She cried out, back arching, and Avery barely stopped herself from doing the same thing as phantom twinges pierced her own nipples.

"It's okay," Carson whispered. He slid a hand up her ribs, rubbing under the curve of her breast. "You can react."

She was definitely reacting. Her body was on fire from head to toe and not from embarrassment. He was tempting her beyond anything she'd imagined. It was like he was wrapped around her, absorbing everything. Her nipples ached for his touch, to be caressed and sucked like the woman's.

She slid her hands back until she gripped his thighs, desperate for something to hold on to. His low hum buzzed over her neck before he nuzzled the juncture of her shoulder and neck. She wanted to touch him and be touched everywhere.

Carson lifted his head, teeth scraping her shoulder before he straightened. "Put her in a chair."

The threesome moved almost immediately. The lean guy rolled a chair to the end of the table and then turned it to face them. The other guy helped the woman off the table. He touched her the entire time, slow caresses, teasing grazes over her skin. She drew the bigger guy into a long kiss as he lowered her into the chair. Were they a couple? The lean guy hadn't kissed her on the lips. Was that one of their rules?

"May I?" Carson asked by her ear. He pressed on the underside of her breast to indicate what he meant. She nodded, warmed that he'd asked even though she'd approved it when they'd talked. He could touch her anywhere, but no one else could.

"Please," she whispered when he only traced the underside of her breast. Her nipples puckered tighter, her focus going to his touch. Her back arched, longing pushing her breast out in a silent plea. She needed his hands there.

"Are you enjoying this?" he asked as his fingers grazed her nipples. She gasped, a wave of hunger racing to her pussy. Her legs dipped. The hard ridge of his erection rode the curve of her ass in a delicious torment.

"Yes," she breathed, almost forgetting there were other people in the room. Yet they were in her line of sight, just twenty feet away.

The bigger guy kneeled before the woman and slid her panties off. Her breasts rose and fell with each deep breath, and Avery was fascinated by them. Perfectly round and large, they had to be fake. Yet they appeared soft, and she wondered if they felt that way. Her fingers curled on Carson's legs as she imagined exploring the swells of flesh.

His muscles flexed, breath hitching. He rocked his hips, and her focus jerked back to his hard dick riding the crack of her ass. She rocked with him until he pressed down on her hips, stopping her.

She whimpered in protest, but he skimmed his other hand up to finally cup her breast. A relieved moan purred up her throat to flow between her parted lips. He held the weight in his palm, fingers coming together to pinch her nipple. Prickles of sensation spread outward. She was so damn happy she'd opted to go braless. He switched to her other breast and brought that nipple to a peak with only a few tweaks.

It was so good. All of it. Wild and free. Crazy. She wanted to feel his hands on her skin and in that moment, she didn't care who saw her.

"Please," she begged, back arching again to bring his hand closer. Her head fell back, eyes closing as she got lost in the humming sensation overtaking her entire body. Her pussy ached for attention. That manly woody scent of his filled her senses, and she turned her head to get more. Her lips brushed his jaw, the light stubble tickling over them in the most sensual way. She snaked her tongue out a second later to experience the same sensation.

His curse was soft, damning but not at her. Her smile curled against his jaw as her own power burned to life.

"Lick her," Carson said.

The command shot through Avery's haze and she jerked up, eyes wide. Fascination held her riveted as the guy spread the woman's legs, rested each foot on the edge of the table behind him, then dipped his head.

Avery's pussy clenched in anticipation of the hot lick that wasn't for her. Her abdomen contracted, and Carson's chuckle vibrated near her ear. He caressed her stomach, the heat sinking deep into her core. He plucked her nipple, the fingers on his other hand grazing the top of her mound as the guy's head rose in one long swipe upward between the woman's legs. The details of his actions were blocked from Avery's sight, but the woman's expression said everything.

Avery's soft whine was overshadowed by the woman's louder cry. Her head arched back, and the lean guy stepped behind her. He caressed her breasts, then pulled on her nipples as his partner took another long lick of her pussy.

Oh God. Avery couldn't focus on anything now. She was a mass of sensation, want and building explosion. Her pussy pulsed with the need to be filled. Her wetness dampened her panties to a state that should've embarrassed her, yet she couldn't care. She craved to be filled. Her clit begged for attention. Just a touch. A stroke.

Anything.

The woman squirmed, a hand going to the bigger

man's head to hold it between her legs. Her other hand gripped the leaner man's arm, her gaze locked on his as he stood over her.

"Are you wet?" Carson asked, his whispered words barely breaching Avery's fog. They drifted into her awareness and she nodded. Her "yes" slipped out on a long sigh that sounded more like a moan.

She grabbed his hand, the one that still teased her mound, and urged it lower. He resisted, another low rumble of amusement grazing her neck.

"Do you want something?"

She turned her head toward him, frustration boiling. She nipped at his chin only to hear that damn chuckle again. He increased the pressure on her nipple, twisting it. A bite of pain choked her as it burst through her chest. She whimpered, legs trembling. Her mind protested, head shaking. Then the pain changed. Morphed.

The burning heat reached her core. "Touch me," she begged, squirming in his hold. Her legs spread in invitation. "Please." She'd lost every ounce of shame. This was decadent. Erotic beyond anything she could've imagined.

Her reserved shell was shattered beneath the freedom Carson released.

His hand slid lower. Her breath stopped.

"Don't come."

The order could've been directed at her or the other woman, but her ability to parse it out was lost when he found her clit. "Oh my God." Her pelvis tipped forward, knees bending. She needed more. Her orgasm coiled in a hot bundle just below his finger.

"Watch them." His hard insistence was punctuated by a sharp tug on her other nipple.

Her eyes snapped open, mouth parting to suck in air.

The men had switched places. When? The leaner guy was now between her legs, face buried in her crotch, head moving up and down in a quick rhythm.

"Fuck." The curse ghosted from her lips.

"You have no idea how much I want to do that," Carson murmured, his tone even lower, sexier. Damning. He pressed her to him, the line of his erection rocking against her as both evidence and torment.

Yes. The demand screamed through her mind but not out of her lips. She was almost desperate enough to fuck him here. Almost, but...

He stroked a finger over her clit, a slow rub that sent waves of need through her. But it wasn't enough. The heat of his touch simmered through the material of her clothing to tease her with promise before he slid his hand beneath her dress. The fluttering caress seared her thigh where he trailed his fingers upward, like the men had done to the woman. A light tease that made Avery squirm, her leg rotating outward in hope, invitation, desperation.

The woman in the chair was panting heavily now, her head swiveling. The bigger guy stood to the side and he ran his fingers down her neck before he cupped her chin, forcing it still. The woman's eyes flew open to land directly on Avery.

In that exact moment, Carson shoved his fingers beneath her panties to stroke his fingers through her heat.

Avery's cry came out as a hoarse whimper that sounded foreign to her own ears. Hunger shot from her clenched pussy to her aching breasts. She leaned fully on Carson, totally incapable of supporting herself in the rush of overwhelming stimulants.

The woman stared at her, and Avery couldn't look away. The woman's eyelids were heavy, lips parted, passion etched in each little gasp before a long groan bled out.

Carson penetrated Avery on a perfectly timed thrust of two fingers to yank an echoing groan from her. *Oh, God.* She fumbled for something to hold her steady when her world was detonating around her. This was too much and not enough. She clung to Carson's hips and silently begged for more.

The thickness of his fingers stretched her, the wet slick of her own arousal allowing each stroke to slide in and out of her with ease. Embarrassment was nowhere to be found, not even when she noticed the bigger guy watching her, appreciation clear on his rugged features.

A glorious wickedness raced free, and she slowly traced her tongue over her lips in a blatant return of lust. Carson chuckled near her ear. The vibration snaked through his chest to sizzle down her spine.

"That's it," he encouraged. Avery rocked her hips, impatience urging her to move faster. Get more. Find that crest that lingered so close. "Show me how wild you can be. How sexy. Hot."

He pulled his fingers out of her. A whimper of protest leaked from her lips before he flicked a wet digit over her clit. Her back bowed, heat bursting to race outward. Her eyes fell closed as she got lost in the erotic pleasure running rampant through her system. Gasps, groans, slurps and kisses all blended together to create a hedonistic soundtrack.

She turned her head to Carson, her voice weaker than her legs. "Please," she begged. She was so ready to come.

So close. He rubbed her clit, each small circle nudging her to the edge but not over. "I need to come."

She did. Truly. She squirmed in his arms, mindless with sexual energy, uncaring of everything except reaching the end.

"Come," he demanded. The command shot through the tension to shatter everything. He rubbed harder, faster. "Watch her."

Avery's eyes sprang open on the order, hazy recognition flowing into the last of her awareness. The woman stared back with the same passion-crazed look that engulfed Avery.

Two fingers thrust in hard, jarring her. A grunt burst out. The world narrowed, darkness tunneling her sight to the other woman.

Pressure returned to her clit, but his fingers still penetrated her in long strokes. Carson nipped up her neck, little bites that stung and retreated before the next one. His hot breath snaked down her ear, trembled over her jaw. His beard stubble grazed the sensitive skin in another tease.

The woman's toes were curled tight, her calve muscles straining. She gripped the arms of the chair, hips thrusting wildly. The bigger guy kissed up her neck in an echo of Carson. The shared experience heightened Avery's own in a dizzying swarm of feelings. Too many. Not enough.

"Come for me," Carson said, each word a clear staccato note that ignited everything.

Her orgasm burst over her in a flash of need, release, hunger and pleasure like she'd never experienced before. She came. For him. For the woman writhing in her chair, her cries meshing with Avery's. For her own wild freedom.

She closed her eyes, lights bursting behind her eyelids as she lost herself to the ecstasy.

Chapter Nine

Carson gathered Avery close as she rode his fingers, hips rocking, her walls clamping down in sharp spasms. She was beyond beautiful. Her head thrown back, lips parted in lost invitation he barely resisted.

He pushed her too, rubbing her clit until he felt the last hard contraction of her muscles. Her gasping breaths stalled before she went lax. He eased up, caught her weight as she sagged in his arms. He slid his fingers from her, a twinge of regret pinching his chest for what he longed to finish but couldn't here.

His dick ached with the need to sink into her heat, to make her scream again. She'd responded to the scene with a wild abandon he hadn't been prepared for. Not fully, at least. Gone was the shy hesitation. In its place was a lush sensuality that was absolutely stunning on Avery. Pure in its newfound freedom.

He ran his teeth up her neck. The urge to suck, bite and leave a mark scraped at his control. He scooped Avery up. Her eyes flew open on a shocked gasp as her arms came around his neck. Wide, deep blue eyes still dilated with passion stared up at him.

He strode forward without answering her unasked

question. Jacob met him at the door, swung it open. His smirk was knowing.

"You can let yourself out when you're ready," Jacob said. He glanced back at the table. "We'll be a while."

Carson nodded and left. He didn't look back or give another thought to what the three of them would do. Avery stayed silent in the short walk to the smaller conference room. The front of her dress was skewed to display the rounded flesh of a breast and the darker edge of her areola.

It tempted him, just like her doe-eyed look that screamed of innocence even though she'd just shattered every concept of that.

The warm drizzle of his precome stuck to his abdomen and his balls ached for the release he'd barely withheld. His temper simmered on a low burn directly connected to his frustration. She'd done nothing wrong. No, on the contrary, she'd been exactly right.

"Carson?" Her brows pulled together in a slight frown, doubt sucking the afterglow from her expression.

He stepped into the smaller room, breaths coming too quickly despite his attempt to slow them. He lowered her feet to the floor, holding her close to ensure she didn't fall. Right. That was exactly why he couldn't loosen his hold when she tried to step back.

The questions were back in her eyes, her pupils smaller now. A flush held on her cheeks, the sultry woman from the boardroom still visible.

He shook his head, tried to deny the recklessness urging him to act. She wet her lips, and his focus went to the pink tip before it slid back inside. Blood roared in his ears, and he leaned down, mesmerized. His lips were on hers before he could stop himself.

Soft. Warm.

Her short inhalation left an opening he plunged into without thought. He cupped the back of her head and deepened the kiss with one stroke of his tongue. His groan rumbled up his throat as he plundered her mouth. His frustration poured out in a wild battle of tongues, nips and gasps. He tumbled into the haze with a blindness he rarely allowed.

The heavier scent of her arousal merged with her lighter perfume to form a sexy musk he couldn't get enough of. Like her heavenly taste and wild abandon.

She clutched the back of his neck, drawing him in as he did the same. He wanted closer to her. His erection raged its desire in a throbbing ache he was so close to easing. Yet…

He ripped his mouth from hers, gasping breaths rushing through the silence. "Fuck." He squeezed his eyes closed, held her tight when she started to protest. "Don't," he snapped, his tone sharp with everything he was holding back.

He pressed his cheek to her head and drew in long, slow breaths. She remained still, her breaths slowing with his until the quiet hush of the office returned. It was another long moment before he eased away. She blinked up at him, that frown line back between her brows.

His low snicker was totally inappropriate. "I'm not laughing at you," he quickly said when her retort previewed across her face. "Honestly." He stroked his thumb down her jaw, thoughts scrambled.

He didn't get involved. He stayed on the peripherals, out of the conflicts. And Avery was a huge conflict. *His* conflict.

"What'd you think?" he asked, thrusting the focus onto her. "About the scene?"

Her brows dipped. A corner of her mouth turned up. "I thought that was kind of obvious."

His balls drew up. *Fucking...* He forcibly shoved back the lust that refused to be denied. He managed a weak smile, too aware of how much she'd enjoyed it—physically. "Tell me what you liked." He kept his voice even while trying to be encouraging. He really did want to know what, exactly, had turned her on—so he could do it again.

She glanced down, but he immediately forced her chin up until she looked him in the eye. He wouldn't let her hide. Not after she'd let herself go so beautifully.

"Did the scene make you hot?" he prompted. "Was it too tame?"

She nodded, then shook her head, eyes widening slightly. Her nostrils flared on her inhale, but she didn't pull away. He stroked a hand up and down the small of her back in calming passes. The silky softness of her dress skimmed over her skin in a mocking reminder of what he couldn't touch.

She swallowed, throat working hard. "It was...hotter than I'd expected. Different." She glanced away, but that determination flashed when she brought her gaze back to him. "I liked all of it. The watching. You touching me. The sounds. The scents. Your commands. The entire experience was..." She searched him, eyes darkening again. "Amazing."

She drew his head down, and he let her. Her lips brushed his, the tentative sweetness so her yet not. He knew better now, and that knowledge was scored into his memory. He deepened the kiss in one controlling swipe that ripped a moan from her and sent his frustration to warning levels.

He jerked back, cursing softly. He pressed a kiss to her temple, his breaths ragged once again. "We need to go," he said, regret heavy.

"Why?" The confusion was so clear in her breathy question.

He stepped away and reached for her coat. "Because I'm going to fuck you over this table if we don't leave."

Her brows sprang up, mouth forming a silent O. His smile was tight as he held her coat out for her to slip into.

She slid her arms into the sleeves before she turned her head back to glance at him over her shoulder. "You could." Her gaze slid to the table, then back to him.

The image of her splayed on the light wood, dress rumpled under her arms, everything bared to him, almost did him in. Her musky scent still lingered on his fingers, and he caught a hit of it with his deep inhalation. Fuck, how he wanted to taste every damn inch of her.

He dropped his hands from her shoulders, grabbed her purse from the table. "The scene is over, Avery." He turned in the doorway and waited for her, hand extended. "It's time to go."

Her jaw dropped before she snapped her mouth shut. Her eyes narrowed, chin rising. He tensed, but she stayed silent as she swept by him. Her strides were brisk, spine straight through her march from the building.

The cooler night air was a welcome refresher when they stepped outside. Avery didn't pause in her hurry to escape him. Not until they reached his car. She spun around so quickly he almost ran her down. He froze, prepared anew for her attack.

"I don't understand," she bit out. Anger radiated from

her. No. That was hurt camouflaged by anger. She shook her head, arms crossed. "How can you just cut it off like that?" She sliced a hand through the air.

He almost winced at the unintentional implication. The shadows softened her features despite the hardness that'd slammed over them. She was wild again. The fire that'd blazed so clearly in the boardroom reappeared to call him on his dickish behavior.

His smile grew in small increments. He raised his hand slowly, giving her plenty of time to duck away. She remained still as he brushed her bangs away from her eyes. "There are rules," he explained. So many rules, both defined by others and himself. "The Boardroom works because they're followed. Our arrangement was limited to there." A flash of hurt blazed in her eyes before she smothered it. Her lips compressed, her nod one short bob. "This isn't more." The reminder was for her, or so he told himself. "I loved every second of what we did," he added to reassure her.

Her frown deepened, doubt clear. She didn't believe him.

He grabbed her hand and pressed her palm to his erection. A gasp accompanied her frown, but he held her hand there when she tried to jerk it back. His frustration buzzed too close to anger with no clear definition of what or who he was mad at.

"This is what you do to me." He forced her palm down the length of his boner before he let it go. Her hand lingered for a moment, one breath too long, before she pulled it back. "Don't doubt my intentions nor my words." He stepped around her to open the car door, his temper plucking at his control. It happened so rarely, he wasn't prepared for it now.

And that irritated him even more.

They rode back to her place in silence, the night passing on a glare of headlights that eventually shifted to streetlights. She remained tense beside him, but he resisted the urge to reach out to her.

He pulled into the small driveway beside her building, stopping once he cleared the street. He shifted into Park, flicked the headlights off, then turned to her. She stared straight ahead, hands clasped in her lap. She didn't move to get out, so he waited. He could give her that much.

"Can we do it again?" she asked, her voice so soft he almost missed it.

Shock nailed him. His hand tightened on the steering wheel. His pulse kicked up. His mind screamed, "fuck yes."

"You'd like to?" he asked instead, voice purposefully level.

Her eyes closed. The faint glow from the street and over the building doorway provided enough light to catch her hesitation before he heard a soft "yes."

Indecision warred. The battle of desire and logic wrestled for victory. "This isn't a relationship," he clarified. Again.

She whipped her head around, her glare cutting through him. "Trust me. I get that."

He raised a brow, a deliberate action to hide his own cutting retort. Damn, he almost wanted to fight with her. He loved the fire when she let it show as much as the quiet restraint. There was so much more to her to discover...

"And you still want to do another scene?" he asked. She nodded and he clarified, "With me?" Another nod, this one very careful and slow. The darkness hid so much of her expression, but he felt the challenge, caught the same defiance she'd shown him the first time she'd asked for this.

He shifted his leg to give his overactive dick more space as he hardened again. That body part was on board with doing everything with her. But he'd never allowed that head to do his thinking for him. Not even when he'd been a horny teenager. He savored the feeling, though. That building want and smoldering desire that curled in his gut and eased through his system.

"Would you like something different next time?" His voice had dropped, bringing the intimacy with it. The small space seemed to shrink, the tension circling them.

She sucked in a breath, eyes closing for a moment. Her hands were fisted on her lap, but they slowly relaxed as she lifted her eyelids. "I don't know what else there is," she finally admitted. "I have to trust you on that."

Power surged through his chest and spread downward to mix with the desire he was finding hard to control. She'd given her trust to him completely tonight, and he treasured the gift for how special it was. He let the corner of his mouth curl up. "So you'll trust me past tonight?"

Her shrug was small. "You haven't lost it, yet."

The ending implied that he would at some point. Would he? Maybe—if he forgot his rules. "Next Saturday?" he asked. He should say no. He should but couldn't.

She looked away, brows dipping. "Yes. That should work."

A week. He had an entire week to wait before he could touch her again, make her come and fall apart in his arms. Could he handle that? Control himself? "I'll make the arrangements." His tone was brisk and he kicked himself when she flinched. Damn it. He didn't want to hurt her.

He cupped her jaw and turned her head toward him. Again, she didn't resist, and he was so tempted to follow her upstairs and show her everything he thought of doing to—with—her.

"You're beautiful, Avery." In so many ways. "But we work together. This can't get awkward."

Her sigh was low but heavy. "I know. It won't."

Could he trust her on that? He had to, unless he was willing to walk away.

He gave in and pressed a kiss to her lips. He lingered there, her lips soft on his, want crashing against reality to ignite his frustration once again. It churned in his gut and beat at his mind. He was playing with fire, and a part of him hoped to get burned.

"I'll pick you up at nine on Saturday," he said when he eased back, his thumb making one last swipe over her cheek before he lowered his hand.

Her "okay" was soft, a resignation to it. His eyes narrowed, but she shoved the door open and was out of the car before he could stop her.

He was out his side and around the front of the car in the next moment. "Hey," he said when he reached her side, a hand going to her back. "I can walk you to the door."

"And I can walk there by myself," she shot back. "I've done it plenty of times before."

He grinned. "I'm sure you have." He stayed at her side until they reached the building entrance. "But my mother would kick my ass if I didn't ensure that my date was safely home."

She turned to him, brow raised. "I thought this wasn't a date."

She had him. His smile grew, spreading within him to set off another round of warning bells. "Touché."

Her lips pursed, a bemused gleam shining as she shook her head. "Goodnight, Carson." The formality felt false yet somehow appropriate. "I had an interesting evening." She stuck out her hand. "I look forward to our next one."

Damn. She's... He couldn't finish that thought, not if he wanted to walk away. He gave a low laugh, accepting her offered handshake. His voice was formal like hers when he responded. "Goodnight, Avery." He brought her hand to his lips to kiss the back of her fingers. "Until next time."

Her shoulders shook, but her laugh was silent. He let her fingers slip free of his grip and stood back while she typed a code into the access box by the door. The latches clicked, and she swung the door open. She gave him one last smile over her shoulder before ducking into the building.

The night was suddenly loud when the door clicked shut. A car passed on the road, a cable car bell clanged in the distance. He jerked around and strode to his car.

He'd give Avery every sexual experience she desired. Hell, he longed to open her boundaries and see her embrace every aspect of her sexuality. But that was all he could have.

All he *should* have.

All he *would* have—if he stuck to his rules.

Chapter Ten

Avery walked into the meeting behind Gregory and took a seat along the back wall with the other assistants. The quarterly meeting of the West Coast managing directors was usually a long and tedious event for those stuck taking notes. She never looked forward to them, and this one even less so.

She glanced down the boardroom table, a smile breaking free. There was no way she'd ever look at that object in the same way again. Her mind went to the last boardroom she'd been in, just five days ago. She scanned the men and women mingling around the room, some standing, others already seated. How many of them were a part of Carson's secret club? Did she really want to know?

No. She shook her head. Definitely not. But would she if she kept going back?

"What?" Maurine asked.

Avery jerked her thoughts back, smile growing. "Nothing." She shrugged when Maurine shot her a dubious look. "Just thinking about something."

The other woman gave a low humph and turned away. Avery barely resisted the juvenile urge to stick her tongue out at her. There was no way she'd tell the snooty woman what she'd been thinking, even if it'd been PG.

Closing in on fifty and staunchly protective of both the company and the West Coast president, Maurine was the hawk who oversaw the executive assistants. Or at least she acted that way. Avery really didn't know if that was part of Maurine's job description, but *everyone* deferred to her. In many ways, she ran the office from her perch outside Trevor James's door.

Did Maurine know about the evening activities that took place in this very room? Avery gave the woman a once-over. The black pencil skirt ended below her knees, her white blouse a simple button-down with no adornments. Her brown hair was always pulled back in a tight bun at her nape, and she wore minimal makeup—if any. With her hands folded on her lap, ankles crossed and tucked under the seat, Maurine could've been a poster model for the proper fifties secretary.

Nope. Maurine would most definitely not be in on the office sexcapades. Would she?

The air seemed to suck from the room when Carson strode in. He glanced around, his gaze skimming over Avery without acknowledgment. Her held breath released when he set a stack of folders before an empty chair at the table.

Instantly hot, Avery sat back and tried to calm her erratic heartbeat. This was nuts. Jean hurried in a moment later, set another folder on the ones Carson had put down, then sat in the open seat on Avery's other side.

"Morning," Jean said. She glanced past Avery and nodded.

"Morning," Avery replied.

"Good morning, Jean," Maurine said, leaning around Avery. "Did you get the technical specs printed?"

Jean's smile faltered just a bit before she forced it wide. "Of course."

"Good."

Maurine turned back to the front of the room, and Jean made a very non-motherly face at the back of Maurine's head.

Avery muffled a laugh, grinning. Jean shot her a wink before opening her laptop. The meeting was starting, and they had jobs to do.

Her gaze landed on Carson as he took his seat. His brows were drawn slightly together, his smile pleasant if not warm. His business front wasn't that different from what she'd experienced, yet she'd seen the cracks in his cool shell.

And she wanted to see beneath them.

There was more there. She'd felt it when he'd kissed her so gently. He could be a complete dick, but then, who couldn't? The hard part was finding a man who didn't feel threatened when he exposed his cracks.

She smiled at that and opened her own laptop. She could be just as professional as him. They'd had...not intercourse but sex. And they were going to again—hopefully. Her stomach flipped as her pussy clenched. Maybe intercourse?

She snuck another look at Carson. His focus was on Trevor, who stood at the head of the table, his authoritative presence ruling the room. Carson exuded a different power than Trevor. A quieter one that appealed to Avery more.

Did Trevor know about the sexcapades? Her eyes narrowed, speculation running in tangents from how could he not to what if he did. Would Trevor know about her then? No! God, that would be too embarrassing. Her cheeks grew hot just thinking of it.

She wasn't that woman, the one she'd been in the other boardroom. Not normally. She was willing—no, she wanted to be that woman again. But she definitely wasn't ready for anyone to know about it.

Maurine jabbed her elbow into Avery's side. Avery whipped her head around, glare in place. Maurine scowled, eyes motioning to Avery's computer. Avery glanced down, another wave of heat rushing up her neck. She'd not taken a single note. In fact, she had no clue what Trevor had said.

She refocused on the meeting and schooled herself to avoid looking at Carson. Fortunately—at least for today—the quarterly reports were a big topic that held her focus as they picked apart the data.

The meeting broke before lunch, and Avery hurried from the room as soon as it wrapped. She was at her desk, computer plugged back in when she took a moment to check her phone. There was one missed text— from Carson. Are your rules the same?

Her grin formed instantly. She sat back and opened the texting app, anticipation and worry rushing in. She snuck a glance down the hallway, like she was hiding something. She was but wasn't. Gregory didn't care if she checked her phone.

She contemplated Carson's question. Were her rules the same? Would she want him to fuck her in the room, in front of others? Her stomach did another flip thinking about it. Yes and no. It would depend, really. She didn't want to be laid out as the main show like the other woman had been. But in the corner, as the sideshow, maybe?

If he kept it respectful. And she couldn't explain what that meant. She just didn't want to feel cheap when it was over.

She'd experienced that a few times in college. The private acts had always been consensual, but the guy's actions during and afterward had left her chilled with a sense of being used.

Are yours? she typed back. He'd never clarified anything beyond their interaction being strictly limited to the scene. *"This is not a relationship."* She snorted, remembering his words. He'd assumed, of course, that she'd wanted one.

It irked her that he'd been right.

But this was good. Better actually.

She was an independent, modern woman. And commitment-free sex was completely acceptable.

She jumped when her phone vibrated. A secret smirk snuck out. Mine stand.

She bit her lip, the detachment offered through texting emboldening her. Do you ever physically participate?

You know I do.

Well he had, technically. She clarified. As the main show?

No.

Why?

Not my thing.

What is your thing?

Have you forgotten already?

No. Not even slightly. She toyed with another response, the office slipping away. Would you go farther?

Explain.

He was going to make her say it. Or type it. She
scowled at her phone. Could he interpret that? Would
you fuck me in the room? There. She tapped the Send
with force, a bit of satisfaction singing through her.

No.

Her jaw dropped. Why not? Was she that objection-
able? Don't you fuck? she added just to push.

Yes, I fuck. But I don't share that.

Why? Now she was really curious.

Again. Not my thing.

Did that mean they'd never do it? Disappointment
settled in swift and hard. Ouch. She set her phone aside,
unsure what she was feeling. A weight pressed on her
chest. Her stomach churned on the last piece of information. She should be relieved, right? She didn't have
to worry about being pushed that far.

But she'd wanted that. To be pushed. To be lost to the
moment. To feel him thrusting into her.

She squeezed her eyes shut along with her legs. The
desire sprang up swift and hot from just thinking about it.

"Avery."

Her eyes flew open, spine snapping straight. "Gregory." She forced a smile, that damn heat spreading over her chest and up her neck.

He frowned. "Is something wrong?"

"No," she quickly assured him, head shaking. "I'm fine."

He eyed her skeptically but didn't push. "I'll need those report notes. AP should be sending their updated numbers this afternoon. Can you roll them in and run a new report when you get them?"

"Will do." She held her breath until he entered his office and shut the door behind him. She sagged forward, relief forcing a giddy laugh to squeak out.

She picked up her phone and sent one more text. Would you fuck me outside of the room? Could she be so bold? Her thumb hovered over the send button, caution warring with irritation. Was she being a pushy bitch? Did it matter?

They weren't a couple. This wasn't a relationship.

He'd told her to ask for what she wanted.

She sent the text with one sharp stab at her screen. And then promptly stuffed her phone into her purse and closed her desk drawer. She strode to the bathroom, determined to forget about the text until after work.

Like that wasn't five long hours away. Could she hold out?

Yes.

She shoved through the bathroom door, the force smacking her palms. Just sex. Not intercourse, but out-of-the-norm sex. Still hot, amazing and so much more than she'd probably have a chance to try again.

No matter how he responded to her question, she'd still make another trip to the Boardroom with him. That reality irritated her, but she couldn't deny the giddy rush that raced through her.

* * *

Would you fuck me outside of the room?

Carson stared at the text. His fingers tingled with the memory of her clenching down on them when she came. The thought of fucking her hadn't left his mind since he'd watched her reaction the first time she'd walked into the boardroom.

Damn. He set his phone down and spun around to stare out the window. The real question wasn't *would* he fuck her, but *will* he. The answer to the first was "hell yes." He'd fuck her just about anywhere if the circumstances were different.

And that was an excuse.

He scrubbed his face, indecision scrambling his normal calm. The truth was he wasn't sure if fucking her once would be enough. Her unfolding passion had been so incredible to watch. And she wanted to explore more.

There was no way in hell he'd say no to being a part of that.

His phone buzzed with another text, and he swung his chair around, dread mixing with anticipation. Had she taken his silence as a no?

That'd be good, right?

His snort shot out sharp and quick when he saw the text from Trevor. Do I need the details yet?

No. Carson left it at that. No one needed the details. A twinge pinched his chest, and it took him a moment to recognize it for what it was: jealousy. He frowned. Where'd that come from? There was no room for jealousy in the Boardroom.

What was his problem? He frequently fucked women. Not during a scene, but after. There were a number of women in the Boardroom whom he played with during a scene, much like he'd done with Avery, and fucked after or hooked up with randomly. All of them had the same view on sex as him. The physical release was their only goal.

And now there was Avery. A gorgeous, smart woman who knew about his sexual desires and wanted more. But for how long? When would it be too much for her? How long would it take before she expected him to give up the Boardroom?

He'd seen it happen with too many men and women who drifted away from the Boardroom once they'd settled down with a single person. Yes, there were couples in the Boardroom, but it wasn't the norm.

And he was getting ahead of himself—way ahead.

Would she seek out another guy to help her explore if he walked away? The thought of someone else showing her how sensual voyeurism could be turned that twinge of jealousy into an angry green monster. What if the guy forced her to do things she didn't want? Would he fuck her in the room? Would he treat her with respect?

Would he cherish every sigh and moan? Each gasp and sweet plea for more?

"Fuck."

He snatched up his phone and texted one word to Avery. Yes.

Chapter Eleven

The building was downtown this time. A high-rise that soared into the night just blocks from the Faulkner offices. Avery stared at the elevator numbers as they rose to the fortieth floor. She took a long, slow breath that did nothing to quiet her racing pulse. She was doing this again.

She glanced at Carson. He'd been the perfect gentleman since he'd picked her up. Courteous. Polite. His hand rested on the small of her back, tempting her to step closer to him.

And she couldn't read anything into it.

He looked down at her, that half smile of his appearing. His eyes were almost a smoky blue that matched the color of his tie. "You okay?" His voice rumbled through the small space. That sexy purr deepened the more intimate he became. Had his voice always been like that?

She gave him a small smile back. "Yes. Just nervous."

He rubbed her back in soothing circles. "The same rules apply. We can leave whenever you want."

She nodded. The bell dinged their arrival, the doors sliding open on the top floor. A tall man in a gray suit wearing black-framed glasses that matched his hair stood behind the large glass doors. Cummings, Lang & Burns was etched into the glass in large script. Avery had to work to keep her shock from showing. Was she really going to watch sex at one of the most prestigious law firms in the city?

Maybe have sex?

She'd been thinking about that since she'd found Carson's one-word response to her text. *Yes.* Yes, he'd fuck her outside of the Boardroom. Would he tonight?

The other man let them in and then stepped into the lobby.

Carson frowned. "You're not staying?"

The guy shook his head. "Not tonight." He glanced at his watch. "I'm late for a meeting. Dan is here. Cleaning arrives at midnight."

Dan? Cleaning? Another wave of nerves settled in Avery's stomach. She tucked her hair behind her ear as she followed Carson past the empty reception desk and down a hallway lined with closed doors. The lights were dimmed. A sense of déjà vu settled over her. Only this time she knew what she was walking into.

Carson led her into another small conference room. He kept the light off, the moon and skyline providing enough to see by. The view of the Bay Bridge was stunning, and Avery stared at it, a quiet falling over her.

She wanted this—whatever it turned out to be.

"Doubts?" Carson asked. He stood behind her, his presence simmering down her back on a wave of awareness.

"No." She set her purse on the table, undid her coat. Her nipples pebbled when the cool air hit her bare back. His inhalation was audible, a long drag that said he approved. The dress cut in a swoop to the hollow of her back, exposing a display of flesh she'd be embarrassed to wear outside of this environment. The silky material teased her skin in a caress of sensual expense that ended high on her thigh in front and cut almost to her calves in the back.

His palm slid beneath the low back to glide around her side. Her abdomen contracted, breath holding. Heat raced in the wake of his touch, sinking deep. "Nice choice." His voice rumbled by her ear.

She basked in his praise, a smile curling her lips. "Thank you."

He ran his hand up her spine to thread his fingers through the ends of her hair. "So is this." He lifted the ends only to let them fall in a feather of tickling glides. "It's as beautiful as I'd imagined."

Another wave of warmth unfurled in her chest. He'd been thinking about her. Her nerves retreated to a low churn as her own power took over.

She turned in his arms and ran her hands up the lapels of his suit coat. She wasn't helpless nor was she completely naïve. And damn, how she wanted him. "Should we go?" she asked. She smoothed her palms down his pecs, images of his bare chest springing up. He was fit, that was obvious. Would he have chest hair? A treasure trail?

His soft tumble of laughter was another sultry rumble that did all kinds of strange things to her insides. He ran his fingers up her jaw, appreciation and lust showing. "You are dangerous." He claimed her mouth in a hard kiss before she could respond.

She froze for an instant, then sank into his demand. He plundered her mouth with a controlling crush that bordered on desperate. It was hard, intense and a little overwhelming until she gave herself over to him. Only then did she lose herself in the hot press of his tongue and reckless abandon.

He wrenched his mouth from hers. "Fuck." His low curse penetrated the fog that'd overtaken her mind. "We need to go." He grabbed her hand and led her from the room a moment later.

She was still catching her breath when he opened another door and led her inside. The skyline was the first thing she noticed, a mirror of what she'd seen from the other room. The woman lying facedown over the table, feet on the floor, was the second.

She blinked and followed Carson as he led her to the opposite end of the table, her focus on the woman. The lighting was once again provided by the moon and surrounding city. The shadows lent a mystery to the atmosphere along with a sensuality. She was quickly learning that impressions were more powerful than blatant detail.

The woman's dark blond hair was draped to the side, her eyes closed. Her arms were spread wide, wrists bound in black straps that disappeared beneath the table. A moan filtered into the room, and Avery's focus went to the man crouched behind the woman. His hands were braced on her butt cheeks, head moving in an obvious rhythm as he licked her. The woman writhed on the table, her gasps plucking through the room on sharp notes.

Confusion swirled in Avery. The scene was more intense and apparently well underway. The sense of invading something private prickled over her skin in a wave of taboo sinfulness. Wrong but so very right in this room.

Carson rested back on a credenza that ran the length of the wall and guided Avery until she stood between his legs. The woman cried out, hips bucking with the little leverage she could gain.

"Give her what she wants," Carson said.

The man swatted her ass. The sharp smack rang through the room before it was drowned out by the woman's cry. Another crack landed on her other ass cheek, the flesh jiggling beneath the impact.

Avery flinched, frowned, understanding hitching over comprehension. She'd asked for more without being specific.

This was definitely more.

She squirmed in Carson's arms, unease twisting in her chest. He urged her back until she rested against him. Her sigh came out immediately. *Trust him.* He slid his hand over her stomach, his touch firm, possessive. Her muscles relaxed in increments from her shoulders to her toes.

The guy stood and proceeded to rain a series of solid, hard swats to the woman's bottom. Each strike vibrated through the room and into Avery. Her breaths shortened, chest rising and falling in time with each strike.

She turned her head toward Carson, eyes still glued to the scene. Doubts swirled, but they collided with her fascination.

"She likes it rougher," Carson said in her ear.

Avery swallowed. "How rough?" she managed to whisper.

"Nothing more than she wants." He kissed her jaw, ran his hands over her hips and down her sides.

And how much was that?

The pinched look on the woman's face morphed to one of pleasure, lips parting, muscles relaxing. Her whimpers turned into moans, her butt thrusting upward as far as she could stretch.

"Please," the woman said. "More." She sucked in a breath, squirming in her restraints. "I need more."

Oh my God. Avery had never witnessed anything close to this. Harsh yet wanting. Wrong and yet so right in this setting.

Carson slipped a hand between them to rub Avery's bottom. An undeniable ache spread over her ass to reach her pussy as her imagination latched on to the possibilities. She wanted to deny the allure, but couldn't. Questions raced through her to mix with the illicit intrigue. What did it feel like? How could it be pleasurable?

A sharp pinch to her ass cheek made her jump. She tensed, but clamped her mouth shut on the instant objection that sprang up. Confusion rushed in yet again. The sting spread in hot waves over her cheek before it sunk deep. The shock of it lit up her nerve endings on a contrary note that somehow meshed with the desire already pulsing through her.

How is that possible?

Carson rubbed soothing strokes over Avery's bottom until the ache morphed into want. But for what? Another bite of pain or pleasure?

She squirmed in Carson's arms, shoving her hips back in search of a firm touch. Would he know what she wanted when she didn't?

The guy slowed, landed one more hit, then stopped. The woman sagged to the table, her back heaving with each breath that matched the intense pace of the man's. The beauty of the visual stunned Avery. There was nothing glorious about it, but she was glued to the erotic savagery of the scene.

A low moan eased from the woman, her eyes fluttering open. Avery was trapped in the unknown once again. Desperate to know what was next, yet uncertain about what was coming.

"Release her." Carson's voice broke through the room without warning.

Two shirtless men at the opposite end of the room stepped forward to release the straps from wherever they were tied beneath the table. One had a coat of hair covering his pecs that trickled down to a thin trail that disappeared beneath the waistband of his slacks, while the other man was hair-free from his neck to his pants. Three men?

They worked together to turn the woman over. Her soft pants peppered the air. Her eyes were closed, a flush painting her cheeks red.

"Tie her hands over her head."

The two guys on the sides followed Carson's direction without a glance their way. Carson had claimed control of the scene the second he'd stepped into the room. The power of that buzzed over Avery. He controlled them all.

Understanding came the moment the two men stepped back to reveal the full picture of the woman on the table. Her arms were stretched over her head, wrists bound, the ends of the long straps draped over the table. Her knees were bent now, legs spread wide. Black stilettos graced her feet, which were braced on the edge of the table.

Avery's chest tightened, the image before her overlaying with the one from that first night. When she couldn't look away.

Oh, God. She leaned heavier into Carson, breaths shortening. Had he done this for her? The idea of that sent a wave of heat from her pussy to her breasts.

"Make her come."

Avery gasped at the same time as the woman on the table. The men dipped their heads almost in unison, one on each breast, the last between her legs. Her back arched in time with her cry. It pierced the air and drove a knife of want into Avery.

Carson slid a hand beneath the back of her dress. Heat spread when he slipped it around to cup her breast as he smoothed his other hand down to grip her mound. Her "yes" was said beneath her breath. He tugged her hard against him, his breaths ragged on her neck. His erection rode that delicious line up the curve of her ass once again. It taunted her with what he wouldn't give her. Not here at least. But maybe later. Soon.

God, she ached to feel him in her. She shuddered, want clenching her pussy.

He surrounded her, his touch seemingly everywhere. On her breasts, between her legs, up her sides. Her nipples became aching buds beneath his deft fingers, each pinch a cross between too much and not enough. His breath warmed her skin as he kissed and nibbled his way over her shoulder and up her neck.

She silently begged for him to touch her aching clit. She needed relief from the building pressure that centered beneath the sensitive nub. But he avoided it, his fingers grazing over the inside of her thigh, along the crease of her leg, the edge of her thong.

The other woman was lost in passion, mouth parted to release an almost constant stream of moans and whimpers. Her head jerked up, eyes wide for one tense moment before she fell back, a high cry signaling her release.

Carson penetrated Avery at that exact moment. His

fingers skimmed beneath her thong to thrust deep, once, twice, again, and she almost lost it too. "Yes." She trembled, the edge so close. If he would just touch her clit.

"Not you," Carson whispered. He pulled his fingers away, and she grabbed his wrist to keep his hand there. His rumbled laugh buzzed her neck before he nipped her earlobe. "Not yet."

Frustration burned where it coiled in her core. She turned her head and attempted to nip his ear right back, but he ducked away. That damn smirk added another level to her annoyance. But pain blazed through her nipple before she could do anything.

She gasped, hunched forward but couldn't escape it.

Carson twisted the tender tip more, pinched until there was nothing but the pain. It spread through her chest, throbbing in time with her heartbeat. She whimpered and tried to escape his hold, but he held her tight. She clawed at the back of his hand in an attempt to pry it from its hold.

"Breathe, Avery."

She sucked in a breath, tears forming. "Please," she begged. The pain was so much worse than a little pinch to her bottom.

"Look at her," he growled.

She complied with his order without thought. Her head whipped up, her eyes wide. The woman squirmed on the table, her nipples pulled taut and twisted within the fingers of the two men at her sides.

Oh my God. The shared experience both sharpened and numbed the pain. The woman's back was arched impossibly far, mouth open to release her panting breaths. A mix of pain and pleasure shifted over her features in a confused state of want and rejection Avery understood.

Personally.

She sucked in a ragged breath, thoughts skimmed past the pain to center on the dull buzzing that'd floated in to neutralize what had just been intolerable. How?

Carson released her nipple, and she sagged in his arms. She'd barely processed the relief before he stroked her clit. She arched back, gasping at the shock of pleasure. Her nipple still throbbed, yet it seemed to intensify the desire racing through her. Every nerve ending vibrated with countering responses of good and bad. Right and wrong. Yes and no.

And oddly now, her other nipple ached for the same hard treatment.

"Carson," she mumbled, lost once again to his deft touch.

"Fuck her," Carson commanded. Avery's eyes snapped open. She hadn't realized they'd closed.

Yes. Please.

Her leg quivered and she tried to widen her stance. "Don't come," he said by her ear. "Not yet."

"Why?" The question came out as both a plea and a demand. She nuzzled his jaw, his woodsy scent triggering another rush of want. She gripped his legs, slid her hands down his thighs, unable to stay still. She couldn't think of anything but finding release.

A loud grunt followed by a high-pitched "yes" yanked Avery's attention back to the table. The other people. There were others in the room. Of course.

The bare-chested guy was fucking the woman, his pants shoved down just far enough to free his dick. Long, hard drives that slapped with each impact. He held her hips in place and sank deep with a thrust that jarred her.

"Can you feel that?" Carson asked Avery. He tapped

his fingers over her entrance in time with the man's thrust. The thin piece of her thong provided an annoying barrier, preventing even the little relief of his skin on hers.

The small impacts became magnified by a thousand, need morphed to a blinding hunger. Her pussy clenched around the emptiness he teased her with.

"Each thrust. Every plunge. He's filling her. Driving her crazy," he whispered.

"Yes. God, yes." She didn't care if the others heard her or if they watched her either. And they were. The two other men at least, who now stood to the sides of the table. Their gazes traveled between the other couple and them. There was no mistaking the lust on their faces or the prominent outlines of their erections beneath their pants.

In that moment, she felt truly decadent. The hunger in the other men's eyes fed her own growing power that was new and freeing in a way she'd never expected.

Carson traced the shell of her ear with his tongue. Hot waves slid down her chest. "Are you wet?"

He knew she was. "Yes." So damn wet and ready.

"I can feel it," he murmured. Yet he didn't penetrate her. No, he kept up that insistent tapping that created an insane want to be filled, like the woman on the table. Hard, deep drives that would stretch her walls and make the ache go away.

"God, I want you, Carson." The truth spilled out in a blind tumble of breathy words. "Please. Please fuck me." She was begging and didn't care how it sounded. She was focused on one thing right then, and that was getting Carson Haggert's dick in her.

Chapter Twelve

Christ, how he wanted to fuck Avery. So damn much.

Carson clamped down on his own need demanding to be set loose and focused on the gorgeous woman slowly falling apart in his arms. "Soon," he rasped. His dick was so hard it threatened to burst through his pants. And Avery rode the length of it in a swirling, wiggling bump and grind of her hips that was pure reaction.

"Make her beg," Carson ordered.

"Please," the women said in unison. The high lilt of Shelly's voice blended with Avery's breathy tone to create a beautiful chord.

Carson reveled in the power they'd entrusted him with. Any of them could object at any time, but he worked damn hard to ensure everyone was pleased. That was his job. Hell, that'd always been his job.

Dan slowed his pounding pace, his grunts quieting. Shelly protested with a half whine, half sob. She lifted her arms, but Drake quickly stopped her. "But…" Shelly twisted her head, back arching. "I need more."

"Me, too," Avery said. She rocked her hips, but Carson only moved with her. He'd slowed his tapping beat to match Dan's, even though his own hunger was urging him to bury his fingers deep into her wet heat.

She grabbed his wrist and tried to shove his hand where she wanted it. He laughed softly against her neck and pinched her nipple in rebuke. Her low growl only added to the need he barely held in check. There was a fighter beneath that shy demeanor of hers. A passionate one who showed there was so much more to her than the demure image she presented.

"Tease her," Carson said to the other men. He caught their gazes, smirked. They'd both been eyeing Avery just as much as Shelly. Was it because she was with him when he'd never brought a woman with him before or simply because she was beautiful in her passion? "Shelly," he clarified.

No one touched Avery except him. That'd been her rule. He was just keeping his promise to her, right?

That damn twinge in his chest called him a liar.

Avery panted in his arms, tried to twist from his hold. "Please." Her head fell forward, a wave of hair trailing down to shield her face. He brushed it back, then brought her chin around to claim her mouth. Her whimper tickled his lips, and he dove in for more. Another brush. A slow swipe. A trace of his tongue over her soft lips. She tried to shove up to deepen the kiss, but he backed away.

The drive to haul her from the room and fuck her senseless hovered on the edge of his control. He had to maintain it, though. Want clamored at his chest. His balls ached in the confines of his pants. Precome coated his abdomen and had probably left a wet spot on his slacks. And all of it, every little discomfort and ache, reminded him of the power he held.

But for once, he lost track of what the others were doing as his focus shifted solely to Avery. Her soft moans and sighs were notes of wonder that whispered her need. Her breasts were heavy in his palm, the nipples hard beads. Her wetness coated the thin cloth of her thong and slicked his fingers. The musky scent teased his senses with the memory of how it'd lingered on his fingers the last time.

She was beautiful. Hungry. So damn open to him. Just him. For him.

How had that happened?

The low pleas and incoherent babble from Shelly slowly broke through Carson's focus. He lifted his head and blinked at the table, dazed. "Give it to her."

He reclaimed Avery's lips in the next breath. She'd turned in his arms, and he dove deeper with the improved angle. This was crazy. Hot. Intense in a way he'd never experienced before.

He jerked away, swung Avery back around. "Watch her come," he growled, his own orgasm simmering so damn close.

Dan powered into Shelly, and Carson kept up the tapping beat on Avery's pussy. The muscles flexed and clamped beneath his fingers. It took very little imagination to picture them clenching around his dick. He groaned his own protest but didn't give in. Not yet.

"I'm… I'm…" Shelly tossed her head back. A loaded pause hung in the air. The tension prickled over his skin. She curled forward right before her cry filled the room with her release.

He slid his fingers beneath Avery's thong and sunk them deep into her heat. *Fuck.* The muscles grasped his fingers, her wetness soaking them. Her shudder trembled into him. Her little gasps and hiccups of breath matched the pounding rate of her heart where it thumped beneath his lips on her neck.

She was close too. Begging for release even if she was silent.

Indecision clawed at his resolve for a breath of a minute before he ushered her from the room. He didn't think about what he was doing. Didn't worry about what happened after.

No. His only thought was of feeling her clench around him. Of her coming on his dick, not his fingers.

The small conference room was only a few steps away, yet seemed to take forever to reach. He set her on the table and claimed her mouth before she could speak. He caught her cry on his lips and drove his tongue in to find hers. She clutched the back of his head and rose up to meet him in a wild dance of tongues and gasps for air.

He scrambled to release his belt and pants. Her hands bumped his as she rushed to help him. She shoved his underwear down and grasped his dick. He choked out a hoarse groan, his peripheral vision going dark. "Avery."

"Yes," she urged. She stroked his length in long, firm pulls that felt so damn good. Too good. Everything about her was too good.

"This is only sex," he said against her mouth. The reminder was for her. Just her.

"I know," she whispered back. She swiped her thumb over his tip and smeared the precome over the head. "I know. Just fuck me. Please."

He ripped her hand away and dug a condom from his pocket. Sweat plastered his shirt to his back and his tie was suddenly constricting, but he couldn't take the time to remove it.

He rolled the protection on in one quick move before he hauled her leg up, shoved her thong aside and finally slid into her. Their mutual groans rang through the room as her heat and wetness surrounded him.

"Fuck." He gripped her hips and dragged her to the edge of the table. He had to get deeper. He needed more of her. All of her.

He bent his knees and drove into her, every thrust hard and fast with the need threatening to spill over. She gripped his nape, clutched at his shoulder. Her breaths were hot and fast near his ear. He buried his face in the crook of her neck and fucked her hard. Each snap of his hips ended in a slap of skin.

He'd never been this desperate. Never this lost.

Her fingernails bit into his neck. Tension strung around them. His balls drew up with the pressure building in his groin. He squeezed his eyes closed and held back that last surge. Her whimper was one of desperation.

He shifted forward, lifted her leg higher and drove in again.

"Yes." Her head fell back, breasts thrusting up. "Right there." Lust covered her expression. Her lips were parted, the pink stain muted. Her cheeks were flushed a beautiful red that spread over her exposed chest. Pride raced through him. He'd done this to her. Drove her to this state.

He gave her everything then, letting go of the last of his restraint. Her release burst from her on a gasping sob that cut off as her muscles contracted around him. *Fuck.*

He thrust harder, savored the clench and release that stroked his dick. Avery yanked him down and sank her teeth into his neck. Pain, sharp and distinct, stabbed the tender area. It jolted his system and unhinged the last thread of control he clung to.

His hips bucked, euphoria exploding in a flash of darkness and light. Every muscle tensed, then relaxed in a last grinding jerk. He emptied himself within the sweet heat that still squeezed his dick so tightly. Her pussy milked every drop of frustration he'd held back since that first sight of Avery hot and turned-on had been lodged into his memory.

The stillness slowly penetrated his awareness as he came back to himself. Avery's raspy inhalations near his ear echoed his own ragged attempts to breathe. He sucked in deep gulps of air in his hunt for the stability he'd lost. His head spun and churned with emotions he didn't want to acknowledge.

A low grunt and the distinct slick and slap of skin jerked Carson from his floating fog with a nasty punch of reality. He jerked his head around and glared at Drake. The man was braced against the hallway wall, eyes heavy-lidded, dick in hand, stroking himself off.

"That was so fucking hot," Drake growled.

The fucker.

Carson stretched back and whipped the door closed. The slam reverberated through the room. Avery jumped, tensing in his arms.

No. He hugged her close and ran soothing circles over her back. "It's okay." He refused to let that fucker ruin the night for her. This was her moment. Her freedom, and Drake wasn't taking it from her.

Her laughter started small. A short hiccup. A jerk. Then a bubbling tinkle that vibrated through her shoulders. Relief swept away his worry and released his own amazed chuckle.

"Why are you laughing?" he asked. He brushed her hair away from her face and couldn't resist placing a kiss over her smile. She giggled against his lips before pulling back to release a full laugh.

Her beauty showed in another stunning revelation of pure freedom. The shadows hid little from him in that moment. The moonlight lent a soft glow to her hair that gave her an almost mystical sense. Her lips were puffy from their kisses, cheeks flushed, eyes dancing when they met his. She cupped a hand over her mouth and visibly tried to control her laughter.

He shook his head, bemused. This was better than tears or anger. Much better, even if he didn't understand it.

"Sorry," she muttered around another giggle.

He pressed a lingering kiss to her temple and grabbed the base of the condom before he eased out of her. He looked around, frowned. What the fuck was he supposed to do with the condom? There were supplies in the Boardroom for this. Tissues and wipes and an obvious garbage can. But here? There was nothing in sight. Not even a napkin.

Avery must have caught on to his dilemma, because she opened her purse and held out a couple of tissues. "Here."

"Thanks," he mumbled, grateful yet embarrassed at how unprepared he was. He was the one who was supposed to be in control here, yet he felt very far from it.

He scrambled to find his bearings in the jumble of emotions Avery had set free. His stomach twisted with nerves that had never appeared in this environment. What was going on?

He stepped away and cleaned himself up in quick swipes before redoing his pants. A dark stain left a tell-

ing spot on the front near the zipper, and he scowled at
it like his dick had betrayed him. Stupid.

Avery sucked in a loud breath, blew it out. "I'm not
laughing at you."

His brow flicked up. "I didn't think you were." *Until
now.* And that was an insecurity he refused to have.
There was no reason for it, especially not here.

She smoothed her dress over her legs, a wad of tissues visible in her fist. He took the tissues from her,
crumpled them with his and dumped them in the trash
can he spotted by the back wall.

The Bay Bridge twinkled over the water, a stream of
headlights forming a chain as cars threaded their way
over it. He took a moment to steady himself. The silence highlighted the tension slowly twisting into his
afterglow. He straightened his suit coat and tried to get
some air circulating over his sweaty back. It didn't work.

Avery still sat on the table when he turned back to her.
She gave him a tentative smile that showed the nerves
she was attempting to hide. Her hand shook, just a little,
when she ran it through her hair. Her fingers snagged on
a tangle and she winced, a frown following.

He couldn't stop himself from stepping up and re-
placing her fingers with his. He ran them through the
silky strands and gently worked the small knot out. Her
breath hitched, held. He swallowed, refusing to give in
to the other, stronger urge he had to gather her up and
bring her home.

"Are you better now?" he asked instead.

She nodded, eyes averted. "Yes. Thank you."

He slid his fingers over her brow to brush her bangs
away. They should leave. He never lingered after the

Boardroom. And they weren't in the Boardroom now. Not technically.

"I'm sorry about that." He motioned to the doorway, hoping she'd follow his meaning. Drake had overstepped his bounds.

"Oh." She glanced up at him, a small smile in place. "That, ah… That was okay."

"Are you sure?" He stroked his thumb over her cheek, slightly fascinated by the softness.

She held his gaze, that determination he admired blazing dark blue in her eyes. "Yes. I'm sure."

Could she get any sexier? She was owning her sexuality exactly as he'd hoped she would, and it was so damn hot on her.

He swallowed, cursing his spiraling control. "Was there anything about tonight you didn't like?" He could stay on track. Keep this…about sex. That was it.

Her laugh came out in a soft snort. "Ah, no. Not really."

His brow went up, thumb stalling on her cheek. "Not really?" he repeated, his question implied. "Then what was the laughter about?"

Her eyes sparked with humor and her lips quirked. Her laughter obviously itched to burst free again. She bit her lip, took a breath. "I'm not really sure," she finally admitted. She shrugged, fingers fiddling on her lap. "I guess it was nerves and…" She glanced away, then back after a beat. "Relief? Amazement maybe?" Her brows dipped, and he found himself smoothing the frown lines away before he consciously thought to do so. Her smile softened, shoulders lowering, and he cursed himself for sending the wrong message. Whatever it was. However, he couldn't get himself to regret it. "I didn't expect to feel so free," she added, wonder in her voice. "This is so far out of my realm of experience. I mean, I've obviously had sex before, including a few drunk events that pushed the normal boundaries. But absolutely nothing like this."

"And?" he prodded when she didn't go on.

She lifted her hand to grasp his wrist, eyes filling with that same wonder that'd been in her voice. "I fucking loved it."

His laughter burst free in a wave of shock and his own wonder. What the fuck? He gathered her into a hug, grin huge. "You are something else, Avery." Something amazing and fresh and so damn dangerous.

Her laughter was muffled against his neck, but he didn't loosen his hold. He couldn't. Not yet. Not until he could shove his desire back and do what he had to do. He squeezed his eyes closed, took one long drag of her addicting scent.

He eased back, left a last kiss on her temple and stepped away, hand held out to help her from the table. "We should get going."

"Oh." Her eyes went wide. "Of course." She turned back to him after he helped her with her coat. Her chin was lifted and he had a second to mentally prepare himself before she spoke. "Can we do this again?"

Yes. No. Fuck. He shouldn't. God, how he shouldn't. "Next week?"

Her lips pursed. "Friday? I have plans on Saturday."

Plans? A date? The twinge stuck in his chest, but he refused to acknowledge it. The green bastard did not control him. "I'll see what I can do," he said, voice brisker than he'd intended.

Her frown deepened and this time he managed to

keep his hands to himself. "Okay." She tucked her hands in her pockets. "Thank you."

"This is still just sex," he responded on reflex. "Just the Boardroom." But was the repeated reminder for her or himself?

Her sigh was heavy with annoyance. "Did I ask for more?" She blew out a small puff of disgust. "No. I didn't," she answered for him. "So you can stop reminding me. It's just about the sex. I get it." She opened the door, a sly grin on her face when she looked back. "And it was really damn good tonight."

She winked and sashayed out the door. His bark of laughter shot through the room before he followed her down the hall.

Avery Fast was going to be the death of him if he wasn't careful. And he was always careful. Always.

Chapter Thirteen

"Earth to Avery."

A hand waved in front of Avery's face. She blinked and jerked away, scowling. "What?" She glared at her friend.

Karen rolled her eyes. "You've been in Neverland all morning."

"I have not." Her retort was too quick and defensive to ring true, even to her own ears. She sighed, leaning into Karen's side as they walked. "Sorry. You're right."

The sun glared off the water in a welcome burst of vitamin D that baked into her skin and reminded her of why she loved the area so much. Or one of the reasons anyway. The distance from her family was another, one she both relished and mourned. She missed her family, yet she didn't think she could ever live close to them again.

A warm spring breeze blew off the bay to ruffle Avery's hair. She tucked it back, only to have it whip across her face a moment later. She weaved through the crowded promenade to a quieter spot near the water and set her reusable grocery bag down. A quick plundering of her purse uprooted a hair band at the bottom.

Three loops later, she had her hair under control, if not her emotions.

Karen set her reusable bag next to Avery's, propped her hip on the railing and eyed Avery. Her sunglasses blocked her eyes, but Avery didn't need to see them to know she was being scrutinized. Great.

The clang of a streetcar rumbling past on the nearby track drowned out the group of seals barking in the distance. An array of food booths at the farmers' market scented the air with the spicy tang of burritos, stir fry and a number of other ethnic cuisines. Thankfully, it overrode the murkier fish and seaweed stench from the bay.

Avery turned around to stare at the Bay Bridge where it stretched over the water, purposely ignoring Karen. She wasn't ready to talk—about anything. There was nothing to talk about. She shook her head, scoffing at her own blind insistence.

"What's going on?" Karen asked.

"Nothing," Avery answered automatically. Nothing she *could* talk about.

"Liar."

She shrugged. She couldn't deny that truth. "I'm fine." She tried to reassure her friend. "Just work stuff." Sort of. Carson was at her work, and he was driving her crazy.

Karen's low "hmm" said she wasn't buying what Avery was dishing out. She turned around to lean back on the railing and scanned the crowd milling through the stalls of the farmers' market. The local Saturday morning crowd had given way to the tourists as it closed in on noon. They'd wasted time wandering through the booths, enjoying the weather instead of doing their usual grab of items from their favorite vendors.

"You've been off for weeks," Karen prodded. Her tenacity was one of her assets and all too often an annoyance. Like now.

Avery frowned, grateful for her own sunglasses. "I hadn't noticed."

"Don't lie to me, bitch."

"Cunt," she countered.

"Whore."

She cringed. The last dig hit too close to her fears even though the lighthearted jibes were ones they'd blasted at each other in the past. Was it wrong to be fucking around with Carson—literally?

She hadn't lied when she'd said she loved having sex with him. She did. Every hot second of it. But she couldn't shake that pesky guilt lodged deep from her upbringing.

A family trudged by on the sidewalk in a wave of giggles and cries. The two younger girls wore matching sundresses, their blond pigtails bouncing as they skipped down the sidewalk.

A pang of longing snuck up and kicked Avery in the chest. She shook her head and shoved the stupidity aside. She refused to be one of those women who based her happiness on her fertility. Children wouldn't make her whole, nor would a husband, even if her mother insisted they would.

Yet her gaze still lingered on the happy unit as the family was swallowed up in the crowd. Thirty didn't make her ancient by any means. She had years before her eggs shriveled up. *What is wrong with me?*

"I don't care what you say," Karen said, yanking

Avery from her thoughts. "Something is going on, and it's more than just work."

Avery tipped her head up and basked in the warm slash of sun on her face. Could she confide in Karen? Like the last time, there were parts she could and most that she couldn't. Not according to that NDA she'd signed. She'd scrutinized every line after Carson had sent her a copy. There was no wiggle room in the terms.

Karen shifted sideways until her arm touched Avery's in a comforting press. "Does this have anything to do with those sex questions you brought up at the bar last month?"

Last month? It seemed like ages ago.

Avery gave a noncommittal hum along with a small shrug. She'd had four "dates" with Carson since she'd last talked to Karen about this. She'd changed in so many ways since then. At least, she felt different. Wiser in some ways, naïve in others.

"Have you ever had a fuck buddy?" Avery asked, keeping her voice low. She didn't look at Karen, couldn't really. She just kept her eyes closed and focused on the sun hitting her face. The sense of disconnect freed her tongue.

"A few," Karen confided. "You?"

"No." She couldn't really classify Carson into that category. He was less and more than that.

"Do you want one?"

Did she? Could she be that carefree sexual woman? "Not really." She was meeting Carson every week for sex, but he wasn't her buddy by any stretch of the word. He was pretty much a distant ass at work.

Wrong. She shook her head, wincing. She couldn't do that to him.

He was normal at work. Professional and distant like he'd been since she'd been hired at Faulkner. She'd gone into this arrangement with her eyes wide-open, and she wasn't going to blame him for keeping the rules she'd agreed to.

"Can I ask you a question?" Karen said after a moment.

"Sure."

"Are your parents ultra-conservative or something?"

Avery snorted. "No." Her head dropped to hang in heavy embarrassment. She couldn't blame them for her hang-ups either. "Not really. Not in the over-the-top way." However, their conservative values had managed to mesh their way into her soul. "But they're very…traditional. My mom didn't talk about sex—ever. They had a family, worked hard, raised their kids to respect others and value what they had. *Sheltered* might be the word for them, but they're not dumb."

Karen gave a slow nod. "So the exact opposite of my family then?"

Avery smiled, nudging her friend. "I've met your mom. She's not dumb." Karen's mother was a respected scientist working on a cure for cancer.

"You're right," she conceded. "She's not. But sex was never taboo. The flower-child still lives beneath her lab coat."

What would it be like to have zero inhibitions or fears regarding sex? It sounded foolish labeling her issues as fears, given the expectations placed on modern women today, but she had to be honest with herself. They were fears.

The fear of being labeled by others and herself. The fear of shame. The fear of admitting how much she loved everything she was exploring with Carson.

"I wish I had your outlook on sex." Avery sent a weak smile at Karen, hoping she took her comment in the way she intended. "I just—I want to be—I—" What? What did she want to be? "Crap." She shook her head. "I don't know."

And that was issue number one.

"Come on." Avery shoved away from the rail, swiping up her bag before Karen could grill her further. "I need to head home." She started down the walkway, glancing back when she noticed she was alone.

Karen hadn't budged. Her hard scowl and crossed arms reminded Avery of a petulant child refusing to move. She could leave her, just keep walking and pretend she wouldn't stew on their conversation the entire way home.

She was going to do that with or without Karen at her side.

Avery heaved a sigh and returned to her friend, steps heavy. "What?" she bit out.

Karen's brows winged up behind her sunglasses. The wind ruffled the tiny spikes of her short hair without disturbing its precise styling that was meant to look imprecise. She unfolded her arms, straightening in slow measures that warned of her building retort.

Avery braced for Karen's takedown, at once mad at herself, yet unable to give in.

"What is going on with you?" Karen's voice was moderated, concern there but tempered with confusion. It kicked at Avery's guilt and only added to her own mixed-up thoughts.

Her shoulders dropped, her defenses draining. "I don't know," she admitted, letting the defeat in. "I really don't." Not about Carson or the sex or what she wanted from either.

Karen stepped closer to wrap an arm around her shoulders. Her side hug was welcomed and comforting when Avery was the one who should be apologizing. She leaned into Karen, taking every ounce of strength she could absorb.

"Something's got you wrapped up inside," Karen said. "And that usually means there's a man involved."

Avery's snort was harsh and cutting. She squeezed her eyes closed and shoved back the derision that tried to bite at her. She had nothing to be ashamed of. Nothing.

"And," Karen went on, "based on your recent round of questions, I'm going to guess it has something to do with sex."

Ding, ding, ding. She got it in one. "So much for my stealth questions," Avery snarked.

"Oh, sweetie. There was nothing stealth about them."

She sighed, accepting the truth. "I'm freaking thirty years old and can't talk about sex without stumbling over my own inhibitions. God, that's so pathetic."

"To whom?" Karen asked. "The nun or the hooker?"

Avery frowned, confused. "What are you talking about?"

"Who gets to judge your feelings?" Karen was completely serious. "You have a right to feel whatever you do. And," she added, lifting her finger to make the point, "the only judgment that counts is your own. So don't be too hard on yourself."

Avery held in her snort for a moment, proud that she managed that before it burst out. She slammed her fist over her mouth, her laugh bubbling behind it. "Is that your mother talking?"

Karen sniffed, chin lifting. She glared at Avery in fake affront before relenting with a shrug and smile. "Maybe. But it's true," she added. "I told you before, as long as you own your wants and feelings, no one can make you feel badly about them."

Was it really that simple?

A sneaky, dirty smile slid over her lips as she gave Karen the side-eye. "But my wants are very, very dirty." She waggled her brows, another laugh bursting free a moment later.

"Do tell." Karen grabbed her bag and looped her arm through Avery's as they started to walk. "And don't skimp on the details."

A secret smile formed in Avery's chest and wormed its way to her face. The giddy lightness that popped up whenever she thought about her evenings with Carson bloomed to flutter in her stomach.

She ducked her head, peeked at Karen. "I've been seeing someone." She waited a beat, then added, "For sex."

Karen whipped her head around. "What? Wait." She came to a stop, forcing people to scurry around them. She grabbed Avery's arm. "Like how seeing?" She scanned the area, leaned in. "Are you paying for it?"

"No!" The denial shot from her on an annoyed shout. "Why would you think that?"

"Hey." Karen held her hand up in apology. "There's nothing wrong with it if you are."

"I'm not!" Avery shoved forward, dodging between people until she was free of the market crowd. Her speed accelerated when she hit open pavement, her annoyance driving her faster.

"Avery." Karen grabbed her arm. "Come on." She slowed, forcing Avery to do the same. "I didn't mean anything by that." Avery faced her, scowl firmly in place. "Honestly." Karen shrugged, an impish smile growing. "I might've asked for their information if you were."

"Oh my God." Avery rolled her eyes, unable to maintain her anger. "Like you'd ever need to do that."

"Who knows?" She shrugged again. "There's still plenty I haven't experienced." She started walking, and Avery paced her. "So tell me about these liaisons."

A part of Avery had hoped Karen would let the subject go, but a bigger side of her wanted to share. Not everything. Just enough to let the giddy out.

"Well..." She bit her lip and shot Karen a secretive glance. "He's been helping me explore a few fantasies." Her laugh trickled out at Karen's shocked expression. One that quickly morphed to interest.

"Really?" Speculation dominated the word. "Are you going to share the details?"

"No." Warmth raced up Avery's neck, and she couldn't blame it on the sun. "But I can tell you it's been amazing." Beyond it, really. She inhaled, a rush of desire and want stirring in her chest. "Really, really good."

"Now I *do* want the details," Karen insisted.

Avery shook her head. "I can't. Seriously," she added when she saw the doubt on Karen's face. "I'm—" Saying the truth would only bring up more questions. "It's just sex," she said instead, trying to sound casual. "We're not buddies or anything." Not out of the Boardroom at least.

"Who is he?" Karen frowned. "Or is it a she?"

"It's a he." A handsome, sexy, confident, strong, kind he. One she was becoming attached to when she shouldn't. No, couldn't.

"So, what's wrong?"

They waited for the crosswalk signal to change and wove through the oncoming swarm to the other side. What was wrong? Avery pondered that, knowing exactly what was wrong.

"I like it too much," she admitted once they cleared the street.

"The sex?" Karen's incredulous tone said exactly how crazy she thought that was. "How is that a problem?"

Avery ducked her head to avoid the startled double-take from a woman passing by. "Shhh," she admonished her friend, smacking her arm. "Not everyone is as open as you."

Karen glanced around, shrugged. "Sorry?"

"No you're not."

"True." Her unapologetic smirk was exactly why Avery loved her so much.

She shifted her bag on her shoulder and tucked a lock of escaped hair behind her ear. "I can't get attached," she said, returning to their discussion. "It's a huge no-strings arrangement."

"Oh." Karen tipped her head, lips pursing. "And that's not working for you, right?"

Her snort was soft and derisive. "Yeah." It both helped and didn't that Karen understood without her having to explain. "I thought I could do it. I *want* to. God, how I want to."

"Avery," Karen started, her name filled with gentle patience. "You adopted both of your cats within two minutes of seeing them in the adoption crates at the pet store."

"But they were so cute," she defended.

"And how long did you stay at that call center job you

hated because you didn't want to leave the manager in a bad spot?"

Way too long. "What does that have to do with anything?"

Karen turned to her when they came to their bus stop. Her smile was warm and just a little sympathetic. "You get attached." Avery scowled. "There's nothing wrong with that," her friend rushed on. "In fact, it's a wonderful attribute. It makes you loyal and kind when so many of us—" she pointed to herself "—are detached from everything."

"You're not detached," Avery countered, more than ready to take the focus from herself.

Karen waved that off. "My point is, you like to connect with people. It's a part of you."

"So?" Avery turned away to look for the bus. She wasn't enjoying this deep analysis of herself.

"There's a reason why you've never had a fuck buddy before."

She hung her head, mortification sweeping over her. There was an easy dozen other people waiting for the bus, and she could feel every one of them staring at her now. She shot a glare at Karen. "Thanks for announcing that to everyone."

Karen glanced around. A few people ducked their heads to avoid her scrutiny. Others smiled openly at her. "Oops." She winced. "Sorry."

Avery stared down the road, relieved when she spotted their bus. She pointedly ignored Karen until they were seated, their bags tucked between their feet, her thoughts spinning even worse than before. A part of her acknowledged that Karen had a point, but another part of her refused to accept it as fact.

She could change. In fact, she was changing with every delicious scene Carson introduced her to. She was alive during those scenes. Free like she'd never been before.

And she wasn't ready to give that up. Not even close.

"What time are you leaving tonight?" Karen asked. She swayed with the rock of the bus, her shoulder nudging Avery's.

Avery sighed and gave up on her silent treatment. Her annoyance was gone now anyway. "Seven," she answered.

"Are you going with anyone?"

"No." She could take a date to the Faulkner party, but the only guy she wanted to go with would already be there. Maybe with his own date. Her stomach soured on that thought. She closed her eyes and forced the flash of jealousy down. She had to be prepared for that possibility.

"I have a date tonight, so I might be out late." Karen waggled her brows, a cunning grin in place. "Or not until morning."

Avery gave a disbelieving laugh. "I won't wait up for you." She pulled out her phone and made a quick check of her texts. There was nothing from Carson, not that she'd expected a message. He'd been busy last night and they both had this damn party to go to tonight. It was an appreciation dinner thrown by the company for a profitable quarter, and normally she looked forward to them.

But now, with the prospect of seeing Carson and pretending she didn't know the low growl he made right before he came or the sensual touch of his fingers on her pussy was going to suck. Big-time.

Their secret sex life had been almost naughty at first.

Just something between them. That feeling had worn off somewhere between them fucking for the first time and her increasing desire to have sex with him away from the Boardroom environment. To hear his rumbled laugh over dinner and see his warm smile in the morning.

And that would never happen.

The hard reminder ground into her resolve. She'd do this. She'd ignore him tonight and simply have fun with the friends she'd made at Faulkner. Like she always did.

Nothing had changed. Nothing except her.

And she couldn't let Carson see that. Not outside of the Boardroom.

Chapter Fourteen

The clinking of china rang in soft notes over the chorus of voices that filled the small banquet room. Carson stood to the side and tried to focus on the conversation with one of his managers. The man gestured broadly, a deep frown indicating his irritation with the code his team was working on.

"I'm sure you'll figure it out," Carson said. Hopefully the generic response covered his disinterest. "In the meantime, have another drink and enjoy the evening." He motioned to the bar and prayed the man would take the hint.

"Right." The guy gave a depreciative chuckle. "Sorry about that. I'd better find my wife." He wandered away with a tug on his collar, his lanky frame giving him height over the milling crowd.

Carson breathed a sigh of relief and discarded the prickle of regret. He didn't usually dismiss his employees like that. In fact, he normally would've gladly indulged in a detailed analysis of the code specifics, especially here. Anything to keep him from the tedious job of mingling.

Not tonight, though. Not when he'd yet to spot Avery. He emptied his glass of scotch and handed it off to a passing waiter. The Faulkner affairs were casually nice events hosted by Trevor and the managing directors at the end of particularly good quarters. Or that was the reason given.

In truth, he believed Trevor just liked having them. It brought the team closer, showed a generosity that was often lacking in today's businesses and minimized turnover. The San Francisco office consistently had some of the highest earnings and morale within Faulkner Worldwide.

A flash of red at the entry had him straightening, neck stretching. His breath caught, and his heart clenched around the shot of awe and want that sprang up in the next beat.

Avery stood just inside the doorway, hands clutched before her around her small purse. She was absolutely stunning. Her hair was wound up in some arrangement that left a mass of curls to fall to her nape. The rosy flush on her cheeks reminded him of the glow that rose after she'd come apart in his arms.

He swallowed and wished he'd kept his glass if only to hunt down a last sip to ease his parched throat.

She turned toward a group of women, her smile softening her features. The hem of her dress flared out and the wide skirt swished around her calves. The bodice hugged her form, the tight sleeves ending at her elbows. But it was the deep, plunging V of her neckline that turned the rather demure dress into upscale sexy.

Damn fucking sexy.

It showed a deep line of skin that worked perfectly with Avery's shape. Her breasts were nice-sized but set farther apart, which minimized cleavage, but enabled her to wear the risky neckline with class.

His dick twitched with the need to feel her heat surrounding him once again. He'd almost canceled his meeting last night just to see her. And that was precisely why he hadn't.

She tipped her head back with a laugh he strained to hear but couldn't. Not from where he stood. But it still danced in his mind, the sweet notes tugging a smile to his face. She set her purse on a table and joined a couple of other assistants in the line at the bar. He was moving toward her before he realized it.

What the fuck?

He came up short and abruptly turned in the opposite direction. He wound his way through the people, smiling and stopping to greet different groups as he did. Normal. Everything was normal.

Except his skin prickled with an awareness he never had before. As stupid as it sounded, he could sense where Avery was in the room. When she got her drink. When she mingled with the other assistants.

When she spent too long talking to a guy in his IT group.

He clenched his jaw and grabbed another scotch from the bar, damn his one-drink rule at these events. He took a long swallow and let the burn slide down his throat. There was no getting away from her, though, short of leaving. And that wasn't happening. Not while she was still there.

She took a couple of hors d'oeuvres from a server, never pausing in her conversation with his soon-to-be ex-employee. *Christ.* He couldn't fire the guy because he talked with Avery.

He rubbed a hand down his jaw and forced himself to turn away. He lasted a minute, probably less, before his gaze landed on her again. She nibbled on a cheese puff, a small bit of the filling catching on her lip before she licked it away.

And there went his dick again. He was walking around at half-mast in the middle of a fucking work event. How professional of him. Thank fuck for suit jackets.

He caught sight of Trevor working his way toward him and used that as a distraction. Trevor had an easy smile and nod for everyone he passed. His natural charm reminded Carson of his brother Jack. As the middle son, Jack had carved out his place by being the social extrovert of the family. Everyone loved him, and Carson had been happy to let him have that spotlight.

"I see you've found your usual spot," Trevor said as he came to stand next to him by the wall. He shrugged, but didn't respond to the dig. Trevor flicked his chin in the general direction of Avery, drink paused before his mouth. "That dress is beautiful on her."

Carson bit back the growl that snapped in his chest. He was not jealous. Fuck, right. Trevor's sly smile was too damn knowing before he took a sip of his drink. Bastard. "There are a lot of beautiful women here," Carson said. The diversion sounded lame even to him.

Trevor's slow nod didn't fool him. He scanned the gathering, and Carson could practically see the calculation and appraisal happening as he did. The attendance was always high, and this time was no different. "Why are you resisting her so much?" Trevor asked in a casual tone without looking at Carson.

He sighed, head shaking. "There's nothing to resist."

Trevor's snort edged near disgust. He lifted a brow, his disappointment a sharp stab at Carson. "Bullshit."

Irritation grew in little digs of heat that crawled over his shoulders and contracted into tight knots. He refused to acknowledge the arrogant ass or how right he was. Trevor's ego didn't need the extra strokes.

Carson focused his glare on the room, determined to not find Avery. He failed almost immediately. She was at the edge of the small dance floor, her wineglass half full, the red liquid swirling with every movement of her hand. She caught his eye, paused for a moment to smile slightly before turning away. Her dismissal launched another jab at him when there was no reason for it. He winced, but managed to hold most of the hurt behind his clenched teeth.

This was fucking ridiculous. He was the one who'd insisted on keeping their distance at work, and here he was beyond frustrated because she was doing exactly that.

"I'm thinking it's time for details," Trevor murmured at his side.

"No," Carson bit out. He cooled his glare when Trevor raised that damn brow again. *Fuck.* He took a long drink of his scotch and focused on the burn as it drained down his throat. No one needed to know any details about Avery. No one except for the Boardroom members who already knew too much about her.

Like how she whimpered so sweetly with her need, or how her cries were always breathy and hoarse.

His jaw tightened until his teeth hurt, and he clutched the glass with a force that threatened to shatter it. She was so damn gorgeous in those moments. He loved knowing she was all his then, that no one else could touch her even though he saw the obvious longing in the others' eyes.

And now? Any man in this room could have her if she agreed.

Fuck. He took another drink. She could've brought a date tonight.

The realization nipped at his anger. He tried to ignore it. Hell, he'd been refusing to address it for weeks. She brushed a hand down the IT guy's arm, her mouth open with another laugh he couldn't hear.

And there was nothing he could do except silently fume.

This was his own damn doing.

"There's nothing in the HR rules that prevents you from dating her," Trevor said. His cocky smirk was damn irritating. "But that would require you to admit that you want her."

"Of course I want her," Carson countered without thought. He closed his eyes and cursed his weakness before attempting to dismiss his admission. "What man wouldn't?" Yet somehow, she was still single. But for how long?

"Really?" A devious glint sparked in Trevor's eye. "Then it's okay for me to engage with her on the app? Maybe suggest a scene? See if she's interested?"

"Who's interested?" Gregory butted in as he approached, his gaze shifting between them.

Dark frustration slithered with the ugly green jealousy Trevor was intentionally stoking. Why? What was the bastard playing at? Carson sucked in a long, slow breath and found the calm he'd honed through years of taking his father's rants and digs meant to motivate. He wouldn't rise to the bait Trevor had laid out.

Trevor made a pointed look toward Avery, and Gregory shifted to follow his gaze. What the fuck?

"This discussion isn't for here," Carson ground out. They were by a wall, the nearest guest far enough away to provide some privacy. But that didn't make it okay.

Not when so much was at stake.

Gregory turned back, a knowing smile lit with speculation on his blunt face. "I was wondering how that turned out." He leaned in, voice lowered. "Her profile is pretty sparse on the app. Is that intentional, or is she temporary?"

"She is not a member," he snapped. A protective possessiveness raged up to destroy that thin line he'd been balancing on. "She is not available for anything that doesn't include me." Each growled word spewed his intent even if he hadn't acknowledged it.

"Is that so?" Trevor challenged. He made a pointed look at Avery, who was on the dance floor with that fucking IT guy. "I wonder...does she know that?"

There was a group of people dancing, mostly women, but a few of the younger guys were in the mix. The hip-hoppy song had a deep beat that Avery swung her hips to. The fucking IT guy matched her moves in a clear nonverbal communication of his desire, and Avery wasn't discouraging him.

"I'm thinking no," Gregory quipped. Each note of his laughter dug into the cracks that threatened to expose Carson's fears. The very ones Avery had started with one innocent stumble into a room she shouldn't have entered.

And they both would've missed out on so much if she hadn't. What would he miss if he continued to insist on just sex between them? Boardroom sex.

He was being a stubborn ass.

"Fuck. You. Both." Carson reverted to his teenage

response to just about everything. Only back then, he'd never said it aloud.

Trevor tipped his head back and released a full laugh that had more than a few heads turning their way. The sound was familiar to Carson, but it was apparent from the wide eyes and gaping mouths that most didn't know it.

Gregory heaved a sigh, finished off his beer and set the glass aside. "I'm tempted to whisk Tam upstairs to a room and sleep until we have to go home."

"What?" The statement yanked Carson from his own stewing to stare at Gregory. "Sleep?" It wasn't that long ago when Gregory and Tam had been active participants in the Boardroom, and now he wanted to rent a hotel room to sleep?

"Christ, man." Gregory scrubbed a hand over his face. "Twins are exhausting."

"And precisely why I'm never having kids," Trevor said, a slight disgust in his tone.

"Aw, but they're beautiful," Gregory countered, his love for his kids clear.

"I'm sure they are." Trevor finished his drink, brows drawing together. "To you. But some of us know better than to travel down that road." He looked to Carson as his comrade in the baby ban.

Carson lifted his glass in agreement. He'd never wanted kids, a point they'd discussed in their twenties and held strong through their thirties. But his gaze wandered to Avery even as he toasted Trevor. Any child of hers would be beautiful. Blond curls and blue eyes or maybe green. With her fresh face and courage even when she doubted herself.

Sexy. Bold. Innocent. Daring. Kind.

She'd be an excellent mother too.

He hung his head and finally accepted defeat. He was so damn drunk on her, it was edging on pathetic. Which meant he had exactly two choices: abstain, or consume until he crashed.

Chapter Fifteen

Avery set her clutch on the ledge over the sink and washed her hands. The bathroom door swung open, and she smiled through the mirror at the woman who passed to the stalls. Her smile fell immediately after she was gone. The pretending was harder than she'd estimated.

But she'd keep doing it. She had no choice.

Carson Haggert wouldn't break her.

Not that he was actually trying to do so. He was just being himself, and that was the hard part. She wanted every part of him. Even that distant, cool veneer he plastered on in the office.

She checked her lipstick and reapplied a fresh coat. Her stomach had been in a state of upheaval since she'd stepped from the cab. She could only hope she was hiding her nerves. The two glasses of wine had helped with that, along with her dignity.

She flat-out refused to let him see how he affected her. Not out of the Boardroom. There, she could give him everything—and had.

But this wasn't the Boardroom.

Asshole.

She laughed at her scowl, but let her annoyance fire the anger that was holding her pride strong. Carson had opened a whole new sexual world to her, and that was the only part of her he was getting. She *could* fuck just to fuck, just like him.

The toilet flushed and that was her signal to bail before she was forced to make polite conversation. She'd taken two steps into the hallway when she was grabbed from behind. Her yelp shot free as she was swung around and hauled into the recess of another set of doors.

Her pulse raced with her reeling thoughts and the fear that'd launched her heart into her throat. She stared up into Carson's stony face and tried to process what was happening. She sucked in a deep breath and got a heavy dose of his masculine scent. Sweet heaven.

His eyes blazed dark with things she couldn't process. Want. Desire. Anger.

"What are you doing?" she managed to snap, confusion blending with her own anger.

He inhaled, nostrils flaring as he cupped her jaw, angling her head as he lowered his. "I have to have you."

His mouth crushed over hers before she'd untwisted his words. He plunged in deep with a forceful swipe of his tongue that left little doubt to his desire. Any thought of struggling was snatched away beneath his ardent demand. He consumed her instantly, every stroke of his tongue and harsh gasp dragging her deeper into the spell he wove.

Her head spun, and her brain shut down until there was nothing but him. God, how she wanted him. This. Everything he was doing to her.

He bound her to his chest with his arm, her own arms trapped between them. He controlled the moment. The kiss. Her. If he let go right then, she'd crumble to the ground.

He forced her head back, and she arched to give him what he wanted. Every insistence she'd had fled with his heady touch. She could only think of getting more. Of feeling him in her, thrusting until she came.

She was alive with want, every cell burning to get closer.

The world went on around them, and she couldn't get herself to care. The party was just down the hall. Anyone could walk by. Find them.

He spun them around, and her back hit the wall before she'd registered the move. He pressed in, his thigh spreading her legs, and she gave him everything. That wild freedom unleashed beneath his demand. *Yes.* She struggled to release her arms, her purse getting lost in her bid to hold him.

She dug her fingers into his hair and returned his kiss with the dark passion he'd released. Everything was adrift. Nothing else mattered but this moment. This heat. This man.

His groan was a low rumble that got consumed by their kiss. He inched back. His breaths heated her lips with quick gusts. He searched her, his eyes stormy with the lust he'd dragged from her.

Her chest rose and fell in a rapid pace, before he reclaimed her mouth. *Yes.* Her silent cry slammed through her on a desperate note. This wasn't her. She didn't attack a man in public.

But she *was* this woman with him.

And she loved it. Every gasping, naughty, wild second of it.

He ripped his mouth from hers to drag her closer. His breath cut over her ear. His whiskers scraped her jaw with each kiss down it. She struggled to land her own sloppy kisses, yet couldn't break away from the line of fiery kisses he layered up her neck.

"I want to see you fall apart," he mumbled near her ear, his tongue tracing a line around the shell. "Swallow your cries as you shatter."

"Yes," she whispered, the deep rasp tearing at her raw throat. Her hips undulated in a slow grind against his leg, but it wasn't enough. An ache grew in waves from her pussy and demanded fulfillment.

He'd done this to her. He'd shown her how great sex could be. How thrilling it was to break from her own confining mold. And she didn't want to go back.

Ever.

A door banged nearby, the vibration trembling through the wall behind her. The tactile reminders of their location added another layer to her lust. They could get caught at any moment. By anyone. Including someone from work.

He reclaimed her mouth, and she fell back, giving him everything. She trusted him, even here. Now.

He shoved the hem of her dress up, his fingers snaking between her legs to find her pussy. She whimpered at his touch. A hard, pressing swipe that dipped into her on a firm thrust before sliding up to her clit.

Oh, fuck yes. She shivered with the need that shot from aching to volatile in a heartbeat. He stroked her hard and fast right where it drove her crazy. He knew her body and used his knowledge to bring her orgasm crashing over her.

She clenched down, muscles constricting before her release broke free. It ignited from her core to shudder through every nerve ending before tingling out her toes and fingers. She gasped, her cry halted by his palm. He clamped it over her mouth, cutting off her voice and air.

Her eyes flew open as another ripple of passion clenched through her womb. He stared down at her, eyes crazy with desire and awe, his want so clear. He didn't hide anything, and she soaked up every addicting drop of his focus.

Their connection strengthened her release until the last raking spasm mellowed into a languid drift. She sank into the wall, and he slowly removed his hand from her mouth. Her first deep inhalation was snatched away by his kiss. It was firm yet slowly gentle. A soft brush. A peck. Another. And then another until he rested his forehead to hers.

His breath rushed over her cheek mimicking her own. Her pulse raced, the rhythm pounding in her ears. He nudged his nose against hers in a tender touch of lazy want. He kissed her again, his hand coming up to cup her cheek.

She floated in the buzz that ripped logic from her head and filled her with hope. It was dangerous and scary and impossible to stop. Not that she wanted to. Not now.

The door slammed again. A pair of women's voices drifted down to break their bubble. A small sound of protest leaked from her lips when he eased back. He stroked a thumb over her cheek with those tender brushes that eased down to flutter through her chest and circled her heart.

He was so dangerous to her, and she couldn't get herself to care.

She drew in a long breath and caught the musky scent of her own arousal. There was something so very naughty about that. Was it on his fingers, or had she come that hard that it filled the air? Either one was raunchy and delicious at once.

He swiped his thumb under her lip, his eyes tracking its path. "Did you bring a coat?"

It took a moment for her brain to catch up to his question. "No," she answered on a raspy croak.

"Fix your lipstick and then meet me outside." He sealed his command with a soft kiss that had her stomach fluttering again. That mix of hard and soft was totally her weakness. One she'd never realized before him.

Her slow nod was an automatic confirmation she didn't question when she probably should have. But she wanted to go with him, and that was all that mattered right then.

He bent down to retrieve her dropped purse. Her hand shook when she reached to take it from him. "Thank you," she whispered, her voice lost behind the silly fantasies spinning free with the hope that'd escaped.

His smile was warm if small. He ran a hand through his hair, straightened his tie and jacket before stepping up to place another kiss on her lips. She closed her eyes and savored the unspoken promise that remained. The gentle confirmation flowed down to eradicate any doubt that'd tried to sneak in. He was giving her something and she'd take it, whatever it was.

"Go," he murmured.

Her eyes fluttered open, her strength returning at the nugget of truth sprouting to life. This wasn't the Boardroom. This wasn't prearranged.

This was something else. Something more.

She reached up and used her thumb to wipe away the ring of pink that stained the edge of his lips. Heat blazed in his eyes as his tongue snaked out to lick the pad, the tease both a reminder and a temptation. Need swelled swift and hot to crest over her chest and clench her pussy. She wanted him again. Right now. Here.

He cleared his throat, stepping away. "I'll get my car." He glanced down the hallway before looking back. "I'll see you in a few." Promise burned in his gaze and seared her lust with every intention outlined within it.

He strode away, back straight, composure in place when she still doubted if she could stand without the support of the wall behind her. Wow.

A smile curved over her lips in a secret slide of wonder. This was happening—had happened. Her stomach flipped, and she pressed a hand to it, inhaling. There were so many risks involved. Her job, her dignity, her heart. And every one of them was worth it if it meant she could keep feeling like this. Wild. Free.

Powerful.

Understanding dawned in a spark of awe followed by an amazed giggle. She'd never applied that word to herself and sex before. Not before Carson. Not until he'd shown her how her sexuality affected him and other men. Not until she'd owned the sensual side of herself— and set it free.

And I'm not going back. She shoved away from the wall, shoulders pulled back. A sense of ownership trickled down from her full breasts to her damp panties. She lifted her chin and stepped from the alcove. She smiled at the women exiting the bathroom, a delicious wickedness igniting at their quick double takes.

She waited for the flash of shame that threatened only to find none. Not even when her reflection confirmed that she looked as thoroughly debauched as she felt. Her lipstick was smudged in a telling smear of pink, and more than a few strands of hair had escaped the clips that held it up.

Her grin was knowing and wonderful. This woman staring back at her was someone she'd never dared to be—until Carson.

And Avery really, really liked her.

Chapter Sixteen

The streetlights flickered by on a consistent bloom and fade as Carson drove through the San Francisco streets. He glanced at Avery, his gaze lingering longer than it should. The shadows played off the curve of her jaw and line of her nose. Her mouth was parted, lips still puffy from their romp in the hotel hallway.

He'd almost fucked her right there. Pants down, dick in, propriety lost to her.

Almost.

His grip tightened on the steering wheel, and he refocused on the road. His erection ran a hard line over his lower abdomen fueled by the desire simmering just below his guise of civility.

"Where are we going?"

Avery's soft question cut through the silence to remind him of how abnormal this was. Her, him, where he was taking her. "My place."

"Oh." Her response was more of a sound than a word. It whispered through the air to dance over his nerves.

Nerves. Why the fuck was he nervous?

"Is that okay?" he asked.

He could feel her studying him, her gaze singeing

those sensitive nerves he'd thought long gone. Her low "yes" came without preamble and no follow-up.

The weight pressing on his chest lightened, and he sucked in a long, slow breath. Visions of her sprawled across his sheets, hair splayed around her head, eyes heavy with passion almost had him groaning aloud. He'd never imagined a woman in his bed before, and now the thought of Avery in it was seared into his brain.

The air crackled with a note of promise tied to the unknown. In many ways, this car ride with Avery was the same as the ones they'd taken to Boardroom events. Yet it was very different. It was just them. No pending scene or audience.

And that was both frightening and exciting. He was making a big leap here. Hopefully, he wouldn't fuck up their arrangement by doing so.

The car coasted down the hill, dipping with each flattening for a cross street. The darkness of the bay was a pitch of oily black and gray visible at the end of the incline. His place was tucked into the Marina district, just a few blocks from the water and the Palace of Fine Arts.

His headlights flashed over the front of his building, highlighting the gray stucco and crisp white trim on the three-story structure. Avery's low giggle caught his attention as he pulled into the garage, which defined the first floor of the building.

"What?" he asked, a smile pulling at his lips. Her laugh was contagious, especially when paired with that open smile of hers.

"Nothing." She shook her head, a teasing mischief twirling in her tone. He lifted a brow and cut the engine. The dome light came on to reveal the same amusement sparking in her eyes. "Really," she insisted with a small shrug. "I was just envious of your garage. Which is silly."

"My garage?" That pricked at his ego for some strange reason. "I have no idea how to respond to that."

"Right?" She squeezed her eyes shut, that adorable red flush rising over her cheeks. She was nervous, and the understanding eased his own.

He cupped a hand around her nape and drew her in. Her eyes sprang open to trap him with the purity of her emotions. Want and fear. Desire and hesitation. "Only what you want," he told her, his lips hovering a breath from hers.

"What?" Her brows dipped.

"I won't push you, Avery. Into anything."

She searched him, more questions flashing before the dome light faded out to leave them in the hazy glow of the garage light. "What if I want you to?"

His dick twitched a leap of want that matched the twisting lurch of his heart. That one question opened so many doors. Ones that led to things he'd avoided for so damn long.

Ones he suddenly wanted to set free and explore.

"I trust you," she whispered.

Her words nailed his heart as her lips closed over his. She pressed in, taking the kiss into a deep clash of tongues and heat. Her brazen honesty twisted every burning want that dug through his groin and ran rampant over his logic.

He dug his fingers into her hair and slowly forced her head back, following her movement until he had control of her and his wild thoughts. He kissed her until she gasped for breath and he ached for her heat.

He reluctantly released her with a last nip at her bot-

tom lip. He could suck on it all night, taste her peppermint flavor and get lost in the sweetness. But not here.
He exited the car before he acted like a hormonal teen
and tried to fuck her in the front seat. Not when there
was a king-size bed waiting for them two stories up.

Her smile was weak when she met him at the back
of the car. He took her hand and led her up the stairs to
his unit on the top floor. The one-bedroom condo was
spacious and maxed with the upgrades he'd demanded
before moving in.

He flicked on the entry light and led her straight
into his bedroom, which was off the foyer. Their shoes
clicked on the hardwood floors and echoed through the
room. He took her purse from her free hand and set it on
the dresser. Her grip tightened when he turned to face
her, but there was no hesitation in her eyes. No doubts.

The light drifted in from the entry to cast a halo
around her blond hair, leaving her face in shadow. His
heartrate kicked up with the sucker punch to his chest.
"You're so damn beautiful," he whispered before claiming her mouth yet again.

He couldn't get enough of her, still. Even after weeks
of having her, tasting her, watching her grow and explore and revel in her desires.

The kiss deepened immediately. Passion and fire and
lust exploded in a rush to escape. It was always like
this with her. Crazy, heated, intense beyond a normal
hookup.

She clutched at the back of his head, her fingers digging into his skull. The bite was familiar now and set
off a chain reaction to his balls. He swung her around
and backed her up to the bed, never breaking their kiss.

He swept his tongue over hers, each stroke a mirror of

what he wanted to do to her pussy. The memory of her musky scent assaulted his mind, and he groaned with his hunger. He tore his mouth free to nibble up her jaw before trailing his tongue down her neck. She hummed in approval, drawing him closer. That fresh peppermint scent of hers was missing tonight, replaced by a sultry heat that matched her red dress.

One he wanted off, now.

She slipped her hands beneath the collar of his suit jacket to shove at the material. Yes, damn it. The need to feel her skin against his, to finally touch every part of her unhindered after weeks of fucking half-dressed, overrode caution and any remaining patience.

"I want you naked," he said near her ear. "Sprawled on my bed. Legs spread wide and open for me." He scraped his teeth over her neck, her throat working with her hard swallow.

"Yes," she whispered. "Please." She ground her hips into his, and he bit down on her tender skin. *Christ*. His dick had been hard for what felt like years, his need at a boiling point.

Her cry drove him even more. He had to have her soon, yet he wanted to do so much more too. The rush to reach fulfillment was tempered by his first chance to fully play with her.

To tease and nurture her desire like he'd been able to do in the Boardroom scenes, but this would be just for them.

For her.

The slash of her zipper broke through their rough breaths as he eased it down the back of her dress. The material loosened, the front sagging when he straightened. Her eyelids were heavy with lust, her passion so visible he could've drowned in it.

She lifted her chin to him, lips parting on a slow exhale. "You, too." She ran her palms up his chest, a trail of fire and want sizzling in their wake from that simple caress.

He stepped back, and her lips curled up in a wicked tease that was so damn sexy. She kept her eyes locked on his as she reached up and removed the little clips holding her hair up. Curls tumbled down to fall around her shoulders in a waterfall of silky temptation. And she knew it.

She bit her lip, let it slide out before slicking her tongue over the same spot. The move was obvious yet so damn hot coming from her. This was the dangerous, wild Avery who'd emerged in the Boardroom. The one who owned every part of herself along with the wanton desire she harbored.

And she was all his.

He loosened his tie, tugged it off. His jacket followed, his eyes glued to hers as he tossed it over his dresser. Her smile turned sultry when she drew her dress down her arms. The bodice fell free to reveal full breasts beneath a lacy pink bra. Dark nipples were outlined under the design.

His mouth watered as his throat went dry. He undid his cuffs before working his way down the buttons on his shirt. She tracked his movements, a flush darkening her cheeks when he tugged his shirttails free and tossed the material to the side.

Cooler air swooped in to caress his heated skin. Anticipation prickled over his chest and swirled in his stomach. Her breast rose and fell in telling beats with each inhalation. The tension strung between them on a note of promise based on past knowledge. He could already feel her clenching around him, hear her shortened gasps right before she came. His neck and shoulders tingled with the coming crescent-bites of her nails.

A little nudge was all it took to have her dress falling in a pool of red material at her feet. She opened her hand and let the collection of hair clips tumble to the floor. He swallowed hard, his gaze traveling from her saucy red heels, up her long legs to the matching pink lace of her thong. He licked his lips, the thought of her taste whetting his palate.

Two steps, that was all it took to reach her. He hauled her to him, breath hitching when skin met skin. Her lacy bra teased his nipples, sending sparks racing to his groin on a train of lust.

He ran his fingers through her hair, the silky strands tickling his hand before he cupped the back of her head. "What the fuck am I going to do with you?" he mumbled.

That slow smile of hers worked its way over her lips. She drew his head down, pausing a breath away in a trick she'd picked up from him. His pulse raced as she looked into his eyes, the heat and want mixed with an honesty he couldn't reject. This was more for her too. Not just another fuck.

His heart did a clench-and-hold that tightened his stomach and nipped at the longing he'd blocked years ago. He was heading into the unknown and he couldn't get himself to stop. Not with her.

She lowered her gaze, her lips brushing his as she whispered, "Fuck me."

He was on her then, his mouth claiming hers in a desperate drive to stake his ownership when he had none. Not yet.

But there was no way he'd be satisfied with one night. And there was no damn way he'd let another man fuck her. Not after this.

Whatever the fuck this was.

Chapter Seventeen

Carson kissed her like a man possessed, and Avery gave herself over to him. His tongue teased and stroked with every little dip of his head, and she met each one without thought. No, she couldn't think. Not now. Not in the moment.

If she thought at all, this entire night would be too overwhelming.

His erection ground into her abdomen, his skin hard yet soft against hers. Her senses were overstimulated with everything about him. That masculine, woody scent of his swirled through her head to spin with the dizzying stroke of his hands down her back, and lower, over her ass, beneath the thin line of her thong.

Yes. Her cry was silent, the want climbing with every heated second that passed. Would she ever get close enough to him?

Her moan was muffled by his mouth when her bra loosened. His hands skimmed over her back, one slipping to her side before it slid beneath the fabric to cub her breast. She heaved a sigh of relief that hitched when he tweaked her nipple, but it was only a tease. *More* chanted in her head as she sucked in deep breaths through her nose. *Touch me. Pinch me. Please. Please. Everywhere.*

He pulled back, removing her bra as he did. His eyes were dark with lust and promise. "Lay down on the bed."

His authoritative tone sent a line of goose bumps down her back. His distinctive rumble deepened into that sultry husk from the Boardroom. Her nipples tightened impossibly more, sending a wave of tingles over her chest that raced to her clenching pussy.

She'd never been ordered around in the bedroom. And she'd never had a man look at her the way Carson was. Like he wanted to consume and savor her at once.

And that was her power. It flared through her to ignite a confidence she'd never had in this situation.

A sly smile curved over her lips as she crawled onto the bed. Every move was deliberate, including the sway of her hips and the peek of a glance she sent him over her shoulder.

His low growl urged her on even more. She could tease him, taunt him with what she had and he wanted. This newfound strength was heady and so damn amazing.

She turned to her side, her smile shifting from sly to knowing when she caught his fiery gaze. She had him. And for right now, in this moment, he was all hers.

Just hers.

She reached down to remove first one, then the other heel. She tossed each one over the side of the bed before rolling to her back, knees bent, legs spread. The pose was decadent and blatantly smutty. And she loved it.

His nostrils flared on his inhalation, lips compressed with the hard clamp of his jaw. He wanted her, and she reveled in that knowledge. She truly felt beautiful under his gaze.

"Play with your nipples," he rumbled as he undid

his belt. Her heart jumped, but she complied without thought. This time she was the show, and there was something thrilling about it.

She slid her palms over her abdomen before cupping each breast. They were heavy and full in her hands, and she savored the delicious sensation of simply experiencing her own touch. Of how her breasts molded and compressed when she squeezed, waking a want she'd never bothered to explore before. Not with herself.

She tipped her head back, eyelids lowering when she finally pinched her nipples. The bite was gentle until she squeezed harder. Her back bowed as a nip of pain burned into desire.

"That's it," he encouraged. "Pinch them harder."

And she did. Her whimper eased out when she rolled the tips between her fingers, twisting like he'd done. The sting shifted to breath-stealing anguish, but she didn't let go. This was his show, and she'd give him whatever he asked for.

She squeezed her eyes closed and tried to breathe through the stabbing digs flaring from her nipples. It wove over her chest and dove deep as it spread in a languid thread to her pussy. She tracked it, a part of her enthralled by the path.

The bed dipped, and then Carson was between her legs. His breath ghosted hot over her pussy through the thin material of her thong, wrenching a shudder from her. "Fucking gorgeous," he said on a low note before he shoved the slight covering aside and swiped his tongue through her heat in one long stroke.

She gasped and curled up, her stomach muscles clenching as the pleasure ripped through her. "Oh, God," she cried, opening her legs wider.

His chuckle tickled her clit before he flicked his tongue over it. Her moan was long and filled with the amazing warmth spreading from her pussy. The pain was gone, replaced by an intense bliss that hovered in her core.

Her hands fell to her side as her focus zoomed to his attack. He was relentless. His assault on her pussy was just as intense as the one he'd made on her mouth. He paused long enough to yank her thong off her legs before diving back in. Each hot lick, flick and suck drove her deeper and deeper into the haze of lust and need. Her pussy clenched, demanding to be filled, but he didn't heed her pleas.

Her hips jerked up in a desperate quest to get him to fill her. A finger, two, more—anything. She ached with the emptiness while pleasure coiled and tightened beneath her clit.

"Please," she begged.

He shoved her hips down, his rough purr of satisfaction vibrating over her tender flesh. She sucked in a gasping breath, legs quivering with the unfulfilled need that had become an aching want.

"Please what?" he coaxed. He slid his tongue down to circle her opening. Just circle. A slow glide that edged the rim without dipping into her heat. Her mind blanked to everything but getting that last plunge. Of having her walls finally stretched and filled.

She squirmed, trying to get closer, but he held her hips in place. Her whine was just that. A pitiful plea for what she couldn't seem to say.

"Please what?" he repeated, his voice stronger, more demanding. He was going to make her say it. Again.

There was no logic to why she was resisting. She'd

told him before. She'd said it—begged for it—in front of others. Yet now it stuck in her throat, trapped behind the last outcropping of resistance.

For some damn reason, she didn't want to give in to him. She could hold out. She could control her own wants.

His tongue skimmed over her opening before returning to her clit to torture her with more flicks and just enough pressure to bring her orgasm so close but not over. It hovered right there, until everything pulsed with the need to explode.

"Please," she finally begged again, head tossing. "God, please just fuck me." The words tumbled out on a rush of courage and acceptance. She wanted this and so much more from Carson.

Her plea was a sweet note of undoing—both hers and his.

Carson surged up and took her mouth in a kiss that said more than he could voice. He devoured her, sought out her sweet flavor and let it blend with the musky saltiness that lingered on his tongue. The combination was perfect and delicious.

He wanted more. So much more.

She gripped his shoulders, legs winding around his hips to hold him close. Avery's passion was so beautiful when she unleashed it. Damn how he wanted to please her. To make her fly. To see her smile and make her cry out with pleasure.

And he had to have her before *he* went crazy.

He shifted back and waited for her eyelids to flutter open. The want and need flared in her enlarged pupils, but there was also something else. Something he was afraid to define, yet a part of him craved it.

He adjusted his hips until the tip of his dick nudged her opening. Her lips parted, breath holding with his as he slid into her on one continuous glide. Heat and wet and tightness surrounded his dick in a torturous yet amazing clench.

She tightened her hold on his neck, mouth opening on a silent gasp until he was buried within her. He sucked in a breath and savored the connection. It was different in ways he couldn't articulate, but it simmered over his senses and prickled down his spine in awe.

She held his gaze as she drew him down. Her breath hitched, the warmth gusting over his lips before she pressed her mouth to his. The soft, gentle glides countered the wild tension hammering to break free. It crept into his chest and wound around his heart to pluck at the denial holding it captive.

His groan tore from his chest in a brazen escape. He jerked his hips back but halted. A breath. Two. Her eyes were wide, expectant.

His arms quivered as he struggled with the needs of his body and the will of his mind. He closed his eyes, a sense of defeat and acceptance flowing over him when he slid back home. Her sigh was soft, her legs contracting around his hips.

He was lost. So damn lost.

He buried his face in the crook of her neck and gave in to nature. He set a sweet, rolling pace that nurtured the desire spreading from his groin. The warmth flowed through his limbs and meshed with the longing cresting from his chest.

Avery surrounded him. All of him. Every sense was focused on her. Her soft cries. Her firm grip on his nape. Her addicting scent that'd deepened with her desire. She ran her nails down his spine, and he trembled with the goose bumps that followed.

He rocked his hips, the pace increasing without thought. He was nothing but instincts now. Need drove him. The need to hear her cry out with her release. To feel her come around him. To catch those small hitches and aftershocks that trembled through her.

To taste her sweetness and see her amazement in eyes heavy from the endorphins flooding her system.

His dam of restraint broke on a hard crash of primal ownership. He crashed his hips to hers, driving deep and hard into her. He couldn't get close enough. Deep enough. And she met him on every stroke. Drawing him down, clenching around him until he grunted from the sheer glory of it.

He gasped for air, dragged sloppy kisses up her jaw, then pressed his temple to hers. Her breath hitched. Her nails dug into his back. He drew his knees up to change the angle. She cried out, and he nailed that same spot over and over.

"Come," he demanded. "Fuck. Please come," he mumbled, eyes squeezed tight. *Come now. Come before I explode. Come for me. Please.*

Her orgasm burst free in a wave of clenching muscles, a breathy whine and hard spasms. Pain laced through his shoulder blades from her nail bites to trigger his own release. His harsh grunt ripped from his throat as he ground into her, seeking every last clench and ripple that stroked over his dick.

He emptied himself into her, relief and awe floating through on the ending wave that left him gasping for air. Dazed, drowning, lost. He sucked in air, unable to move or even think.

This...this wasn't a fuck. Not *just* a fuck.

He rolled his head against hers, brushed a kiss to her cheek and wrapped his arms around her as he scrambled for the control he'd somehow lost.

There was no controlling this, though. Not anymore.

And for once in his life, he didn't care.

Avery floated in the warm afterglow of bliss and contentment. That had been amazing. So much more than just sex.

At least for her.

Held tightly in his arms—their breaths still heavy, skin still heated, connected in the most intimate way possible—she wanted to believe it was for him too.

She laid a kiss on his jaw. The stubble tickled her lips, but she held it there, believing he would understand her meaning. She couldn't say what was churning inside her, not if she wanted any chance of experiencing this with him again.

After another long moment, one where her arms grew heavy and her legs slid down to rest on the mattress, Carson reached between them and eased out of her. The loss was tangible, but she clamped her lips tight to stay silent.

He held the condom in place as he rolled to the side of the bed. Her brain hitched, a frown forming at her own lack of awareness. She'd totally forgotten about protection. "Thank you for putting that on," she told him. She had an IUD, and she assumed his Boardroom membership meant he was STI-free, but they hadn't discussed going bare. Hell, she didn't remember when he'd gotten rid of his pants either.

His lips quirked. "Of course. I need to take care of this." He pointed out the door before he stood. She turned to her side and openly ogled his taut butt cheeks and muscled legs as he left. How could she have missed admiring that before?

She debated if she should get dressed or crawl under the covers. Was this where it got awkward? If this was just sex, then he'd take her home, wouldn't he?

And she shouldn't assume it was anything more, no matter how it felt to her.

With heavy limbs and heart, she shoved herself up to sit on the edge of the bed. A chill swept over her skin and she shivered. Indecision had her still sitting there when Carson walked back into the room.

He stopped in the doorway, blocking the flow of light from the hall. His expression was concealed by the shadow, but she could tell he was staring at her. What was he thinking? The urge to cover herself brought a wave of heat up her neck.

Damn it. Why now? Where was that brave new woman she'd embraced earlier tonight? At least she didn't look away from him.

"Do you need to go home?" he asked.

That low rumble of his floated across the room to caress her. Her shoulders lowered, the tension fading. "No. Unless you want me to leave."

He flicked off the hallway light. The room plunged into a haze of dark outlines. He came toward her, each step a slow stride that seemed almost predatory. Another shiver raced over her skin, but this time she wasn't cold.

He stopped before her, and she kept her eyes up even though his dick was right there. The musky scent of them filled her nose on her next inhalation, and she couldn't stop the smile that formed. She definitely wasn't used to being so casually naked around anyone.

She knew now that his chest was free of hair, his muscles firm and defined from his abdomen to his shoulders. He was fit and strong and everything that made her feel protected even when he loomed over her.

He cupped her chin, dipped to kiss her. "Will you stay?"

Her heart jumped, hope springing forward yet again. She swallowed it down before saying, "Yes."

"Good." He kissed her again. Longer, deeper, oh-so thoroughly that she forgot about being naked. Forgot about remaining distant. Forgot about tomorrow and all that would come.

He pressed forward until she fell back, his lips never leaving hers. She wrapped her arms around his neck and made the choice not to worry. Not when she was here with this amazing man who'd changed her life and was becoming so damn important to her.

Maybe it *was* just a night, but it promised to be a very, very excellent one.

Chapter Eighteen

Carson woke with a start. His eyes sprang open, senses on alert. Why? His pulse raced, his brain coming online with the squeal of breaks. A stream of muffled curses filtered into the room from outside to slowly bring the world back to him.

Christ. He flipped to his back, rubbed his eyes. His yawn stretched his jaw. *What time is it?*

The sun blazed through his thin curtains, and he squinted at the ceiling as he adjusted to the brightness. He didn't sleep this late—whatever time it was. He was usually up at dawn no matter when he went to bed.

He shifted to his side and froze. The previous night raced in with all the heat and passion that'd accompanied it. The other side of the bed was rumpled but empty. Had Avery left?

He shoved up and scanned the room, breath held until he spotted traces of her belongings. Her red heels still lay in the middle of the floor where she'd tossed them, a scrap of pink lace was bunched on the floor by his dresser and her red dress was folded neatly over the back of the chair in the corner.

He flopped back down, breath gusting out. Why did it

matter so much that she was still there? If she'd been any other woman, he would've been relieved that she'd left.

But she wasn't any other woman.

If he was honest, she'd never been.

He tugged on a pair of nylon shorts and a T-shirt before making a quick stop at the bathroom down the hall. He glanced in the other rooms as he passed them, but didn't spot her. *Where is she?*

A mug sat waiting for him on the counter next to his one-cup coffee machine. A dirty spoon was in his sink, but other than that, nothing was different. He made himself a cup of coffee and sighed heavily after the first sip. Maybe his brain would function now.

Coffee cup in hand, he took the hallway stairs up to the shared rooftop deck. His smile broke free when he spotted her. Avery was curled up on a deck chair beneath the shade of a table umbrella. Her feet were tucked under her, one of his T-shirts hanging loosely off a shoulder. Her hair flowed in loose waves over her shoulders as she focused on something on her phone.

His heart did another one of those weird twisting things that aligned so clearly with the happiness flowing through him. It was just the day. The beauty of the morning. That was it.

And he wasn't fooling himself.

The sky *was* a stunning pale blue with a few wispy clouds streaking through it. The Golden Gate Bridge stretched in the distance, one tower clearly visible through the foliage. A slight breeze ruffled her hair and swayed the palm fronds on the surrounding trees.

The scent of breakfast teased the air, along with the ever-present freshness of the bay. His stomach growled, and he paused to take another hit of his coffee. He needed something to clear the wild thoughts from his mind.

Avery lifted her head, smiled when she saw him. "Hey," she said as he approached. "I hope it's okay that I'm up here." She motioned to the deck.

"It's fine." He pulled out a chair and took a seat next to her. He glanced at the view, which also included the dome from the Palace of Fine Arts and the surrounding hills both behind them and across the bay. "I forget this is here." He said that more to himself. He couldn't remember when he'd last used the deck.

She set her phone on the glass table and turned toward the water. "The views are gorgeous."

"Yeah," he agreed distractedly. *She is beautiful.* The cheesiness of the thought didn't bother him like it should. "Sorry I slept so late," he said when she remained silent.

"It's fine." She shrugged, her smile still there. "I thought you might need the sleep."

"You could've woken me up."

"And then I would've missed this." Her tone was light as she extended her hand to encompass the surrounding vista, but her smile fell as she stared at the view.

"Hey." He leaned over and touched her chin until she turned her head to look at him. The hesitation and doubt in her eyes kicked at his guilt even though he wasn't sure why. What he did know was he didn't like seeing it. "I'm glad you stayed last night."

She blinked, the doubt still there. "Me, too." Her admission was soft and contained more of that hesitancy.

He urged her closer until he could finally kiss those lips he couldn't seem to get enough of. He meant to keep it short, light, but one touch blew his intentions to hell. He shifted closer, licked her lips and found the wet heat

when she opened to him. Coffee and that sweet underlying flavor of Avery flowed into him, and he forgot
about thinking.

Slow swipes, lazy circles of his tongue, a free fall
into things he had no grasp of. He pulled back after one
last pressing touch. Her eyes had softened, that hesitation erased. He brushed his thumb over her lips, lost
on what to do next but so damn content in the moment.

He sat back, took a drink of his cooling coffee simply
to let his thoughts and emotions settle. She leaned back
in her chair, tucking his shirt around her legs. Her movements were more relaxed, and he was glad about that.

"I hope you don't mind that I borrowed this." She
plucked at the shirt she wore. He'd had that gray T-shirt
with the stretched-out neck and faded baseball logo for
years. He'd never look at it again without picturing her
in it. Just like this.

"It's fine." He ran a finger down her bared shoulder.
She shivered, her gaze flirty when she glanced at him.
He dropped his hand and jerked his thoughts away from
the path of taking her back to his bed for the rest of the
day. "Do you need to get home for anything?"

"No." She shook her head. "Sundays are usually laun-
dry and random errand day."

He nodded in agreement. He also used the day to
catch up on work or to simply program. But he was in
no rush to do anything today. "Do you have family in
the area?" There was so much he didn't know about her.

"No." Her expression warmed. "They all live back
in Ohio."

He raised a brow. "They?"

She shrugged. "Parents, older brother, grandparents,
cousins… You get the idea."

"You're the only one who ventured away." And that in itself was intriguing. But it matched that underlying courage that hid beneath her reservations. "How come?"

Her brows went up. "What? That they're still there or I left?"

"Both?"

Her soft laugh drifted through the air to tease a smile from him. "I don't know why everyone remained close to home. But me…" She shrugged again. "I had an opportunity and figured why not?" She stared into the distance, voice lowering. "What did I have to lose? I could always go back, right? But if I'd turned down that initial job offer, it would've been a fear-based decision, and I refused to let that rule me." She glanced at him, her determination stamped on her face. There was so much unsaid in that statement, but it was clear how proud she was of herself for making the move.

And damn, he was proud of her too when he had no right to feel it. Yet it still spread on a wave of impressed admiration. "Do you miss them? Your family?"

"Yeah." She tipped her head. "But it lessens the longer I'm gone."

He nodded in understanding. "I get that. Your lives become separate where before they were linked."

"Exactly." Her grin flashed. "And I love them dearly, but they don't really know me anymore." She leaned on the table, posture relaxed. "They're all the same. Their friends haven't changed or their routine or their beliefs. But me? I don't even feel like that girl who left home five years ago."

"Five years?" He crossed his arms on the table and leaned in like her. "Is that how long you've been out here?"

"Yeah." She glanced at the view. "And I don't see going back. Ever."

Yet another thing they had in common. "I get that." He'd had no desire to return to Southern Cali after graduating from Stanford.

"What about you?" She flicked her chin at him. "Are you local or a transplant?"

"Transplant." He puffed out a laugh at how that sounded. "But not as far as you. I was born and raised near LA." She looked at him expectantly, and he gave in with another laugh. "Fine." He sat back, stretching his arms over his head before he let them drop. "I have two older brothers. One who still lives in the same town we grew up in and another who's in Seattle. My parents are divorced, but they're both in Southern Cal." And that was the short version of his family tree.

How long had it been since anyone had cared enough to ask? For the most part, guys didn't dig beyond the surface unless they'd known each other for years.

"What do your parents do?" She propped her head on her hand and studied him. Her hair fell over her shoulder, her face mostly makeup-free—and she was even more beautiful. Was that possible?

"My dad's a high school football coach," he said, jerking his thoughts back to their conversation. His dad loved and had sweated that job into his sons through years of practice, lectures and demands. "And my mom's a college math professor."

"Really?" She reached out to run a finger over the bump on the side of his nose. "Did this happen playing football?"

"Yes." His bemused smile flowed in an easy stream, relaxing the tension that still lingered years after the event. "My junior year of high school. I was hit by an illegal blind tackle that knocked my helmet off and slammed my face into the ground." His swallow was reflexive as he prepped for the next part. "The guy had his arm around my neck when we went down." He shrugged at her frown. There was nothing he could do about it now. "The damage to my throat, along with the concussion, left me in the hospital for over a week and my voice like this." He motioned to his mouth in vague reference to the rumble that accompanied every word he spoke.

"Wow." Her brows were raised in impressed shock. "That must've been traumatic."

The husky rasp was a part of him now, but for a long time it'd been a reminder of what'd almost happened. He gave another shrug. "For my mom more than me, I think." He smiled at the memory. "She declared my football career over right then, and my father didn't try to argue."

"And you were okay with that?"

"For the most part." He tried to remember back to that time, but history had a way of mellowing emotions. "I focused on school after that, which worked out well." It'd gotten him into Stanford and where he was today. "What about your parents?" he asked, both interested and ready to change the subject. "What do they do?"

Her lips twisted. "My dad's an accountant. My mom stayed home with us and then worked in a day care center once we were both in middle school."

"That must've been nice."

"What?" She sat up, stretched her shoulders back. "Having my mom home?" He nodded. "It was." She frowned. "Yours wasn't?"

His stomach sank a little and he focused on the hillside in the distance without really seeing it. This was why guys filtered over the surface. The deeper stuff always stirred up emotions better left untouched. He took a drink of his coffee before answering. "My mom was a high school teacher when I was kid. She took night classes to get her master's and eventually her PhD."

Her nod was slow with understanding. "Which meant she was busy."

He shrugged in dismissal. "She was—is—a good mother. And I'm proud of her for going after her dream."

"But…" Avery dipped her head until he lifted his gaze to meet hers. "You missed her as a kid."

His heart clenched around the truth he'd gotten over long ago. He was a fucking adult and way past his childhood. He stood, hand extended. "Should we go get breakfast?"

Her brows dipped, confusion clear before a smile lifted the corners of her mouth. "I don't think I'm dressed for eating out." She glanced down at her shirt.

His thoughts instantly went to the fact that she was absolutely naked under it. Unless she'd stuffed extra underwear in her purse. "Right." And there were better things to do than eat.

He ducked down to steal a kiss, one hand snaking under the collar of her shirt to cup her breast. She squeaked into his mouth and shoved lightly on his shoulders. Not in real protest, or he would've stopped. He played with her nipple until the nub hardened into a tight peak. Her moan rumbled in her throat and she wove her hands around his neck, any resistance gone.

His dick hardened, heat racing to center in his groin. His mind blanked for a moment until a car horn blared from the street below. *Fuck.*

"We could go back to bed," he said near her ear once he'd dragged his lips from hers. He found her other nipple and worked it into a mirror state of the first, thoughts running to all the things he wanted to do with her. Anyone could walk up here. Hell, there were numerous buildings around them that had clear views of their rooftop.

His kink went wild just thinking about it. The risk. The excess. The wrong of it.

She tilted her head, chest lifting. "What if I'm hungry?"

He nipped at her neck. "I'll feed you later. I promise." He pulled away, her groan of regret tempting his desire. He should've been satisfied after last night, yet he wanted her again. Now.

He sat back down and drew her forward until she straddled his lap. He held her gaze the entire time, and she read his intent if her wicked smile was any indication.

"What are you doing?" she asked as she wrapped her hands around his neck. Her knees were bent, her bottom resting on his thighs.

This was a bit insane, even for him. His heart beat harder and his dick twitched beneath his shorts. The wind rushed in to blow her hair over her eyes. He brushed it away from her face and drew her head down. "Kissing you."

Their position put her at the height advantage, and she made use of it. Her mouth pressed to his, and he let his head fall back, giving her the lead. The thrill of seeing how she'd grown with her sexuality made it easy to give over his power—for a little bit.

She cupped his face, tongue thrusting in to claim him in a fierce kiss. The want and need were front and center even in the light of day. He groaned, the urge to sink into her blazing through his groin, damn their location. But that was out of the question.

At least the full fucking part.

He drew a hand down her back, then up her thigh to snake between her legs. She gasped, her mouth withdrawing from his when he found her clit. He was ready, though. Her eyes went wide. Her objection was on her lips when he cupped her neck and jerked her down into another kiss.

She squirmed on his lap, but not to get away. No, her hips worked to meet his quick, persistent rub on her clit. She rotated them in a circle before changing to a rock in unspoken guidance. She was so damn hot.

His pulse raced, stomach clenching, dick aching for her heat. He dipped his fingers into her and groaned. She was soaking wet. Memories of how good it felt to sink into her raced to his dick, which was already so fucking hard.

She rocked forward, a hand braced on his chest as she kissed him with full abandon. "Oh. My. God," she mumbled, her lips grazing his with each panted breath. Her hair had fallen around them to create a semi-shield against the world. An illusion that wasn't real, not by a long shot.

He turned his head, glanced at the buildings across from them, never stopping his play with her pussy. The wetness slicked his way as he drew his fingers back to her clit. The soft sucking and flicking sounds added to the eroticism when everything he was doing was hidden beneath her shirt.

No one could see anything blatant. She was fully covered, as was he. But there was no hiding her passionate expression or their movements. That knowledge jacked his excitement into the stratosphere.

He nipped at her lip, worked her clit faster. "Someone could be watching us," he murmured. He drove his fingers into her when she stilled. She cried out softly, throat working as her hips rotated to meet his thrusts.

Her eyes were closed, head tossed back, hair draping down to brush the back of his other hand. She was a vision of wanton lust, and he loved it. He dipped forward and bit her nipple through the material of her shirt. He wished he could taste her skin, her pussy, screw who could be watching or if they were caught. But he restrained himself, loving the insinuation almost more than the blatant.

She straightened and dragged his head closer to her chest. She held him tightly, grinding down on his fingers. "Yes." Her soft pant was music to his own need.

He sucked on her nipple and used his thumb to stroke her clit. He kept his fingers in her, pumping despite the cramp building in his wrist. Her muscles contracted around his fingers, and her soft whimpers shortened into abbreviated notes.

She trembled, nails digging into his nape. He forced his head up and hauled her into a hard, claiming kiss. He swallowed her cries, holding her to him as her orgasm crashed free. She rode his hand without hesitation, completely abandoned to him.

That alone drove him wild. Once again, that strange possessiveness reared up to stamp his claim on her. He'd brought her to this state. He'd shown her how gorgeous she was when she let go. How passionate she could be.

How brave and free.

And he wanted more of her. This. Them.

* * *

Her movements slowed, breath releasing on a shuddering sigh. Avery's mind was completely blank, overwhelmed by the endorphin high.

She sucked in a long draft of air, forehead pressed to Carson. Everything tingled, even her toes. She didn't want to think either. Not yet. Not when she could still float in the glow of another stunning orgasm.

Carson's fingers should be enshrined in gold. Or maybe cast into an amazing vibrating dildo.

Her soft laugh bubbled up in a weak escape at her inane thoughts.

He flicked his thumb over her clit, and she shivered, muscles tensing. Pleasure burst on a dagger's edge of too much and more. She didn't know if she should beg for another touch or demand he stop. Was it possible to do both?

He rubbed her slowly. The hard circles on her clit started a wave of sensation through her pussy. She squeezed her eyes closed, both embarrassed and enthralled.

"You are so gorgeous like this," Carson rumbled. His breaths were short, tone so rough it scratched over her skin. "I want to fuck you." He thrust his fingers in her. Her walls clenched, trying to hold on to the fullness. "Right here. Right now."

She nodded, lost in the orgasm building yet again. Her entire body was flushed in heat, the breeze doing nothing to cool it. "Yes," she said on a soft exhale. She'd let him too. Out here. In the open. Where anyone could watch them.

Awareness prickled over her nape, plucked at her

mind. People could be watching right now. She should object. Be horrified.

She wasn't.

She was covered. No one could see anything revealing. Just her response. And his. The wanton freedom of being the show without showing a thing turned her on so damn much.

She opened her eyes to watch Carson's hand where it moved between her legs. Her hips rocked with a mind of their own, following the demands of his fingers. The eroticism of it drove her desire higher. Her lust insane. The combination of seeing the action while feeling and hearing the distinctive sounds lit up that wild side of herself that she'd only set free with him.

She could be this woman with him—and he still respected her.

"See how wet you are?" He slipped his fingers out of her just far enough to show them covered in her juices.

Her blush rose in another wave of heat. The pungent scent of her arousal filtered into the air, and she inhaled even deeper, longer. Her abdomen contracted with the want building below it.

He tilted his head so he could kiss her jaw. "I can't get enough of you like this." He drove his fingers back into her. She shuddered, hold tightening on his neck, every nerve ending buzzing with expectation. "Wild. Free." She whimpered. The pressure on her clit increased with his circling pace. Another shudder raked her. Her release was so close.

Right there, hovering, growing, prickling over her skin.

"Mine," he growled. "Fuck. I can't believe you're mine."

Her orgasm broke on a harsh cry that was quickly

smothered by his mouth. Wave after wave of indescrib-
able pleasure rocked her system until there was nothing but joy.

She sagged against him, head tucked into the crook
of his shoulder, gasping for air and something to ground
her. She was vaguely aware of him removing his fingers,
wiping them on his shorts before he hugged her close.
He rubbed her back in soothing strokes, and she simply
absorbed his presence.

Happiness floated through her on wings of possibilities. She refused to read too much into his declaration
at the end, but she could still hope a little. There was
nothing wrong with that. That little nugget had been
growing since last night. She'd contain it, though. Hold
it close so he didn't shove her away.

This is just sex.

His mantra echoed in her head to dim her glow. The
world crowded back in with the rumbled roar of a mo-
torcycle. This was just a moment. One amazing, beautiful moment.

And she could create more of them, line them up and
make a series of moments that would eventually become
a part of her past. That was how life worked.

She rubbed her palm over his chest, her hum one of
contentment. "Thank you," she whispered on a halted
hitch of laughter. "I seem to be saying that to you a lot."
She'd never had a man give so much without demanding his turn. She ran her hand down to stroke her palm
over his erection.

He snorted an abrupt laugh. His hands tightened on
her back and his hips rocked up, but he placed his other
hand over hers to keep her from stroking him again. His

voice was tight when he spoke. "I'll come right here if you keep that up."

"And that's a problem?" She squeezed his dick to tease him.

His half-groan growl was full of frustration but also humor. "Yes. A huge one." He urged her head up so he could slam a kiss to her lips. His eyes were dark with purpose and mischief when he looked at her. "Because if I come here, I can't fuck you like I really want to do." His eyes darkened, smile falling. "Hard. Deep. Until you beg for mercy."

Her pulse jumped both at his words and the intensity of his look. Was there more here? Could he have possibly meant what he'd said about being his? No. She couldn't go there and stay in the moment.

She raised her brows, a smile curving over her lips. "Well, when you put it that way…" She climbed off his lap, taking his hand to urge him up. *Keep it light. Fun.* She could do that. She waggled her brows, face holding for a moment before she slid the hem of her shirt up, giving her hips a shake.

"You're such tease," he joked as he yanked her in and tickled her ribs.

Her laughter broke over the rooftop in a flight of levity and joy. This wasn't sex, and she wouldn't box it into that little category. She also wasn't going to waste any more energy trying to define exactly what it was.

She squirmed out of his hold, skipping backward, smile bursting. The wind blew her hair over her face and she brushed it away, uncaring of how she looked or what anyone thought.

She was happy. Right then. With him.

"And it's all your fault," she taunted, moving toward the exit.

"Mine?" He grabbed their coffee mugs and her forgotten phone, a devilish glint overtaking his features. "Is that so?"

"Yup." She nodded. "Totally."

He took two long strides that cut the distance between them in half. She shuffled back, laughing more.

"How?" he asked as she reached the door.

She paused in the open doorway, smile falling as the truth slipped out. "Because I was afraid to be this person before you." There it was. Bold. Unvarnished, and she refused to regret it. If nothing else, he deserved to know that.

"Yeah?" He stopped before her, the moment suddenly serious. He searched her before the corner of his mouth quirked up. Her heart raced for no clear reason, but she didn't look away or run. She gave a single nod in response. She'd own her words and actions even if they exposed more than she wanted to show.

He shook his head in a slow show of confusion. "I have no idea why. You're a beautiful, amazing, smart woman." Her heart flipped. "And I can't take credit for that."

She swallowed, unsure of what to say. There were so many directions she could take this conversation, and most of them were littered with land mines. "Maybe." She shot him a wink, smirk forming. "But I can certainly thank you."

His brows drew down. "For what?"

She stretched up, lips ghosting close to his. "Making me come so damn hard."

He sucked in a breath, and her own wanton power

grew. She turned around, threw him one last look over her shoulder before hurrying down the stairs. She flew with her own brazenness even though it was probably minor to most.

His laughter chased her, and her smile grew. This was good. And she was going to enjoy every damn moment of it for as long as it lasted.

Chapter Nineteen

"Good morning, Gregory." Avery smiled at her boss as he stopped by her desk. "Can I get you anything before your meetings?" He had two that morning, one in thirty minutes.

"No, thank you." His smile was tired and went with the bags under his eyes. His suit jacket was undone, and a small orange stain was visible on his white shirt when he lifted his arm to scratch his jaw.

"Are you sure?" She stood, smile sympathetic. "Let me grab you a coffee."

His eyes lit up with his widening smile. "Thank you. I'd appreciate that." He'd never been one to make her fetch things nor had he ever treated her like she was beneath him, which was why she wanted to help him. Getting a coffee was easy.

"You might want to wipe that off." She pointed to the stain in another attempt to help. She winced when he looked down and sighed. "Rough morning?"

He tugged the material out and glared at the offending dab of food. "You could say that." He dropped his hand, blew out a breath. "Madison got sick yesterday, and Adam decided to catch it just when his sister got better. And then Tam had an early meeting today and—" He cut

himself off with a tight clamp of his lips. "Wow. Sorry.
None of that is your worry." He forced a smile. "How
was your weekend? Did you enjoy the party? Tam was
disappointed that you left before she got to say hello."

Avery tracked his quick topic change with a startled
laugh. Gregory only rambled when he was tired, and it'd
been a while since he'd gone on quite this badly. She'd
been a little stunned the first time it'd happened after
his twins were born. Now, it made him human.

"I hope Adam feels better soon," she said with complete honesty. His kids were firmly sectioned in the too-
adorable category. "And I had a nice time at the event."
She willed her blush to stay down, but a secret smile
slipped out. She'd had a very, very nice time both at the
event, and after and the next day.

Gregory arched an inquisitive brow, and she rushed
on. "I'm sorry I missed Tam too." His wife had become
a friend over the last year. Thankfully, she was a logical spouse who chose to work with Avery regarding
Gregory's schedule and job responsibilities. "Can I do
anything to help? Send over supplies for the twins or a
bottle of wine for you and Tam?"

His laugh held a relaxed note that Avery took as a
good sign. "Just the coffee, if you don't mind." He turned
to his office before adding, "And those IT cost reports.
Please." The last was tagged on with a tired smile.

She could almost hear his wife admonishing him for
ordering instead of asking. Tam was a petite woman who
smiled sweetly and clobbered anyone who made the mistake of disrespecting her or any woman. "They're sent
and waiting for you in your inbox," she reassured him.

"You're a godsend."

"Remember that at my next review." She shot him a

teasing wink and laughed. "Go." She shooed him into his office. "I'll bring you that coffee."

Her steps were light, smile genuine as she made her way to the break room. She'd spent almost the entire day with Carson yesterday and she refused to dwell on what that meant. A good deal of the morning had been consumed in bed after their rooftop adventure. But he'd eventually ordered takeout, which they'd eaten while watching a movie. It'd been close to dinnertime before he'd driven her home.

It really had been a perfect day, and she wasn't going to spoil it with questions and doubts.

Even if she had no idea how she was supposed to act if she saw Carson today. She assumed they'd be back to formal association and she'd prepared herself for that. This was work, and he was still her superior.

That was all he was here.

Multiple voices flowed from Gregory's office when she returned. Her stomach tightened when she recognized the distinctive timbre of Carson's voice. Her hand clenched around the paper cup, her steps slowing.

She pressed her palm to her abdomen, inhaled, exhaled. *I can do this.*

Her smile was in place when she tapped on the door. Four sets of eyes immediately turned to her as she entered the room. "Your coffee," she said, focusing on Gregory when she set the cup on his desk.

"Thank you, Avery." His smile held an honest note that was confirmed when he immediately swiped up the cup and took a drink. His eyes closed, a sigh escaping. "You're the best."

"You're welcome." She glanced at Trevor, who stood at the window, before turning to the two men seated in the chairs before Gregory's desk. "Can I get any of you something to drink?"

She swept her gaze between Carson and the other man, her pulse fluttering despite her efforts to remain neutral. It froze, though. Everything froze—her thoughts, breath, even her heart for a beat or two—when she identified the man sitting beside Carson.

He was from the Boardroom.

He smiled at her, his expression neutral. Did he recognize her? Because she sure as hell remembered him.

Her focus darted to Carson, whose scowl skirted between the stranger and her.

"I'm good," Trevor said, raising his silver travel mug. "Thank you."

She jerked her attention to him, smile tight. Her pulse thundered in her ears with the pounding flow of her blood. That dreaded heat rose up her chest and neck in a telling wave she hated. Why had she been cursed with pale skin that showed every speck of her embarrassment?

"Me, too," the other guy said. Dark hair, navy tie and suit on. It didn't help that she could picture him without a tie, shirt removed. He had chest hair, a wicked smile and eyes that'd burned with heat when he'd watched her come.

This isn't happening. Not here. Now.

She refocused on Carson when he remained silent, if only to rip her thoughts from her free fall of doom. His brows were drawn lower, his scowl harder. What was left of her smile fell before she could check her reaction. Was that aimed at her?

Annoyance raced in to admonish her thoughts. It

didn't matter. Not in this environment. She'd done nothing wrong.

Trevor cleared his throat, and the other guy nudged Carson with his knee. Carson jerked his gaze to Trevor, scowl deepening. "What?"

Gregory's laughter rolled free before he covered it with a cough. "Sorry," he mumbled when Carson leveled that scowl on him.

"I think that's a 'no,'" Trevor said. He gave her an apologetic smile. "It's Monday. We'll blame his attitude on that."

"No problem." Her response was void of emotion, and she didn't wait to hear more. She escaped with her dignity in place even if that bubble of happiness had burst. She closed the door behind her, a sigh of relief and frustration gusting out beside the fear.

Had she really expected something different from Carson? *No.* She dropped into her chair as the lie eased in to mock her. She *had* hoped even when she'd insisted she hadn't. Even when she'd known it was foolish. Especially when he'd voiced his claim to her and she'd dared to believe him.

And that other man. What about him? Would he say something? Had Carson brought him here on purpose? To test her or maybe simply to provoke her?

Or to remind her that it was just sex?

She blew out a long breath, eyes closing for a brief moment of meditation. The guy looked like a businessman. He was in Gregory's office—with Trevor too. He was most likely here for a meeting. Plus he'd be bound by the NDA. He couldn't say anything to the other men. To her, privately, he probably could.

A new wave of heat spread across her chest as it contracted with the hit of shame. No. She shook her head, resolve taking hold. She had nothing to be ashamed of. Embarrassed maybe, sure. But she would not be shamed for being a part of the same sexual encounter that he'd been in.

And she was probably making more out of this entire incident than it deserved.

She didn't have time to focus on Carson or whatever they had—if they had anything—going on. And she couldn't think about the intimate details the other man knew about her. Not here.

But why had she never considered that aspect before? That she could someday run into another participant? Forced naïveté? Purposeful blindness?

A simple desire to expand her sexual desires with an incredibly handsome, charming, strong, kind, funny, thoughtful man?

Her shoulders sagged and she sat back. The truth had a way of stripping the lies from her anger. Yes, she wanted more with Carson, but that didn't mean it was true or would ever happen. And she'd gone into this arrangement knowing that.

Every reminder did little to ease the ache in her heart and the disappointment that chiseled away at the shabby barrier she'd erected around her dreams. The odds of Carson being her happily-ever-after were about a million to one.

Even if she wished differently.

And that was enough of her wallowing.

She jerked her chair forward and typed in her computer password with hard, jamming strokes. Work. This was her job. Carson was just a man. She had her pride and she wasn't letting go of it. Her job performance had never slacked because of a man, and it wouldn't now.

She punched in her access code to the finance system and zeroed in on the numbers. Those at least were logical. They all had a place and told a story when properly organized. They made sense and seldom lied. She could trust them and right now, they'd distract her.

Carson didn't belong in her thoughts when she was in the office. And he didn't belong in her dreams either, even if he had snuck into those.

Chapter Twenty

"Details," Trevor stated on two flat notes.

Carson jerked his gaze from the closed door to his friend, a scowl already in place. "What?"

Trevor didn't flinch. If anything, his expression hardened with the authority he wielded with precision. "It's time for the details." There was no leeway in his tone and no escaping the demand. He might be Carson's friend, but he was also his boss.

And this thing with Avery—whatever it was—was thoroughly entrenched in the company.

"What details?" Gregory asked.

Drake sat back, a questioning smirk circling between the other three men.

Carson ignored him even though he wanted to ram a fist in his face. It took his full concentration to control the frustration that simmered and stewed beneath his barely held calm. The irony was, he had no real clue why he was so on edge. But Drake seemed like a really good target to unload on.

And that would be a dick move.

Trevor flicked his gaze to Gregory. "He told you about Avery, right?"

"Is that her name?" Drake asked, motioning to the doorway Avery had just exited through.

Carson's protective growl burst out, but he clenched his jaw and forced his retort back. Avery deserved better than to be discussed when she sat just out of hearing on the other side of the door. Especially when there was nothing more to talk about.

And if that lie was believable, he wouldn't be a ball of anxious energy ready to bite the heads off the three men in front of him.

He dropped his head back, his anger draining from explosive to accepting. What the hell?

A throbbing pain started in his temple and he rubbed his eyes in an attempt to clear his head. But it wasn't his head that was causing the issues. His damn emotions were the culprit. The ones that bristled at Avery's cold formality when she'd seen him just now, along with his irrational desire to jump up and stake his claim on her before the other men—especially Drake.

I'm a fucking caveman now. Great.

He released a defeated snort and sat forward to massage his temples. He stared at the industrial gray carpeting for a moment and gathered what was left of his dignity.

The others were staring at him with a mix of amusement when he sat up. Excellent. He sighed and lifted a shoulder in begrudging admission. Yup, he was fucked up. And they knew it.

And it was over Avery.

Gregory glanced at his watch and frowned. "We've got fifteen minutes before our meeting." He nodded to Drake to include him in the reference. "Can you keep this short?"

Carson snorted a sarcastic laugh. "Sure." He'd just condense everything into a memo and move on with his day. That was the norm anyway. "What do you want to know?" he asked Trevor, voice flat. He shifted into business mode with a swift downgrade on his strange tide of doubts. He preferred action to hesitation. Movement to standing still.

So why was he floundering when it came to Avery?

Fear.

The truth rang clear and unwavering. His conversation with her yesterday raced forward to smack him. He'd never let fear guide his actions—until now, apparently.

"Don't play dumb." Trevor flicked his head toward to door. "I want the details on Avery. What's going on? Why are you being a dick? And do I need to worry?"

Straight to the point. Good.

Carson bobbed his head in slow thought. "I'm still helping her explore via the Boardroom. We've participated in multiple scenes over the last month. Our arrangement hasn't affected our work or jobs." Not until this morning when he couldn't reconcile his own damn emotions. "I wasn't aware that I was being a dick, and no, you don't need to worry."

He sat back, satisfied that he'd checked off each of Trevor's questions without giving away more. For some damn reason, he didn't want to share anything about Avery.

Their relationship was private.

And that meant they had a relationship worth preserving.

The wonder of that settled into his chest and nudged

against his heart. He braced himself for the immediate kick of resistance, only it wasn't there.

"I don't?" Trevor asked, his knowing look only moderately annoying. "Then don't fuck this up."

"What, exactly, shouldn't I fuck up?" There were so many damn things that statement could apply to.

Trevor chuckled before he took a drink from his travel mug. Carson wanted to be mad at him just for the point of it, but he couldn't be. Trevor knew him too well, and that was the problem. He wasn't fooling Trevor, and by the knowing smirks on Gregory's and Drake's faces, them either.

"What I don't understand," Trevor finally said, "is why you're fighting it so hard. She's not your direct employee. Gregory knows about your relationship. You're both adults. And—" He leaned in, obviously setting up for the killing blow. "You're so damn possessive of her you might as well piss a circle around her while you blare your ownership from a bullhorn."

Gregory snorted. Trevor straightened, that knowing smile back in place. And Carson had no idea how to respond. One thought made it through, though. "Is it really that obvious?" Could it be, when he'd only recently acknowledged his feelings for Avery himself?

Drake scoffed, head bobbing in an exaggerated yes. Carson glared at him, but Drake just laughed.

"Seriously?" Drake asked, grin wide, brows raised. "You bring a woman to the Boardroom for the first time ever, no one can touch her but you, and you wonder if it's obvious?" His bemused laugh was full of sarcasm much like his tone. "Her profile is so pathetically thin, I doubt she's even logged into the app after setting it up."

Carson's glare hardened. The thought of Avery using

the app to participate in scenes without him had his
jealous rage flaring hot and fast. She wasn't ready for
more. She didn't want to be with other men. She'd barely
agreed to watching with him.

And every excuse he raised screamed of his own reluctance to share her. The irony of his hypocrisy hit him
like a kick to his heart. He'd been participating in open
relationships for so long that he'd let go of the thought
of ever having a monogamous one.

And then Avery had come along.

"Just to us," Gregory reassured him. "In the office
anyway. Because we know what's going on."

"And what's going on?" Carson frowned, his defenses
holding.

Gregory returned his frown, but there was a hint of
skepticism in it. "You like her." He shrugged. "Now you
need to decide what you're going to do about it."

"And how that works with the Boardroom," Trevor
said.

"If it does," Gregory shot back.

"And if you're okay with her decisions regarding it."
Trevor let that hang.

Carson sat back, stunned. How had they gotten that
far? "We haven't even had a real date," he blurted in an
attempt to apply the brakes to their aggressive schedule.

Trevor flicked a brow up, stepping away from the
window. "Maybe you should try that first."

"And my original statement still holds," Gregory said,
standing when the other men did.

"What's that?" Carson asked, his head still spinning
from their bombardment. Hell, they almost had him and
Avery at the altar. And why didn't that thought have him
shuddering in instant rejection like it had in the past?

"I'll hunt you down and skin you alive if you make her quit." There was a slice of truth behind Gregory's humor. His steady gaze spoke to exactly how serious he was.

"Got it." And he'd been reduced to a scolded school-boy. Awesome. "Anything else?" he asked with a heavy dose of snark.

"Will the assessment on the new software be ready for the two-o'clock?" Trevor asked, deftly changing the subject back to work. Thank fuck.

"Yes." He followed Trevor to the door. "With recommendations." His team had been analyzing it for weeks and they had a number of concerns—and none of them had to do with Avery Fast.

"Good." Trevor opened the door. "I'll see you in five. Gregory. Drake." He nodded to the men and exited.

Carson followed Trevor out, ready to be gone, yet unsure of how to deal with Avery. She glanced up, a tight smile in place. She received a short nod from Trevor as he cruised by her, no doubt already focused on his next task.

Carson stopped before her desk, thoughts colliding with his damn emotions again. The florescent lighting wasn't always friendly in its glaring shine, but it didn't cut from Avery's beauty even slightly. She looked up at him, not a hair escaping from the tight bun at her nape. Her lipstick appeared freshly applied in that pale pink color she favored. Her silky black blouse with the ruffled collar bordered on that prim side she presented in the office.

Yet he knew there was more to her. He'd seen it. Felt it. Held it.

He could have her—all of her—too.

His pulse beat too fast, a wave of heat flaring up his nape. He wanted her. He'd acknowledged that long ago. And he wanted more. He'd decided that over the weekend. So what the fuck *was* his problem?

"Can I help you?" she finally asked when the silence became awkward.

"I think so," he said, decision made. He was in. Period. "Would you like to go out for dinner tomorrow night?"

Her eyes widened, mouth parting in shock. She whipped her head around to Gregory's open door, only to shoot a "what the fuck are you doing?" look back at him.

His laughter flowed from a deep spot of unknown. He really didn't know, but whatever it was, it felt right.

He gave her a smile before stepping back to duck his head into Gregory's office. "Hey, Gregory," he called. The man halted his conversation with Drake and jerked his focus to Carson, question etched on his features. "I asked your assistant out on a date."

Avery gasped behind him, but Gregory gave him a slow smile and nod. "Good luck with that."

"Thank you." He turned back to Avery, resolve in place. "There." He motioned to Gregory's office. "He's fine with it."

Her lips were still parted, head swiveling in slow denial. She leaned in, earnest confusion pulling her brows low.

He rested his palms on her desk and bent down, his grin spreading. He honestly couldn't contain it if he tried. "I'm asking you on a date."

Her mouth fell open again before she snapped it closed, sat back. She blinked, brows furrowing. "You're what?"

"You know. A date." He was enjoying himself now that he'd owned his feelings. "Where we have dinner, talk, hopefully laugh a little. Exchange details about our lives." Like they'd done yesterday over pizza and a movie. He hadn't spent a day doing nothing with a woman since...

Since his parents' divorce, when he'd been shown how hurtful love could be. College then. Maybe grad school. He'd had female friends back then, before he'd placed his focus on his career.

She stared at him for a long moment. The dull drone of the office went on beyond them. A phone rang, chatter hummed and someone walked by at a clipped pace. She didn't even glance at the person, and neither did he.

He didn't care what anyone else thought. Not in this moment.

A corner of her mouth quirked up, fell, rose again. She closed her eyes, and he watched her resistance slide away with a slow sigh. Her smile grew and he buzzed with premature success. "Do you know what you're doing?" she asked when she opened her eyes.

"Yes," he reassured her. He did now. "Do you?"

Her soft laugh held a mix of disbelief and resignation. "No," she admitted with a smile. "But I'm hoping you're worth the risk."

Was he? He wasn't sure of that in all honesty. But it also wasn't his assessment to make. He stole from Trevor's playbook and remained silent, waiting for her, not pushing or retreating.

"Sure," she finally said, her voice low.

It wasn't the firm declaration he'd hoped for, but he'd take it. "I'll text you with the details," he said as he straightened.

Her brows went up, doubt showing. "I, ah…" She swallowed. "You said dinner, right?"

He paused, confused. "Yes." Then he understood. The text. "This isn't a playdate," he said softly. "If that's what you're wondering."

"No?"

"No." Unless she wanted it to be—after they ate. "Dinner and conversation, that's all I'm asking for."

Her smile returned as she sat back. A soft warmth moved in to bring an enticing light to her eyes. "Okay."

The two men exited Gregory's office at that point. A stack of folders was tucked under Gregory's arm along with his tablet. "Carson. Avery." He nodded at both of them and strode by without another word.

Drake followed, his acknowledgment a mere compression of his lips as he passed. He didn't even look at Avery, and part of Carson was too damn relieved.

Avery tracked their departure before looking back to Carson. She tilted her head, contemplated him. "We have some things to discuss." Her gaze scanned back down the hallway.

"Agreed." They had a number of things to talk through. "I'll pick you up at seven tomorrow. Deal?"

She gave him a reluctant smile, but he caught the amusement in her eyes. "Deal."

He left after that. There was work to do, and he didn't want people speculating about them. Not yet at least—if ever.

Chapter Twenty-One

"I have a date," Avery told Karen when she burst into their apartment the next night. She glanced at the clock, cursing silently. She dropped her bag, kicked off her shoes and rushed past her stunned roommate to her room. "In ten minutes." Damn delayed bus.

"Wait. What?"

Karen's call chased her as she slid open her closet door. Guilt nipped at her for keeping the date a secret out of fear of jinxing it. She'd spent most of the last two days expecting him to cancel.

"What's going on?" Karen asked from the open doorway.

Avery spared her a quick glance before refocusing on the line of color-coordinated clothing hanging on the rod. She rubbed Flip with her foot in an attempt to appease the cat as she wound her way around Avery's legs. "I have no idea what to wear," she mumbled to herself. A light sweater? Nice T-shirt? Skirt? Jeans? Slacks?

Karen came forward to stand beside her. "What kind of a date is it?"

"A first, but not first," she tried to explain without details. "Dinner, but I don't know where." He'd given her no further information, not even when he'd texted her last night to ask how her day had gone.

A general text. A "how are you doing?" text. Something simple, almost mundane, yet she'd fallen asleep to the promise of it.

"Is it with the Saturday-night-rolled-into-all-day-Sunday guy?" Karen raised a speculative brow.

Avery ignored the question, but her grin grew despite her efforts to smother it. She pointedly shoved her hangers aside as she assessed and rejected each item. She couldn't verbally acknowledge the positive answer to Karen's question. Not if she wanted to contain that pesky thing fluttering in her chest and dancing beside those silly fantasies of love and a relationship and— Nope. Not yet. Maybe never with him. But maybe...

Karen plucked a hanger from the line of clothing and held up a red top with a deep V-neck and shiny silver buttons. "Wear this with your black skinny jeans and red heels."

Avery bit her lip, undecided. "How about my black flare skirt?"

"Perfect." She swung back to the closet. "Get moving," she commanded. "You have five minutes."

"Oh, God." Avery stripped off her office clothes, uncaring for once where the dirty items landed. She grabbed a matching bra and panty set from her dresser and darted into the bathroom across the hallway.

"So, it's *that* kind of date," Karen said with a laugh.

Was it? She both hoped so and not. Hell, she didn't know what she wanted anymore. Carson had her thoughts and emotions twisted into such a knot that she couldn't define them.

She quickly undid her bun and brushed her hair out.

Her makeup would have to suffice with a fresh coat of lipstick. She raced back to her room, heart speeding along in a flight of anxious anticipation. She didn't want to be late. Didn't want to think too much. Didn't want to dream.

"Is this with the sex guy?" Karen asked, her smirk somewhere between amused and concerned.

A firm knock at their front door saved Avery from responding. She froze.

Karen's eyes went wide before her smile turned devious. "I'll get that," she chirped as she left the room.

"Karen," Avery called in warning, unsure of exactly what she was cautioning her about.

She yanked on the outfit Karen had laid on her bed. A quick look in the mirror confirmed everything was on correctly and free of cat hair. The sleeveless blouse draped over her breasts in an alluring way before it skimmed her form to end at her hips. The midthigh length of the skirt worked perfectly with the top to give it a fun yet dressy feel. Should she add a necklace?

The deep rumble of Carson's laugh drifted down the hallway to spur Avery to move faster. The longer Karen was alone with him, the more intel she'd gather, and that could be dangerous for the coming interrogation. How long could she avoid Karen's questions?

She slipped her heels on, paused, her hand resting on her hip. Could she do it? What would it feel like?

"Have you known Avery long?"

Avery squeezed her eyes closed at hearing Karen's question. She needed to move.

"A while," Carson answered, the deliberate vagueness both a relief and a disappointment.

She shook her head in an attempt to remove the warring emotions. This was just another moment. A chance to own the new confidence Carson had given her.

With a firm nod, she slipped off the scarlet panties she'd just put on. Air swooped over her pussy in silent condemnation. She'd never gone out in public without her underwear or some form of lingerie covering her.

A secret smile lit her face when she turned back to the mirror. She wiggled her hips. Her skirt swished against her thighs, her pussy noticeably exposed beneath the fabric. She soaked up the naked sensation, a secret smile forming. More than anything, it was the knowledge that she was completely bare beneath her skirt that teased her.

And nobody would know.

A spark of that wanton, sexy woman who'd emerged with Carson flared to life. She'd hold on to her secret—or maybe share it early. Taunt him. See his eyes flare with desire.

Her shoulders were back, confidence spreading as she strode down the short hall to greet Carson. His presence seemed to overtake their small space with the calm control he exerted. His dark suit fit him perfectly—like all of his suits did—accentuating his shoulders and tapering to his waist. The only change from his office appearance was the lack of a tie. Was that significant?

"Hi. Sorry I'm late." Her voice was steady, and she praised herself on her casual facade. "The buses were slow."

Carson made a long, slow glance down her and back up. Appreciation blazed when he smiled. "Not a problem." He leaned down to brush a kiss on her cheek. His hand settled on her lower back in a light hold that managed to feel possessive. It ignited her longing as did his whispered praise. "You look beautiful. Like always."

"Thank you." Her heart did that silly flip and plunged without her consent. This was just a date. One date—after more than a month of wild, passionate sex. She cleared her throat and turned to her roommate, her hand falling from his chest. When had she placed it there? "You've met Karen?" she asked him even though he obviously had.

"Yes," they said in unison.

Karen's smile said Avery would most certainly be grilled the next time she saw her. "Have a good night." Her words were polite and neutral, but Avery caught the unspoken implication. *Have some really hot sex.*

If only she knew, and what would she think of Avery then?

Carson helped her with her black cropped jacket and held out his arm for her to take as they left her condo. Her nerves swelled, but she forced them aside. This was nothing. It was just Carson. A simple date.

She was making too much of it.

The night air was comfortable, yet she was acutely aware of it caressing over her thighs and beneath her skirt. Her secret did a naughty dance that nudged aside her conservatism. This was fun, even though it barely registered on the daring scale.

The leather seat was cool on the underside of her thighs, and sent another reminder of her naked state. She crossed her legs, a knowing smile on her lips. Would she tell him? Show him? When? Where?

"Do you like seafood?" he asked once he'd started the car.

She looked to him, her nugget of power held tightly. "Yes."

Dusk was settling in, bringing the gentle softness that

came before dark. It washed the harshness from Carson's features and highlighted the gentler side of him. The little quirk of his lips. That bump on his nose that she'd assimilated into his features but kept him from being too perfect. The deep blue of his eyes that exposed a hint of his own nervousness.

Her shoulders relaxed as the knot in her chest loosened. He felt it too—whatever it was that was growing between them. And that…was too big for words.

She held her purse on her lap and embraced her wants for one brief moment. This could be something. It had the potential to be, if she allowed herself to go with it. Whatever it was. Her stomach dipped, heart too. A wave of warmth flowed through her, fueled by the opportunities she'd set free.

Every moment was a chance at something new, and she'd been scooping them up her entire life. Why was she so afraid of this one?

Because it had the potential to hurt her the worst. Or give her the most joy.

"How was your day?" Carson asked once they were on the road.

"Good. Busy." She tucked her hair behind her ear. "Yours?"

His laugh was a short huff. "The same."

"Gregory's excited about a potential client the firm is courting." Her smile grew from the inside. The mundane day talk was just filler chatter, yet it was another side of normal they'd missed before.

Carson nodded. "Trevor has a way of getting whatever he goes after."

Her short chuckle was one of agreement. "I don't

know him that well, but he doesn't come across as a guy who accepts no as a final answer."

His evasive shrug provided little insight into their boss. "Have you ever been to Carmichael's?"

Her respect for him increased when he changed the topic instead of gossiping about Trevor. "No. But I've heard it's really good."

"My mother introduced me to it," he said. The corner of his mouth lifted. "She's somewhat of a foodie now."

She shifted to face him better, intrigued. "Now? She wasn't before?"

"No." His smile grew before it fell away, the memories obviously filtering by. "Money was too tight, and we were all too busy to be picky about what we ate." He glanced at her, shrugged. "She had three boys in four years. We ate a lot."

She laughed, nodding. "I can imagine. My mother complained constantly about my brother's endless stomach when he hit his teens."

"Pure survival instincts prompted me to learn how to cook," he added, his smile waning again.

"It's a good skill to have." One her brother never learned since their mother had deemed kitchen duties women's work.

They fell into silence as they crossed the Golden Gate Bridge. The fog was creeping in on a wall of dank clouds that seemed to coast over the water. The fog would reach the bridge soon, but how far would it invade tonight? There was no way to tell, and she both loved and hated the mystery.

He took the Sausalito exit into the little nook situated across the bay from San Francisco. The town held that quaint, artsy tourist feel that leaned toward elite without being obnoxious. The window displays varied from sculptures and pricey decorations to baked goods and toys.

Carson stopped at a valet stand before a restaurant built on a dock over the water. The scent of fish and algae floated in the air beside the tantalizing food smells when she exited the car. She inhaled again and appreciated the simple beauty of their surroundings. People strolled on the sidewalks, and bikers utilized the road with the slow-moving cars. Everyone was out enjoying the last of the daylight.

A wind blew off the bay, and she scanned the stunning view of San Francisco in the distance—a mass of staggered monochrome buildings against a pale sky filled with fluffy clouds tinted pink and orange from the setting sun.

"It's nice, isn't it?" Carson asked as he came to her side, gaze on the view.

"It is," she agreed. "Sometimes, it's hard to believe I live there."

"Why do you say that?"

"I don't know." She searched for a tangible reason but only had vague outlines. "Maybe because in some ways I'm still that small-town girl from the Midwest. And that—" she gestured back at the skyline "—is about as far from it as you can get."

"And city kids are that different?" he asked, a teasing note in his voice.

"No. Maybe." She shrugged. "I don't know." She laughed at herself and her own ramblings. "Haven't you ever felt like an outsider only to realize that at some point you'd become a part of the very thing you'd once thought you were separated from?"

"Yeah." He studied her, completely serious. "I get that."

He took her hand and led her to the door before she could dig beneath his meaning. His palm warmed hers and brought with it a sense of belonging.

And yeah, she liked it.

The gust of wind lifted her skirt as he opened the door, and she quickly pressed the material down as she ducked inside. A slow wave of heat worked its way up her chest at her almost exposure.

Apparently, she hadn't thought her daring through with her skirt choice.

Had it lifted high enough to show her nakedness? A quick glance around didn't reveal any sniggers or speculative looks. She was good, but a part of her almost wanted someone to know.

And how strange was that?

They were seated at a table overlooking the bay. Candlelight flickered on the white linen tablecloth. Their food was ordered, wine poured before she sat back to study him. He returned her appraisal, smile growing.

"What are you thinking?" he asked.

"Nothing." She tilted her head, the wine easing through her to loosen her muscles and words. "Just about you. Your life."

"Yeah?" His brow rose. "What do you want to know?"

Everything? And that was overbroad, even if it was true. She went instead with the most pressing question, one that linked to others and would unlock a part of Carson she loved yet didn't fully understand. "How did you get involved with the Boardroom?"

Chapter Twenty-Two

Carson had been expecting that question, or one like it, since he'd picked Avery up. There was so much she didn't know about the Boardroom and even more she didn't need to know.

He took a sip of his wine, let it rest on the back of his tongue before swallowing. The action stalled for time under the guise of appreciating what he barely tasted. Avery waited for him, head slightly tilted, determination lining her smile. She wouldn't accept a blasé answer and she deserved more than that.

"I was invited." He set his glass down before continuing. "A few years back."

"By whom?"

He shook his head. "I can't tell you that. Plus, it doesn't matter."

"Okay." Her brows dipped. "Why did you agree to go and then stay?"

His laugh was light. "Because I liked it." She rolled her eyes, and he leaned forward, voice lowered. "I went out of curiosity. I continued because it set a part of me free." Understanding burned in her eyes. "It was hot, wrong yet right. Wicked but accepted. And for me, it fit nicely into my lifestyle."

"How so?"

"Sex without attachment." He kept his voice flat. She'd asked for the truth, and that was it. "I didn't want a relationship."

"Oh." She nodded, sighed. "I knew that." Her half smile was full of self-deprecation. "You made it very clear before we started."

"But," he said, waiting for her to look at him. "Things change."

"They do?"

He huffed a short laugh. "Always." Even when he wasn't expecting them to.

"So how, exactly, have they changed?" She tucked her hair behind her ear, doubt clear. Her bangs skimmed her forehead in a side part and did little to hide her drawn brows.

Damn. Admiration grew beside his irritation. She wouldn't allow him to be vague, and he adored her for it.

He stared into her eyes and let the truth show. "We're on a date. You spent the night at my place. I haven't done either of those things in years." He let that sink in before adding, "And I've had no desire to sleep with anyone except you since you stumbled into that boardroom so many nights ago." Months now.

Her smile wobbled, that telltale red tinge flowing over her cheeks. She lowered her head, gaze dropping as her smile grew. And there was that almost timid shyness that screamed of innocence. Would it ever recede? He hoped it didn't. Not when it balanced that lusty, passionate side so evenly.

She looked back to him, head tilting as a playfulness overtook her expression. "So you don't make a habit of getting women off on your rooftop?" She lifted a brow, lips twitching.

His laugh rolled out. "No. Not at all." Not ever.

Their food arrived, and the conversation shifted to lighter topics while they ate. The weather. Work. Local hiking trails. Wine tasting. Observations about various areas of the city. Her laughter was quick, smile open as they flowed from one thing to the other.

This was easy, nice and he could've sat there talking to her all night. He'd barely scratched the surface on the things he wanted to learn about her.

Their plates were gone, the wine bottle empty when she sat back, expression growing serious. He let his smile go, prepared for the subtle shift.

"How do you do it?" she asked, frowning. "I mean, how do you handle seeing people you've done scenes with? Like that guy at the office yesterday?" She stared out the window. The sun had set, and San Francisco twinkled in a sea of lights across the black expanse of the bay. Her throat bobbed with her swallow, and she nibbled on the inside of her lip in an absent fashion.

He rested his elbows on the table and thought about his answer. "Can I ask you something first?" She nodded. "What part of that concerns you?"

Her eyes widen. "What part doesn't?" And there was her fear. Or was it something else, worse maybe?

"So you passed a negative judgment on him when you saw him in Gregory's office?" he pushed. "You thought less of him because you'd seen him in a sexual situation?"

"No!" She shook her head, leaning in. "Of course not."

"Yet you assumed he made one about you." He lifted a brow. "Am I right?"

Her lips parted, brows drawing together as she studied him. She snapped her mouth closed a second later. "Maybe," she finally said with reluctance.

"You're not the first one," he tried to reassure her. "But it's not like that."

"Then how is it?"

He glanced around them. The restaurant was pretty full, but the tables were a respectable distance apart, unlike many places in San Francisco where privacy was dismissed in order to cram more people in. "The people in the Boardroom are all there for the same thing," he said, voice lowered. "There is nothing shameful about what happens, because no one sees it that way." He thought back to his initial reaction and the months it'd taken him to be comfortable both in and out of the setting. "And we don't pass judgment on anything that goes on as long as it's consensual."

"Has there ever been a situation when it wasn't?"

He shrugged. "Once that I know of. But it was handled, and the member removed."

She went silent after that, and he signaled for the check. Her cheeks were flushed an attractive shade of pink. From the wine or warmth? Either way, it softened her features while adding a sensual allure. Maybe it was just the lighting or it could be his memory of the same flush covering her cheeks and chest when she came.

And he really shouldn't go there when they were in public.

He cleared his throat and handed his credit card to the waiter when he returned. Avery was still silent, her regard both introspective and undecided.

"What are you thinking?" he asked.

Her eyes narrowed slightly. "I'm trying to believe you, but it's hard to grasp."

"What part?"

"The shame thing." She shook her head, a breathy laugh gusting free. She waved a dismissive hand in front of her. "Sorry. Never mind. It's my issue, obviously."

He reached across the table to grab her hand. She stilled, swallowed. He rubbed his thumb over the back, an almost desperate need growing to purge that emotion from her when it came to sex. "Tell me about it," he said. "Please."

"What?" Her voice was soft, her gaze focused on their joined hands where they rested on the table. "My feelings, or where they stem from?"

"Both."

The waiter returned with the bill, but Carson only spared him a brief smile as the man set the folder on the edge of the table. His tip would reflect the man's deft understanding of the moment and his quick departure.

Avery wet her lips, crossed her free hand over her body to grip her other arm. She raised her gaze, smile pensive. "I was raised with the perception that sex was private. You didn't talk about it, and you certainly didn't do it in public. Or with multiple people. Or anything besides basic positions in bed."

He understood that. It wasn't hard, given the wave of sexual conservatism that gripped a large portion of the country. His Southern Cal roots had been a lot less tethered, largely due to the melting pot of Hollywood, TV and music that wove its way into the fabric of the area. "But you obviously know those perceptions aren't the only ones, nor the correct ones." He wouldn't let her apply an ounce of shame to what they'd shared. "I would never look down on you for a sexual choice you made openly and willingly."

"Never?" Her brow lifted.

"Never," he restated with insistence, meaning it.

"And what if this thing between us becomes serious?" There was no hint of shyness in her now. Her gaze was direct, voice even. "Would you want an open relationship that included intercourse with other people?"

"No." He didn't have to think about that. Her eyes widened, doubt clear. He shook his head. "I wouldn't. Not where you're concerned." He paused before adding, "Why? Would you?" His gut clenched. That jab of jealousy snaked out to bite him once again.

"No," she said with a soft puff of laughter. She sat forward to rest her chin on her fist. Her eyes narrowed again, and he smiled, both in relief for her answer and preparation for what came next. "No. I don't think I'm that...open-minded. Is that the right word?" She squinted in thought. "But," she continued before he could answer, "I don't really know. I'm not really versed in the world of open relationships and sexual play."

Her final admission was pure truth, yet it sucked the air from his lungs. "I won't share you," he stated, just to clarify. Yes, he was being a caveman and he didn't give a fuck.

"No?" she raised a brow, an impish smile tugging her lips up.

"No," he insisted, completely serious.

She stared at him, the mood shifting with the unspoken communication. Somehow, they'd jumped the divide from just sex to serious relationship in the span of a few words. He had no idea how it'd happened, but he didn't want her dating or fucking anyone else. And he sure as hell didn't want to be with anyone but her.

The clink of silverware and the low din of chatter blended with the roaring in his head. His pulse beat a hard pace at his throat, but he wasn't backing down. Not from her or the chance of them.

She was worth the risk. He was positive of that.

"And what about the Boardroom?" she asked, voice so low he almost missed her question.

He frowned. "What about it?"

"Would we—you—still play there?"

"Not without you." His decision was made on the spot, and he knew it was true. "And only if you wanted to."

It was her turn to frown. "But that's not right either. You have a say. It's your kink too."

His kink too. The voyeurism.

His smile grew in slow increments as her words sunk in. She was admitting to it for the first time, and that was huge.

Possibilities washed out many of his long-held positions with each increased thump of his pulse. Could he really have found a woman who complemented all parts of him so well? Who didn't scorn his desires or try to persuade him to change?

"There are other ways we can explore that if you'd prefer to avoid the Boardroom," he said, his mind already racing to the many possibilities.

"How?" Skepticism wrinkled her forehead.

"I can show you." He slid his credit card back into his wallet, signed the bill. "Tonight. If you'd like."

"Tonight?" She straightened, brows lifted. "How?"

A slow buzz of excitement hummed through him at

her interest. "Do you trust me?" he asked, standing. He extended his hand and helped her from the chair.

She stood before him, searching deep. Her eyes were darker in the low light, intense but curious. "Yes," she whispered. "I trust you."

That was so damn powerful. Did she know that?

He cupped her jaw and kissed her upturned lips. "Thank you," he whispered before pulling back. He had to force himself to move away or he'd dive back in and not come up until neither of them could breathe.

And this wasn't the place for that, but he would do it later. That and so much more.

Chapter Twenty-Three

Avery stepped off the industrial elevator into a cavernous room lit by small lamps, wall sconces and the occasional hanging light. People milled about, some fully clothed and, shockingly, some half naked, a few completely.

She clenched Carson's hand, stomach twisting at the unknown. What had he brought her to?

They'd returned to San Francisco, where he'd driven to a nondescript building in the Mission district. He'd given her no details, only slipped her ID into his wallet before tucking her coat and purse in the trunk at the restaurant. He'd reassured her they could leave at any time before she'd completed the membership papers downstairs.

Leave what, exactly?

A slower rock song played over a sound system that intensified the bass and did an excellent job of blanking out a majority of the noise. Rooms were sectioned off throughout the space by a series of rods holding different-colored curtains. Some were completely black, one was boxed in red and another had plain white.

The shadowed outline of a couple in the obvious act of sex showed through the white sheets. The guy was thrusting hard, head bowed, back arching with each jar-ring jerk into his partner.

She sucked in a breath, both stunned and not. She'd assumed he was bringing her to a sex club, but she had zero knowledge of what it would be like. Books and movies didn't compare to reality. Not even close.

The guy behind the sheet reared back, grabbed his partner by the hips and flipped her onto her stomach. He hauled her bottom up and dipped to smother his face in her pussy.

Oh my God. Avery watched, fascinated. The woman squirmed, head tossing, breasts jiggling, and Avery imagined what she was feeling. The wet heat on her pussy. The hard licks and lighter flutters over her clit.

Her pussy clenched, want flaring without heed, just like in the Boardroom.

A swipe of that damn shame washed over her despite her effort to reject it. There was nothing wrong with being turned on by what she watched. Nothing.

Carson turned from the bouncer guarding the eleva-tor and guided her into the space. She stuck to his side, scanning everything but holding on nothing. She refused to stare, even if she couldn't define what that couple was doing along the wall behind the circle of watchers.

"What is this place?" she asked softly when he'd drawn her to an alcove not far from the white sheet room. They had a front view now. The guy had returned to fucking his partner, each thrust rocking the woman forward.

Avery leaned into Carson, needing to be close to him. His reassurance maybe. Definitely his security. She was safe with him, no matter where they were.

"What does it look like?" He urged her around to

stand in front of him, and she welcomed the familiarity of it. Her muscles relaxed, mind loosening as she settled against him. Every part of her screamed yes.

She turned her face up to his, smile soft. "Like a sex club."

His brow twitched in time with the corner of his mouth. "Nothing gets past you."

She elbowed him lightly in the ribs, her laugh releasing a round of nerves. Where had this man come from? How was she even here with him?

The couple behind the sheet finished on one last crushing thrust that forced the woman to her stomach. The man followed her down, his deep cry floating over the music to accent the climax.

Avery sucked in a breath at the visceral show. Her abdomen contracted in time with her pussy, want blazing. She squirmed against Carson, at once uncomfortable and totally enthralled.

"This is another option," Carson explained, his breath warming her ear. His hands drifted over her abdomen, one rising higher to caress her ribs. "More autonomous in some ways, but less controlled."

Her eyelids lowered beneath the languid flow of lust and excess seeping into her. Maybe it was the wine she'd drank, and maybe it was simply the man behind her. Either way, it really didn't matter. Not right then.

"Do you know anyone here?" she asked. She scanned the faces she could see without registering details. She had no idea what she'd do if she actually recognized someone.

"I know people who come here." He ran his thumb under her breasts in a hard line that lifted each one and taunted her for his full touch. He slid his other hand over her hips, tugged her back.

His erection nestled into the spot on her lower back, and she hummed at the rightness. Her pussy clenched in an almost Pavlovian response to the contact.

A couple kissed on a couch. Another couple openly groped each other on the same couch. The displays were countered by the subtle unknowns. Moans drifted randomly through the room, indistinct yet pervasive. And beneath it all was the scent of sex and lust and want. Heated. Predatory. Naughty.

She turned in Carson's arms to draw his mouth to hers. Her moan rumbled through her chest at the first touch of his lips. They were hot, firm and oh-so perfect. She opened to let him claim her, and he did. With deep strokes of his tongue and the hard press of his demand.

He tipped her back, and she simply held on. Her mind blanked, heart pounded. There was nothing besides Carson. And this wasn't just sex. Not anymore. He'd said as much tonight.

She could trust this crazy, spiraling feeling buzzing within her. Finally set it free with the hope she'd been feebly holding back.

He wanted her. Only her.

Her desire jumped from smoldering to inferno in one dizzying moment. She clamored to get closer to him, uncaring of where they were. The music held a solid beat that matched the slow grind of their hips. A teasing pace meant to entice, tempt, incite.

She was vaguely aware that anyone could be watching them. Her neck prickled with expectation. What would they think? Would they be turned on? Think they're hot?

She stretched up and wrapped a leg around Carson's

hip, seeking the touch to her pussy she desperately needed. His growl flowed over their kiss as he cupped her thigh, lifting her leg higher.

"Damn," he rumbled against her jaw. "You're so fucking hot."

She tipped her head back, neck stretched to receive his trail of nipping kisses down her throat. The sharp little bites stung for a blink before merging with the passion blazing beneath her skin. She sucked in air, lost to everything but his touch.

He skimmed a hand up her leg with slow intent. It slid beneath her skirt to cup her ass in a firm grip, fingers spreading, searching. He froze, pulled back and she slowly lifted her head, a coy smile in place.

His eyes were filled with lust, his smile a dark promise. He ran his fingers down the crack of her ass, stopping before he reached her pussy. He ran them back up, her whimper escaping as a low plea. "You've been keeping secrets." He traced his fingers back down to coast the tips through her heat. Her lips parted on a silent gasp. Power and need collided within her as each finger dipped into her, only to slip back out before fully breaching her. "Do you have any idea what this does to me?"

He circled her clit with his pinky, slow soft strokes that shot daggers of want through her core. She gripped his neck, hips jutting forward in a hunt for more. Harder. Anything.

He drew her closer, lust purring in his voice. "I want to fuck you." He thrust a finger into her, and she cried out, pussy clenching. "Right here." He stroked her, hard long plunges that slid over her walls in another tease. She needed more. Something bigger. Firmer. More filling.

She needed him. All of him.

"Yes," she pleaded. "Do it. Here."

Anyone could see them. Literally. She had no idea who was watching, who was even there. But there was an anonymity in that. In not knowing, despite the public setting. She never would've dared to be this wild, this uncaring before Carson.

And she loved it. Wanted it.

She scrambled at his belt, frantic with the desire coursing through her. He growled into her neck, fingers working her pussy. Her standing leg trembled, but he held her up.

His belt slipped free, and she had the button freed, zipper lowered in the next beat. She gripped his dick, shoving his underwear down to stroke the velvet stiffness. God, yes. Need raced through every fiber, buzzed on her skin and tossed out every ounce of rationality.

This was good. Right. Okay.

She whimpered in protest when Carson yanked his hand from her pussy. He knocked her hand away from his dick, pushed her skirt aside and slid home before Avery could complain further. Oh…fuck. Her walls contracted, hugging him within her. Pleasure raced from her full pussy to wrap her in warmth. *This. Yes. This.*

Just him. No barriers.

She should say something, remind him, yet the words wouldn't form.

He jerked her closer, hips rocking to fill her again and again. Music blanketed the room, but she heard only his rasping grunts in her ear. She clung to him, unable to do anything except take his dick. He held her one leg up and her other shook in a warning of potential collapse.

Tension spun through her core, tightened, grew, spread. His fingers dug into her thigh in a possessive, desperate clutch. She loved that too. Loved all of it. Every crazy, frantic, gasping second of it.

She loved him.

Her heart burst open on that nugget of truth, her orgasm shattering on her next breath.

Joy and amazement blasted through her on wave after wave of pleasure. She shuddered, face buried in his shoulder as she rode the sensations threatening to drop her.

He grunted, thrust hard and growled his release into her neck. His hold bit into her thigh as he dipped her back and drove into her one last time.

"Fuck." His curse vibrated over her skin. "Fuck." The second one was softer, less violent. His hold loosened in increments and he sagged back, drawing her with him as he leaned on the wall.

She gasped for air, world spinning as she descended from her high. That was…

Beyond description. Not perfect, even a bit awkward, but so out of this world. The daring alone had her buzzing with adrenaline.

He let go of her leg, and it slid down. She was simply too tired to hold it up. His dick slid from her when her foot touched the ground. Her pussy clenched in an attempt to hold him in her when it was impossible to do so.

He groaned, and she chuckled softly as a sticky wetness coated her inner thighs. The aftermath of sex was never graceful—especially without a condom.

Their surroundings wove their way into her awareness on the familiar words of a song lyric and a rambunctious burst of laughter. She'd just had full-on sex in public. Yes, it was a club meant for it, but it was still public. She waited for the trace of shame or embarrassment, but none came.

She stepped back just far enough for him to tuck himself away. She smoothed her skirt down, distinctly aware of the line of liquid easing its way down her inner thigh.

She squeezed her eyes closed, heart hitching, before she lifted her head to look at Carson. "We forgot the condom."

The condom. Fuck.

"I know." Carson winced. "I'm sorry." He cleared the rasp from his throat and tried to clear his head. "I don't know how that happened."

He never went without a condom. Never. Not even in the heat of passion—until Avery.

"It's okay. I could've said something." She stepped closer to smooth a hand down his chest. "I have an IUD."

A small sigh of relief eased through his chest at her reminder. He'd known that detail about her, from the medical information she'd submitted for the Boardroom. But that didn't excuse his carelessness, no matter how fucking good she'd felt.

She straightened his collar, focused on her task. Her lipstick was mostly gone, and he damned the darkness for hiding the flush of her skin and the lingering heat from her orgasm.

She was waiting for him to respond, and he was fumbling the pass.

He grabbed her hands, halting her fiddling. Her head jerked up, those expressive eyes of hers showing every fear and desire.

He tipped her chin up and kissed her lips. His own

were tender, his dick limp in his pants, yet he wanted to dive right back in for more.

"I should've stopped," he told her. "I'm sorry. But I won't give you anything. I swear."

Her lips quirked, a smile itching to break free. "Like a puppy? Or fleas?"

He groaned at her joke, hauling her in for a hug. He buried his nose in her hair, eyes squeezed closed against the happy flutter around his heart. "You are not funny," he told her around his amusement.

"Sorry," she mumbled into his neck. "But I have come sliding down my leg and you get to tuck everything away."

He snorted into her hair and hugged her tighter. "For your information, I have come plastered to my dick and groin, which is probably going to dry into a sticky glue in my pubes before I get home." Her giggle tickled his neck but he didn't move away. God, he didn't want to let her go.

"I'm good too," she said, a laugh still in her voice. "No fleas, bugs, ticks or puppies to share."

He swatted her bottom, gaining a squeak from her. "The bathroom is down that hall," he said as he loosened his arms. "You can clean up in there before we go."

"Thank you." She shoved a hand through her hair and straightened her blouse.

He smiled at her attempts at modesty in the midst of a sex club—after they'd just fucked against the wall. That dichotomy was so her.

He traced his fingers down her hairline, tucking strands behind her ear. He kissed her again, still awed at the passion he'd discovered beneath that conservative shell of hers.

"I'll be right back," she said before moving away. He tracked her progress down the hallway. Her skirt swayed with each step in a tempting reminder of the secret hidden beneath.

His heart did another of those flighty fluttery things that warned of emotions he wasn't ready to claim. How could he trust it—this? Would it last?

He adjusted himself and contemplated a quick trip to the restroom. They had supplies stocked in there and around the room.

How had he forgotten the condom—even for a moment? *Fuck.* There was a bowl of them on the table not more than five feet from them. But damn, it'd been amazing. That hot, wet heat had gripped him so tightly he'd almost come when he'd entered her.

And he'd known, in that instant, that he was bare.

It hadn't mattered to him then. Not even slightly.

He hung his head, another wave of shame washing over him. He'd been all in at that moment. No panic attacks. No oh-fucks at the undiscussed relationship leap.

Or the potential of a fucking baby—even if it was remote.

He'd never been that reckless, not even when he'd been a teenager. His dad had hammered home the importance of protection, as had his mother. It didn't take a mathematician to count the six months from their anniversary to his brother's birthday.

"Hey," Avery said at his side. She touched his arm and he lifted his head. "Are you okay?" Concern pulled on her brow as she rubbed his arm.

"Yeah." He threaded his fingers with hers, drew her in. "I'm good." He swallowed her response, diving in to taste her again. To find the sweetness and passion. To drive out the emotions racing free in his chest.

Because he had never contemplated having a kid with anyone and now he couldn't shake the idea of having one with Avery.

Chapter Twenty-Four

The scent of freshly cut onions and green peppers teased Carson's nose as he sprinkled the diced vegetables over the egg mixture. He covered the frying pan, slid two pieces of bread into the toaster and took a hit of his coffee before turning back to the omelet.

He lifted and maneuvered the runny eggs to the underside, then layered fresh spinach leaves over the top. It'd been forever since he'd taken the time to cook a big breakfast, but his stomach was growling in anticipation.

"Wow," Avery said as she stepped into the room. "You really do know how to cook." She rubbed her eyes, yawned. Her smile held that lazy morning softness as she shoved her hair away from her face, which was still rosy from sleep. She wore his gray T-shirt again, the one he'd left out for her this time. His dick twitched at the thought of her naked beneath it.

He'd intended to put some distance between them after that night at the private club, only to wake up the next morning thinking about her. Having dreamed about her.

Wanting her even more.

Which had led to coffee that night after work, and

their date last night, along with a few dozen texts in between.

"I'm not promising anything," he told her, refocusing on his task before he burnt everything. The shirt was hers now, really. He'd never be able to wear it without thinking of her. The microwave beeped, and he opened it to take the bacon out.

She inhaled. "It smells wonderful."

"If nothing else, we'll have bacon and toast." He added the pieces to the ones he'd already cooked and turned back to sprinkle cheese on the omelet. "It's almost ready." He motioned to the pods lined up by the coffee pot. "I bought some new flavors." He flipped the omelet in half, success blazing when it didn't fall apart.

Her arms snaked around his waist, and he stilled, a sense of peace weaving through him. She laid her head between his shoulder blades, and he absorbed the sensation of having her pressed to him.

It was simple, nice and way more intimate than a lot of the sex he'd participated in.

"Thank you." Her breath warmed him through the silky material of his athletic shirt. A wave of goose bumps chased the heat, and that crazy fluttering kicked up in his chest. "But you didn't have to."

"I know." He turned the burner off, used the spatula to cut the omelet and then slid each half onto a plate. "I wanted to." She moved with him, swaying with his little shifts as he finished.

"How come?" She pressed a kiss to his back, then stepped away to read the labels on the coffee pods.

He frowned, distracted. "How come what?"

"How come you wanted to cook?" She plopped a pod

in the reservoir and closed the lid. Her smile held nothing but curiosity when she glanced at him.

He waited for the coffee machine to finish its preparatory grind and chug before answering. "Because I haven't in a long time." Not for someone else.

"No?" She quirked a brow at him. "Well, for the record, you can cook for me anytime you want." She took her mug and sat down on the bar stool on the other side of the kitchen island. Her smile grew after her first sip of coffee. Not quite orgasmic, but definitely satisfied.

He cleared his throat and turned to butter the toast. It'd be so easy to forget breakfast and drag her back to his bedroom. "Do you have plans today?" he asked to keep his thoughts away from her in his bed, naked, panting, begging to come.

"I usually go to the farmers' market on Saturday mornings." She sat back when he set her plate before her. Steam still wisped from the omelet, and she inhaled, humming. "This looks really good. What's in it?"

He shrugged her compliment off. "Just some veggies and cheese." She took a bite of bacon as he came around to sit beside her. "Which market do you go to?" There were multiple ones around the city on any given day.

"We usually go to the big one at the Ferry Plaza."

"We?"

"Karen and I." She shrugged. "But I told her I might be busy today." She shot him a side glance, an impish smile in place.

That silly chest flutter started again to spread a wave of happiness through him. How fucking silly was that? But he didn't stop his smirk nor could he resist teasing her. "Oh yeah? With whom?"

Her scowl was about as menacing as a puppy. She hit his arm mumbling, "Jerk."

"Who, me?" He shot her the innocent face he'd perfected before he'd hit his teens. With three boys in the house, one of them had always been in trouble, and he'd done whatever he could to avoid his dad's wrath—and his mom's. Her disappointed glare was worse than his dad's bellow.

"I'm not buying that innocent thing," she told him. "I know way too much about you to fall for it."

She did. He couldn't deny it, and that was yet another step into the unknown. One he had no desire to retreat from.

He turned his focus to his plate and dug into his food. He had no comeback, not even a joking one. This thing with Avery was moving faster than he could control. His stomach did a queasy dip and roll that he'd become accustomed to in the last week. He ignored it though, identifying it for the nervous fear that it was.

"How did you get such good tickets to the show last night?" she asked. She took a bite of the omelet and gave another low hum of approval.

He stared at her, thoughts racing back to the previous night when he'd stripped her slowly before using every trick he knew to hear that exact same sound. He cleared his throat, shifted his legs apart as he took a drink of his coffee. "Trevor," he answered when he could think beyond his dick.

"You'll have to thank him for me." She smiled, touching his arm. "How did you know I loved Broadway shows?"

He shrugged. "Who doesn't?" Gregory had relayed the suggestion from his wife, but Carson would never divulge that. Just add it to the list of things he hadn't told her. The guilt nudged him, but he stubbornly ignored it—or tried to. *Fuck*.

He sat his fork down and turned on the stool to face her. She lifted a brow, her mouth turning up at the corner. "What?" Teasing suspicion laced the word and lightened her eyes to a pale blue instead of that darker, passionate hue.

"Are you okay with this?" he asked, deliberately vague. Where would she go with the answer? How would she define the question?

She sobered, brows dipping as she sat up. "With what?"

His smile tugged at his mouth. He should've known she wouldn't fall for the simple bait. "Where we're at." Another vague answer.

She turned to face him, her knees nestling between his wider-spread ones. Her contemplation lasted a few moments, but he waited her out. "I was," she finally said. "Until you just said something." She clasped her hands on her lap, head tilting. "So what's wrong?"

"Nothing." He trapped her hands in his and stroked the backs with his thumbs in an attempt to sooth. "Honestly," he reassured her. "I just wanted to check. We started off at a very different point than where we are now." Just sex. Wild, passionate, erotic sex.

And now?

"True." Her nod was a slow, contemplative one. "Is that an issue for you?" She tried to tug her hands free of his, but he wouldn't release them. Not when she was retreating so quickly.

"No." He shook his head, ensuring she read the truth in his eyes. "I have no problem with how things have changed." Yet he still refused to articulate exactly *how* it'd changed. He still wasn't ready to admit that, not even to himself.

Her gaze dropped to their hands, and he searched for the words that'd ease the worry he'd placed within her.

"Can I ask you a question?"

She looked up, nodded.

"What did you think of the sex club the other night?" They'd never discussed it afterward. He should've asked her when they'd left, but he'd still been spinning from the idea of a baby with Avery, not to mention angry at his own reckless disregard for basic safety.

Her expression shifted from confusion to honesty, though. Her lips compressed before she spoke. "It was different. Hot in some ways, but…" She frowned, and that lovely pink tinge worked its way over her cheeks.

"But what?" he prompted when she remained silent.

She blew out a breath, mouth twisting. "But it wasn't as intimate."

He held his smile back, nodding in understanding. "As the Boardroom."

"Yes." Her eyes were wide with that innocence of hers, but they included the knowledge of exactly what they both liked about the Boardroom scenes.

"It brings it deeper, doesn't it?"

She nodded in slow agreement.

"The shared experience," he continued. "The implied circle of trust between the group. The sexual acts witnessed and performed in the open yet exclusively private."

Her tongue slipped out to moisten her lips. "Yes," she whispered. "That." She swallowed, her throat bobbing. Heat smoldered in her eyes, darkening them until

he could read every dirty thought simmering within
her. Want. Lust. That edge of excitement. Of loving the
implied wrong.

He released her hand to run his fingers over her jaw.
She closed her eyes, chin lifting to follow his touch. And
there was that soft trust. The trace of naïvety that called
to him and made her passion so alluring. "Do you want
to continue doing scenes there?" His breath stuck in
his lungs, his own wants twisting between yes and no.

Her eyes fluttered open to show the indecision warring within her, so like his own. "I don't know." Her
brows pulled down. "I—" She swallowed. "I like them
as we've done them."

In other words, the rules remain the same. Which was
so damn perfect. "We can do more of that." So much
more of that.

"Is that what you want?"

Driving her mad while others watched in envy?
Touching her? Teasing her knowing he was the only
one who could pleasure her? Make her come? Feel her
clench around him?

Yeah, he could so do that.

"As long as you do," he qualified.

She leaned in and braced her hands on his thighs.
His skin buzzed at the gleam in her eyes and the promises they held.

He cupped her jaw, amazed that she was even discuss-
ing the option, let alone considering it. Could he really
have her and his kink?

"I do," she whispered.

His pulse jumped, heart hitching at the gift she'd
handed him. "Have I told you how amazing you are?"
he asked, the pure wonder escaping with his awe.

"No." Her smile tweaked. "But you can do it any-time."

His laughter tumbled out on two short breaths as he drew her in. "I plan on it." He closed his mouth over hers, contentment flowing with that other emotion struggling to be acknowledged.

There was no need to analyze it, though. Not when he had everything he wanted right here.

Her lips parted, and he brushed his tongue over hers, tasted the dark hint of coffee and lighter cast of the food. She moaned, longing stringing through the rumble.

Fuck. He couldn't draw away from that. Apparently, he couldn't deny her anything. Not that he wanted to.

Not anymore.

Chapter Twenty-Five

"Good morning, Maurine." Avery smiled at the admin queen as she held out a folder to her. "These are the signed payment agreements Mr. James requested."

Trevor's assistant wrinkled her nose in that habitual twitch of disgust. Was it directed at Avery or the reports? Whichever it was, it reminded Avery of a spinster cat lady before she scolded the kids for stepping on her lawn. "Thank you," Maurine said, her distaste dripping from each word.

Avery's laughter bubbled inside her, but she kept it from escaping. "You're welcome." She added an extra dose of sunshine to her voice and smile before turning away. The witch could keep her pissy mood and superior attitude. It wasn't going to affect Avery, not today.

Nope. This happy bubble of hers had been intact since that night at the sex club almost a week ago, and it showed no sign of popping.

"Gregory asked me to drop these off," she said to Jean when she reached Carson's office. She forced herself to focus on Jean and not at the open office door. "He had some questions regarding the proposed budget for the new software."

Jean took the folder, her smile tight. "Thank you."

She glanced at the open doorway before leaning in, voice lowered when she spoke. "Anything I need to warn him about?" She tipped her head toward Carson's office.

Avery frowned. Was something wrong? Carson hadn't mentioned anything. "Not that I'm aware of." But she had zero knowledge of their discussions, which were still in the proposal stages.

"Good." Jean sat back, shoulders falling as she relaxed. "How are you doing?"

"Good, thank you." Saying *fabulous*, *unbelievable* or *amazing* would be too much. "You?"

Her nod was contemplative. "No real complaints. But my brain is fried from all of this data." She motioned to her computer screen. "And the day is still early."

"I get that," Avery commiserated. "Anything I can do to help?" It was basically an empty offer since she had a stack of her own work waiting, but she extended it anyway, just like she'd been raised to do.

"Oh, I'm fine." Jean straightened, a practiced smile moving into place as she glanced behind Avery, standing. "Good morning, Mr. Hanson." She moved toward Carson's door. "Let me check if Carson's ready for you."

She ducked into the office as Avery's smile fell. Her stomach churned, her happiness bubble deflating on a wave of sour embarrassment. She turned around, nerves contracting every muscle when she faced the guy from the Boardroom.

Drake Hanson, CEO of a Silicon Valley software company. She'd looked him up after seeing him in Gregory's office. Highly educated, relatively young and well connected, if his company profile was to be trusted.

"Morning," she managed to say, voice stiff.

"Good morning," he said, smile indifferent. He

looked nothing and everything like her memory from the Boardroom encounter. Same dark hair, only it wasn't mussed. Same predatory stare, only there was no hint of heat. Same sleek appearance, only he was fully clothed.

She flashed a weak smile and moved past him. "Excuse me." She didn't wait for a response before she strode away. Her face was warm, heart pounding with her own damn issues. There'd been nothing improper about their encounter. No hint of secret knowledge or insulting leer.

Nothing.

But she knew what he knew, and that was the convoluted problem. She couldn't shake her own ingrained hang-ups. Would she ever?

She flopped down in her chair, thoughts jumping between berating herself and laughing at her stupidity. Carson was right. She was applying this sense of shame to herself. It hadn't come from that man—Drake Hanson. Not now or the last time she'd seen him.

Yet it still swarmed in her stomach and squeezed her chest. Why? Where was that power she'd embraced before?

Saved for Carson, apparently.

She snorted at herself, her disgust as clear as Maurine's had been. There was no reason for this little panic attack. None.

She hadn't participated in public sex with Carson since that club, and it'd been weeks since they'd been to a Boardroom scene. Was it even crazier to admit she missed it?

Yes. Yes, it was.

And there was no way she could say that to Carson. Going along with what he arranged was very different from suggesting it herself. That was a step she wasn't ready to cross, at least not yet. Her newfound boldness only went so far. But why hadn't he set something up after their talk last weekend?

And she was stewing over a non-issue, making something out of nothing.

She yanked her drawer open and grabbed the bottle of peppermint oil. One deep inhale of the fresh scent had the tension melting from her shoulders. The wonders of aromatherapy still amazed her. She rubbed it on the back of her neck and savored the cool vapors as it tingled over her nape.

She'd been "dating" Carson for almost two weeks. More dinners, strolls through neighborhoods hunting for the best coffee, nights spent in bed that'd bled into a few mornings. Couple that with the prior months of sex and yeah, she was fully invested in him now.

The stupid *love* word floated around in her heart, but she kept it locked up tightly. There was no place for it now, not yet.

"Hey, Avery?"

She snapped her head around, smile in place as Gregory stepped from his office. "Yes?"

He scrubbed a hand through his hair, grimaced. That frazzled appearance was out in full force, and she almost winced for him. "I need to ask you a huge favor."

The overemphasis on "huge" had her tensing. "What?" she asked, dragging the word out.

He heaved a sigh before sending her his best begging puppy-dog expression. "I forgot the papers for the McPherson deal at home." He cringed at her scowl.

"Your meeting with Trevor is at eleven." As she understood it, the financial details were the last hurdle they had to pass to land that big new client.

"I know." He dug his phone from his pocket. "Which is the only reason why I'm asking you to run down to San Carlos to get them for me."

"Umm...what?"

"Don't worry," he rushed on, already tapping at his phone. "I'll pay for the ride. Tam is at home today. The twins both have ear infections now, and they spent the night playing tag on the crying schedule." He made one last jab at his phone before looking to her. "A car will be here in three minutes." He checked his phone again. "And you should make it back in time as long as the traffic cooperates."

Silence settled around them for a brief moment before her stunned laughter burst free. "Wow. All right." She shook her head and opened her desk drawer to grab her purse. His verbal diarrhea convinced her to agree more than the implied obligation of her position. "I'll go get them."

"Thank you." The relief flowed in his voice. "I owe you."

"You do," she agreed, mentally reshuffling the rest of her work to accommodate Gregory's emergency. "Remember that at review time," she added with a smirk as she left the outer office area. "Text me if you need anything else."

She hustled to the elevator, annoyance shifting to happiness when it dawned on her that she'd get to see the twins. It'd been months since Tam had brought them into the office.

The ride down the peninsula was uneventful, which gave her too much time to mull over the morning. Would she ever be comfortable with others knowing intimate details about her sex life?

She snorted to herself. It was a little late to be stewing on that. She should've thought through her initial trip to the Boardroom just a little bit better. But she hadn't wanted to think about the potential consequences back then.

But what were they now?

The car pulled up to the curb before a two-story modern home situated in the hills overlooking Redwood Shores. The beige stucco was accented by dark brown trim in a boxy style with large windows overlooking the brick-paved drive, which rose on an incline to a three-car garage. The lot even had a small front yard that ran along the side of the home. Mature trees provided an established feel, and the view added to the stunning impression of the home.

Tam answered her knock after a few moments. "Hey, Avery." Her smile was tired but warm as she waved her inside. "Come in. The papers are in the kitchen." Her yoga pants and T-shirt were comfortably chic, yet her hair was pulled up into a messy ponytail instead of the stylish bob she usually sported, and her face was makeup-free.

Avery followed Tam past the line of discarded baby toys that trailed across the hardwood floors. The chef's kitchen was straight out of a magazine with its marble countertops and stainless-steel appliances. But the high-end glamor was offset by the collection of empty baby bottles, dirty plates and open boxes of crackers and cereal that littered every surface. Avery smiled when she spotted the magnetic alphabet letters that covered the lower half of the fridge and the colorful swirling "pictures" that dominated the top.

"Sorry about the mess," Tam said, waving at the counters. "Priorities shift once you have kids."

"I can imagine," Avery said. The open living area displayed the large collection of baby trappings attempting to overtake the family room. Everything from Pack 'n Plays to walkers to a stack of primary-colored bins, half of them spilling toys from their confines.

This was a family home. A lived-in reality that made her heart ache and melt at once.

"Here you go," Tam said, grabbing an overstuffed folder from the edge of the island. "And tell Greg he owes you." She leveled a warning look at Avery that made her laugh.

"I already did," she told her, taking the papers from her.

"Good." Tam slouched against the counter. "And thank you. The thought of waking the twins just to drag them downtown to deliver that almost made me cry."

"Really. It's no problem," Avery quickly said. "Gregory told me the twins both have ear infections."

"That's the way it works with two," Tam said with a sigh. "If one gets it, it's only a matter of time before the other does. And if we're really lucky, they have it at the same time." She did a little cheering motion that screamed of sarcasm.

Avery winced. "Sorry."

Tam waved her off. "No worries. It's life, and I wouldn't trade those little shits for the world." Her expression softened with the love shining on every exhausted line on her face, just like Gregory's when he spoke of his family.

Avery's chest squeezed around that display of love as it pressed on the longings she'd tried to ignore. She'd always envisioned having a family. A husband, the proverbial two kids and a dog in the suburbs. She'd been raised in that nucleus and no matter how sheltered it'd been, it'd been good. "At least they're sleeping now," she said more for something to say.

"Finally." Tam's relief was palpable. "I think the medicine is finally working."

"That's good." Even though that meant she wouldn't get to see them. Avery glanced at the clock. "I should be getting back." She looked to Tam, waiting.

Tam frowned before she launched forward. "Right. I'm supposed to get you a ride back." She scanned the counter. "Sorry." She moved to the other side of the island, frown deepening. "Tired mom brain in play here." She scratched her head, turning to the family room. "And I have no idea where my phone is."

"Where'd you use it last?" Avery asked, wandering toward the kitchen table.

"Hmm... I think after Gregory called about the papers." She turned in the middle of the family room, gaze landing on every surface. "But I honestly don't know." She flipped a blanket off the couch, moved the pillows around.

Avery scanned the table. Two high chairs consumed the space along the wall where an array of green, orange and creamy-colored food stains were splattered across the yellow paint. "Is this it?" she asked, lifting a cell phone in the air. She assumed it was, but it could be an older model they used for child entertainment now.

"Yes." Tam grinned as she came forward, taking it. "Thank you!"

Avery laughed at her obvious relief. "No problem."

Even this scrambled, tired side of motherhood called to her.

"Okay," Tam said, tapping at her phone. "One car ordered. It'll be here in five." She lowered her phone and brushed a lock of hair from her forehead. "Thanks again."

Avery waved the thanks away. "It's fine. I hope the twins feel better soon."

"You and me both," Tam joked. She followed Avery down the hallway as they returned to the front door. "I wish you could've seen them."

"I'm just happy they're sleeping." Which was true.

Tam hesitated, her hand on the door handle. Her lips thinned, concern flashing before she spoke. "I hope this isn't overstepping my bounds, but I'm here if you ever need or want to talk about anything."

Avery stilled. "About what?" Warning bells rang in her head for no real reason, but...

Tam tilted her head, frowning. "About the Boardroom." Her voice was clear and flat when she made the statement, all coyness gone.

Avery inhaled, and those bells clanged loud and instant. She blinked, unable to believe what she'd just heard. "The Boardroom?" A clammy heat spread over her chest and neck before flashing down her back.

"Yes." Tam drew out the word, brows dipping. She straightened, caution screaming from her expression. "I feel like I stepped in something here. I don't mean to be intrusive, but Gregory mentioned it and then I saw your profile on the app and assumed you'd pieced together that Gregory and I were also members."

The world blacked out for one long moment. They

were members? Tam and her boss? In the Boardroom? And they knew she was a part of it?

Oh. My. God. How? How! "App?" she managed to ask, thoughts squirreling down to that one nugget of information. She couldn't think about the rest, not if she wanted to walk out of there with any dignity at all. "What app?" Her voice had flattened out to a single note with the cold focus that settled in.

Tam bit her lip, clearly confused. Well, that made two of them. "I'm guessing that explains why your profile's so thin," she quipped.

"So I have a profile?" Excellent. Awesome. "And who has access to this *app*?"

Tam made a few swipes on her phone before turning it to show Avery. "Every member." She touched an icon that had a red B in front of a black outline of buildings. How simplistic. The application opened to show a login page, the word Boardroom stamped in red font across the top.

"And what does it do?" she asked. The full impact of what she was seeing was held off by the simple need to survive the moment. She wouldn't break down. Not here. Not in front of Tam.

Her boss's wife.

Tam lowered the phone. "It's where the scenes are scheduled." Her voice had softened to a patient, explanatory tone.

So that was how Carson did it. Why hadn't she asked that detail before?

Because she'd trusted him.

And she hadn't wanted to know the details. Her actions had been easier to accept when she'd sat back and let Carson make the arrangements.

"And everyone has a profile?" she asked, circling back to that detail. What did hers say? Who'd created it? Carson. It had to have been him. No one else in the Boardroom knew her—or so she'd thought. She shook her head. "I'm such a fool," she mumbled.

"Why?" Tam leaned in, reaching her hand out. Avery shook her head, stepping back. Her stomach soured at the thought of being touched. Tam curled her fingers in and let her hand fall to her side with a weighted sigh. "I don't understand."

Avery clutched the folder to her chest, anger trembling through her on the controlled wave of loathing spreading from her heart. She swallowed, and forced back the tears that burned in her throat. "I'm assuming you can't download the app from the app store." She let the snark blaze in her voice, well past the point of caring what Tam thought of her reaction. "So who gives out access to it?"

"Avery," Tam pleaded. "I'm sorry. I just assumed—"

"Who?" she snapped. She braced herself for the answer, a part of her already knowing.

Tam heaved a sigh, shoulders falling in defeat. "Carson." She took a breath. "And Trevor."

The world dropped out from beneath her yet again. Her heart hitched, then raced at the implications released by those two names. Her lover and her boss.

The big boss.

The president of her damn office.

There was no reconciling the wave of shame and anger flooding through her. Why had Carson kept the app from her? What had Trevor and Gregory been thinking? How long had they known about her when she'd been clueless about them?

"I don't know what you're thinking," Tam rushed to say. "But I'm sure it's not what you're—"

"You're right," Avery bit out, cutting her off. "You have *no* idea what I'm thinking. None. So don't even try to guess." She blinked back the tears welling behind her eyes. Her throat ached with the betrayal, but she wouldn't break. Damn it.

She refused to break.

Tam nodded. She took a step back. "All right. I won't." She crossed her arms and leveled a steady gaze at Avery. "But I'll listen if you need to vent."

She barked out a harsh laugh and stared at the ceiling. Those damn tears collected at the corners of her eyes. Like, right. She could vent—to her boss's wife.

That was so not happening.

A car horn blasted from outside, and Avery praised the universe for the awesome timing. She forced a tight smile toward Tam, not an ounce of sincerity behind it. For all she knew, Tam had been aware of her involvement since that first embarrassing night.

Was she the only one clueless to how exposed she really was? How many other people at work were a part of this "private" group?

And why had she never questioned that before now? She had, right? At some point?

Or was that another detail she'd willingly ignored?

"The car's waiting," she stated. Tam still blocked the door, and short of shoving her aside, Avery was trapped until she moved.

"Avery?"

She shook her head. There was nothing left to be said.

Tam sighed, but she opened the door, stepping back to let Avery leave. "I'm sorry," she said as Avery passed.

She snorted a laugh, not looking back. What did Tam have to be sorry about? For letting the cat out of the bag or being a part of the secret all along?

Avery slid into the car, numb to everything yet screaming silently from the ice that was slowly encasing her heart. How? How had she been so naïve? There was nothing secret about that group. Nothing.

Except what hadn't been told to her.

The driver rattled off the address to the office, half turning to see her. She stared at him as his question slowly registered.

"No," she said. But where could she go? Tam was probably already on the phone with Gregory. "Wait." She still had the papers he needed. "Yes. But can you wait while I run in and drop these off? I'll need a ride somewhere else then."

"Sure," he said. He turned around and jerked the gear shift into Reverse. "Not a problem. But the fare is only paid to the first stop."

Her laughter died in her throat. Of course.

She closed her eyes and sank into the seat, the damn file still clutched to her chest. Maybe she'd know where to go by the time she reached the office.

And maybe she'd wake up and realize this was all a bad dream. And maybe pigs would fly and cows would jump over the moon.

And maybe her heart could be put back together again.

Right. It was past time she stopped believing in fairy tales. Especially the ones with happy endings.

Chapter Twenty-Six

One hard knock was all the warning Carson received before Gregory stormed in. He slammed the door closed behind him.

"What the fuck did you do?" he barked. His rage vibrated through the room to smack Carson. Gregory pointed his finger at him, accusation blasting. "I told you not to fuck with her. I told you not to mess with my assistant. But you had to fuck it up anyway."

Carson jerked up. "What the hell are you talking about?" Avery. That was all he knew. It had something to do with her.

Gregory shook his head, lips compressed in a hard line around the words. He let out a growl, spun around and stalked to the wall, then back.

Carson rose from his chair, a knot already cinched in his stomach.

"Why did you hide the app from her?" Gregory threw up his hands in exclamation, frustration humming over his words. "Why?"

The app?

The knot in Carson's stomach tightened into a firm ball of dread. He swallowed, guilt snapping out to laugh at him. There was only one app Gregory could be talking about. *Fuck*.

"What happened?" he asked, worry already centered on Avery. Was she okay? Where was she? He stepped around his desk. "I need to find her."

"She's not here," Gregory bit out. He gripped his hips as he sidestepped to block Carson's path, the action subtle but pointed. "No thanks to you."

Carson pulled up, anger bubbling. He clenched his jaw and forced back the reflexive instinct to fight. It crawled over his skin and picked at his pride. "You need to tell me what is going on." The words were ground out over the rough edge of grit lining his throat. "Now."

Another knock blasted through the tension before his door burst open. Carson shifted his glare to Trevor as he entered and received an equally cutting one in return.

"What is going on?" Frustration simmered from Trevor as he glanced between the two of them.

"You went to him first?" Carson accused Gregory. His disgust grew with each passing second. And he still didn't know the full scope of what had happened.

Avery. The worry hammered in his skull and twisted through his chest until each breath was a forced effort.

"I had to," Gregory ground out. "You fucked up, and now I have an upset wife and a missing assistant."

"What did I do?" Carson growled.

"You didn't tell her about the app," Gregory shot back, his finger pointed in accusation once again.

"So what?" he exclaimed. Yet his guilt sat on his chest to further impede his attempts to breathe. He sucked in deep gusts of air, but each one came back empty. Possible outcomes spun through his mind in an endless stream. Ones that brought down the entire Boardroom to less dramatic ones that left him without a job and Avery.

Avery. Fuck.

Pain pierced his chest, and he focused on it for one long moment. On the ache that spread through his ribs to pound in his head.

"Enough." Trevor's command cut through the argument in one clean stroke. He glared at each of them in turn, his scowl harsh with reprimand.

Carson stared at the floor, his teeth clenched at the scolding. The added humiliation did nothing to calm the rolling sea of angst, guilt and worry.

"Gregory," Trevor snapped. "Explain."

Carson looked up to stare directly at his accuser. He'd take whatever hits Gregory threw out and deal with them, just like he'd done his entire life.

Gregory took a deep breath, blew it out. "I forgot the McPherson papers at home." He winced at Trevor's silent rebuke. "I know, okay? It was a shit night with the kids." He dug a hand through his hair, leaving the strands in a wild mess of wayward curls. "I asked Avery to run down and get them from Tam, and she mentioned the Boardroom app to Avery while she was there."

"Why?" Carson bit out. Why in the fuck would they talk about it?

"I don't know," Gregory flung back. "The real question is, why didn't you share it with Avery?"

Two sets of eyes drilled Carson, waiting for his response when he had none. The truth laughed at him, though. Hard and bitter with his own denial. He tried to drag in another breath only to fail. Countless possible answers shuffled through his mind, but he could only hold on to one: control and fear.

And he'd let it screw up the one thing that'd come to matter to him the most. His stomach heaved at the realization, a clammy unease spreading over his skin.

"Where's Avery now?" Trevor asked.

"I don't know." Gregory's voice had lowered, a tired resignation filling it. "The papers were delivered to my office from the security desk downstairs along with a note that said she didn't feel well and would be out for the rest of the day."

Trevor looked to Carson. "Has she contacted you?"

"No." Not a word since her "good morning" text before he'd arrived at work.

Trevor's eyes narrowed and he crossed his arms over his chest as he shifted into that full analytical mode Carson recognized.

"There's more," Gregory said, caution in his tone. He jerked his gaze to Carson before returning it to Trevor. "Tam mentioned that she and I were both a part of the Boardroom. That's how the app came up. She told her she was there if Avery had questions or wanted to talk about anything regarding the group." He rubbed a hand over the back of his neck, winced. "She also said that you could give her access to the app, along with Carson."

Trevor's expression flattened into a blank facade. Technically, Tam hadn't disclosed anything that wasn't openly known by all Boardroom members. But… "Let me guess," Trevor said, his gaze boring into Carson. "She didn't know about Gregory, Tam or me."

And there was that good ol' guilt again. It punched Carson in the gut before tightening the winch around his chest. "No." He shook his head in a slow rejection. His guilt lay exposed in his voice. "There was no need for her to know." Not when she doused her desires in

shame when they were exposed to someone she knew—
and she'd been blindsided with that reality.

Fuck.

"Full disclosure," Trevor said, each word clipped with
conviction. "There is no true consent without it."

"I know." Carson met his gaze and managed to with-
hold his flinch. "I fucked up." The admission did nothing to relieve his own shame that was growing into a
hot, sick mess.

Trevor spun around and stalked to the window to
stare out it. He gripped his hips, his shoulders lifting
and falling with his deep breaths. "Every member is en-
titled to all the facts so they can evaluate if the Boardroom is for them."

"You're right." Carson didn't even try to contradict
the reprimand. "The starting circumstances were different with Avery. You know that."

Trevor faced him. "And you told me it was handled."

"It was," he snapped. "In fact, it was going fucking
fantastically until Tam opened her mouth."

"Fuck you," Gregory growled. "You don't get to
blame Tam for your mistake."

Carson cringed, eyes lowering as more of that shame
rushed in. "You're right." He forced his gaze up. "Sorry."

Gregory's eyes narrowed, but he gave a nod. "You
need to fix this."

"I know." Irritation crawled over his neck alongside
the growing sense of desperation and…loss. The truth
smacked him in the face with the clarity he'd been avoid-
ing. "I have to find her." He bolted for the door, moving
before he'd finished the thought.

"Wait."

He froze at Trevor's command, pulse racing, nerves

jumping. An urgency pressed on him now that he had a direction. He needed to talk to Avery and explain his actions—before she made the wrong conclusions. Like that hadn't already happened. His own sharp laugh cut through his mind.

Trevor came toward him, brows drawn low. "I understand this turned personal for you."

Carson couldn't stop his snort. Personal was way too shallow of a description.

"But," Trevor went on, "this is also legal. She can't speak about anything regarding the Boardroom, or I *will* sue her for everything she owns." His voice had shifted to ice, along with his glare.

A cold spear of protective fury raced through Carson. His chest expanded with his mounting retaliation, but Trevor cut him off.

"And there is no sexual harassment case, if she tries for that angle." His gaze included Gregory this time. "No one pressured or threatened her into joining the Boardroom, right?"

"No one was pressured into anything," Carson spit out. He'd made damn sure that every decision had been hers. "And your opinion of Avery is insulting."

"She isn't like that," Gregory defended. His scowl said exactly what he thought of Trevor's assumptions.

Trevor dismissed their words with a shrug. "I have no opinion about her. My responsibility is to this company. And to that end, I will protect it however necessary."

"You asshole." Disgust coiled in Carson's stomach. "There is more to life than this damn company."

"There is," Trevor agreed. His voice rose with each word. "And I have over a hundred employees and millions of dollars in client investments to protect." He took a breath, leaning back. "Avery is a single entity."

A single entity.

The minimal classification didn't fit her. Not when she'd become everything to him.

"I'm calling Burns," Trevor said as he pulled his phone from his pocket.

"You don't need a lawyer," Carson insisted.

"Hopefully not. But he should be briefed." Trevor moved to the door. "I'll hold off on notifying the corporate lawyers."

The door clicked closed behind him. The soft note seemed to shatter through the quiet to nail Carson with a final condemnation. *Fucking A.*

Gregory cleared his throat. "Sorry about that." He motioned after Trevor.

Carson's low chuckle contained every deprecating thought flagging him. "Not your fault." Not at all. This was one hundred percent on him. "And sorry again about Tam." He winced. "This isn't on her."

Gregory gave a tight smile and turned to the door. "I'll let you know if I hear from her."

He nodded. "Thanks."

The silence wrapped around him after Gregory left, yet his ears rang with every condemnation he could muster. Avery had trusted him, and he'd failed her. Completely.

Would she forgive him?

Should she?

He cursed his own stupidity and swiped his phone off his desk. No messages or missed calls. He pressed her number and waited, heart racing with the barest of hope. The ringing rolled to voice mail as he'd expected, but he'd hoped anyway. He left a brief message for her to call him before firing off a text. Are you okay? I'm sorry. Can we talk?

He sent the message and stared at the phone. A long moment passed before he recognized another step on his stupidity trek. Like she would really respond to his text.

He had to find her.

Jean jerked up when he stormed from the office.

"I'll be out for the rest of the day." He didn't spare her a glance or wait for a reply. He was on a mission and he wouldn't stop until he knew that Avery was okay.

Even if that meant he was out of her life forever.

Chapter Twenty-Seven

The sun was coasting on its downward descent when Avery settled onto a stone bench in the Palace of Fine Arts. People milled about, some taking pictures of the architecture, others simply strolling around the grounds that arched along the edge of the man-made lagoon.

She closed her eyes, inhaled. The scent of life mingled with the mucky decay of rot in a subtle reminder that the world went on, revolving, changing, adapting.

A single tear escaped to slide down her cheek. She let it flow, tracking its path until it reached her jaw. She brushed it away with a quick swipe of her hand. Tears never solved anything, but they sure as hell relieved the pressure that'd been trapped inside her all day.

Another tear escaped, and she let this one fall too. What harm would it do?

She glanced around, her anonymity both freeing and isolating.

A toddler squatted on a rock near the water, his happy cry echoing over to her. His mother hovered behind him, her own smile tender.

No one stared at Avery. She was simply one in hundreds—thousands—today. She'd spent the day wandering the pier in a daze. Being lost among many had brought her problems into perspective. In the broad scheme of things, her issues were pretty minor.

But damn did they hurt.

She squeezed her eyes closed, swallowed. The throbbing pain in her chest had dulled to a sore ache. Carson's betrayal had cut deep, but her day of roaming had brought the scope down to size. Like always, time and perspective had eased the shock and allowed other thoughts to temper her emotions.

She sniffed and wiped the tears away—again. They'd been on a slow drain for the last hour, leaking out of her eyes with no rush. She'd waited for the downpour, only none had come. Not all day. She'd been a numb mass until she'd strolled by the little shop in Ghirardelli Square, the one she'd explored with Carson. Had it only been last weekend?

It felt like years ago.

He'd laughed when she'd admired the little sculpted pig set among a collection of animal carvings. It'd been cute, with its upturned nose and tiny curled tail. Trivial and meaningless, but that'd been part of its attractiveness.

She dug the little sculpture from her purse and held it in the palm of her hand. Why had she bought it today?

Because it reminded her of Carson.

Her laugh was wry and sarcastic. He wasn't dead, for God's sake.

Maybe she could use it like a voodoo doll and carve little cuts into it. Her bubble of laughter bordered on loony now. She couldn't do that to the pig.

She curled her hand around the carving and dropped her head back. What was she going to do? She'd outlined a dozen different options over the course of the day, but she had no idea which one to take.

Did she—could she—go into work tomorrow? Her chest pinched, her air choking off at the thought of facing Gregory. He knew about her sexcapades. And Trevor. God. Her face warmed, the embarrassment grounding in deep. What did he think of her?

Logically, she knew they were a part of the same group, but they were men. The standard and expectations were different for women. It didn't matter what people said, they simply were. And women didn't fuck around. They didn't partake in sex games. Not without gaining a reputation.

A bad one.

Her mother would be so disappointed in her. And she couldn't even think about what her father would say.

She snorted at her own dramatics. This was just one of many, many things her parents would never know about her.

She had believed only a very limited few would know about her sex life.

And her naïvety was showing again.

But the truth was very few did. Unfortunately, those few included people she knew. Ones she respected and who were her superiors—at work.

Work. She squeezed her eyes closed again. The mortification only lasted a moment this time. It'd lessened over the day, just like her anger. She wanted to blame Carson for everything, but her sense of moral correctness wouldn't allow her to do so.

Fucking morals.

She sniffed, swallowed. The pig dug into her palm. She returned it to her purse and tugged the last tissue from the little travel packet she'd bought at the dollar store that day.

Part of being an adult was accepting when she was at fault. That included owning the outcome. She'd entered the Boardroom willingly. She'd wanted to experience the decadence and the implicated depravity. She'd locked on the blinders and followed her desire instead of her logic.

And it'd been so damn good.

But now she had to live with the aftermath, and that included owning her part in the fallout. Yes, Carson should've told her everything. And she should've asked more questions. She definitely should've thought about it more.

And if she had, she never would've experienced the crazy, freeing rush of letting go. Of passion as she'd only dreamed about.

Or Carson.

Her head fell forward, hand clenching around the now soggy tissue. Another stab of pain radiated from her heart, but the ache faded as it rippled past her stomach and trickled down her limbs. Her nerve endings had numbed out hours ago, along with her emotions.

Logic prevailed now, and that rarely failed her. There were questions to ask, decisions to be made, actions to take.

She sucked in a long breath, held it. She pulled her shoulders back, forcing a confidence that wasn't there. But there were things to be done.

One, she wanted access to that app, and that meant contacting either Carson or Trevor. Second, she had to decide if her self-imposed shame was worth sacrificing her job for. Third, she needed to face Carson—at some point.

And in order for any of those things to happen, she had to get her ass off this bench and go home. But what if Carson was there waiting? What if he wasn't? She snorted at her conflicting wants.

If he was there, it meant she mattered enough for him to hunt her down. But was she ready to talk to him? And if he wasn't there, did that mean he didn't care? Or if he was there, was it only to minimize the damage to the company and the Boardroom? Like she was going to retaliate against either of them. She didn't think that way, and she hoped he knew that by now.

No matter how she spun it, the entire situation was a mess.

A duck squawked madly, setting off a chorus of angry quacks from the gathered cluster that sent a group of young tourists scrambling from the edge of the lagoon. Laughter and squeals followed the girls' flight from the attacking ducks until the animals backed off.

A smile pulled on Avery's mouth as she watched the antics. The world kept spinning no matter what happened.

She heaved a sigh and pulled her phone from her purse. The temperature was dropping with the sun, and she shivered at the growing chill. She'd have to move soon.

She stared at the phone screen as it went through its restart process. She'd turned it off after the first call and text from Gregory. Even at that time, when the betrayal had been fresh and ugly, she'd still felt guilty over leaving for the day. And she resented that too.

Stupid, damn morals. *Don't be in the wrong. Apol-*

ogize for your behavior. Expect the best of others. Be kind. Be nice. Be quiet. Be, be, be...

When was it okay to be mad? To speak out? To demand better?

To be herself?

Now. Now would be a good time for that.

She typed in her password and sucked in a breath at the screen full of missed messages. She scrolled to the bottom and started reading from there. Her pulse pounded in her head, skin heating as she read through each text. Ones from Gregory, Karen, Tam and Carson. Apologies, inquiries, concern, worry—they were all there.

A laugh broke free at Karen's last text, her frustration apparent even without the line of angry emoticons. Avery's missing-in-action stunt was getting old, according to her roommate.

And she was right.

Her sigh was weighted with resignation. It was time to reengage.

She called Karen first. Her hand tightened around her phone as it rang.

"Avery!" Relief sprang from that single word, as did the condemnation for making Karen worry. "Are you okay? Where are you?"

A wobbly smile broke out at the love that stretched through the line to embrace her. "I'm okay." She squeezed her eyes closed to hold back the fresh wave of tears prickling up her throat.

"Thank God." Karen's sigh gusted through the phone. "I was so worried about you."

She swallowed, and forced her words out. "Thank you. I'm a..." She was what? "I had to think."

"What's going on?"

Everything? Nothing? "What do you know?"

"Carson was waiting outside our building when I got home." Avery's stomach flipped, even though she'd read that in her texts. "He looked wrecked. He said he needed to talk to you. But I didn't let him upstairs."

"Thank you," Avery said softly. At least he wasn't camped out within her home.

"Are you kidding me?" Karen scoffed. "Something was obviously wrong, and there was no way I was letting him in until I knew you were okay."

Avery swallowed hard and tried to speak around her gratefulness, but the words stuck in her throat. What could she say?

"Hey," Karen prodded. "Are you really okay? What can I do?"

A long, slow exhale calmed her and brought a sense of focus back. Her smile was weak when she thought about how to answer. "I'm...working through it."

"What?"

The hurt. The sense of betrayal. The embarrassment. The shame. The self-inflicted condemnations. "I found something out today," she said instead. "I needed some space to process it."

"Did he cheat on you?" Her indignation put another smile on Avery's face. God, she loved her.

"No. At least not that I know of. But we never discussed exclusivity." She thought it'd been implied, but then a lot of her thoughts had been proven wrong.

"Are you pregnant?"

A harsh snort jerked out. "No!"

God, no. She winced. But she could've been. Maybe. She'd been reckless with Carson, in so many ways. But

Karen's question put things in perspective. Nothing in her life had changed, not really. Not unless she made this into something it most likely wasn't.

A horn blared in the distance, but Avery barely registered it as it blended into the backdrop of urban living. It was just another component of the vibrancy that fed the concrete energy. It hummed around her even here, now, when she felt so damn alone.

"Do you want me to come to you?" Karen asked.

Avery could picture her already heading for the door, determined to help. Another wave of gratefulness rushed up to ease the ache in her chest. "No," she quickly answered. "I'm coming home. Do you know if Carson is still outside?"

"Just a second." There was rustling on the other end. One of Avery's cats meowed in protest, which pulled a faint laugh from her. Were her cats perched in the window waiting for her to come home? "I can't see him from here, but I can run down and check."

"No," she said again. "Don't worry about it."

"Are you sure?"

"Yes. But thank you." She couldn't hide forever.

"If you're trying to ease my worry, it's not working," Karen said, sarcasm heavy.

Avery released a dry chuckle followed by a low groan. "Sorry." She rubbed her temple and tried to dislodge the knot of guilt pounding behind it. "I promise I'll be home soon."

"You swear?"

"Yes."

She ended the call after asking Karen to feed the cats, which she'd already done. Avery stared at her phone, thoughts flailing in protest over her next action. Her pulse started that insistent beating that tapped out her nerves and heated her skin. She didn't want to call Carson, but she had to.

She owed this to herself.

Chapter Twenty-Eight

The pealing ring of Carson's cell phone yanked him from his numb stupor. He jerked up, heart racing faster when he saw Avery's name on his screen.

He answered the call, still doubting it was her. "Avery?" His pulse drummed in his ears as his world focused down to the empty silence on the line. Had she meant to call him? Was this a joke? What would she say?

Another long moment passed before he heard, "Carson."

It was her. Relief flushed through him, only to be immediately followed by doubt. Was this it? Would she let him explain?

"Avery," he repeated, eyes closing as he dropped his head back against the car seat. He'd been sitting on the street outside her condo for hours, waiting for her to return. He clutched the phone with a desperate need to stay connected to her. "Are you okay?"

Her soft laugh was soft and cynical. "It's kind of a shame that you have to ask me that."

The jab struck his heart. He winced, cursing himself. "I'm sorry." So damn sorry. "Can I explain?"

The silence stretched, but he bit his tongue when the urge to speak rose up. She had every right to deny him, and he wouldn't force her to hear him out. He'd lost that right.

A low sigh ghosted over his ear. "I need a couple of things from you."

"What?" His voice cracked on that single word.

"First, I want that app." Her voice strengthened with the demand. He could picture her back straightening, those expressive eyes of hers darkening. "I understand every member has access to it, and I want to see what's in it."

An odd quirk of pride flared in his chest. That was the courage he'd found so attractive since the beginning. A strong sense of purpose lingered beneath her surface to hold her steady, and she was tapping it now—to go against him. Right.

"Of course. I'll send you the information tonight." Trevor might be pissed given the recent events, but Carson couldn't deny her request.

"Thank you."

Her reply was so stiff and formal it almost gutted him. "I'm so sorry." He put every ounce of truth and misery in his apology. "You have to believe that."

"Do I?" she challenged.

His stomach swirled with the sick disgust of his actions, but he'd brought this on himself. "No," he admitted. No, she didn't. "But I hope you do. I didn't keep it from you as a way to hurt you."

"Then why did you?" The flatness of her voice told him how bad the situation was. He'd expected a stream of tears or an angry tirade, but her measured emotions meant she'd either locked the others down or was already beyond them. And that gave him nothing to respond to or counter.

"I don't know," he exclaimed on a frustrated burst. He squeezed his eyes closed, grimaced. He had no right to be angry—except at himself. "Sorry. Shit." He released a sigh. He owed her something, at least what he had, even if it sucked. "I didn't think you'd want to know about the app in the beginning. And I wasn't sure if you'd be a one-time attendee. We don't give it out to the occasional participant."

There was a beat of silence before she asked, "And after the first time? Why not then?"

Why not then? Did he tell her the whole truth? "Because I was afraid you'd react just like this." Yup. There it was.

Her sharp inhalation shot through the line to confirm his unintended hit. He rubbed his eyes, desperate for a solution. The last thing he wanted to do was to hurt her more.

"You were—are—so worried about what others will think of you," he said quietly. Maybe it was the exhaustion from worrying about her all day or just the utter defeat plowing through him, but the truth continued to pour out. "And I didn't want you to stop playing." He inhaled, released it. "I was afraid you'd withdraw, and I didn't want that. I lo—" *watching you. Feeling you.* He had no right to use that word now. "You were so stunning to watch," he said instead. "And I wanted to keep watching as you grew into your passion and owned it."

"So it was just about the sex."

"No," he insisted before correcting himself. "Maybe at first, but not even then. Not truly."

"Then what was it about?"

He chuckled at her dogged persistence. She could've

stayed away and simply not spoken to him. But not her. Not Avery.

"You," he answered simply. "It was about you. You were full of surprises. Strong. Funny. Tender. Compassionate. Wicked. Sexy. Beautiful. I couldn't get you out of my head. And I didn't want to share you. I couldn't stand the thought of you playing without me." And he'd become a possessive asshole with that one admission.

"You don't own me," she whispered.

"I know."

Another long beat of silence held before she said, "I wouldn't have." She choked back a laugh that had him cringing yet again. "Would it have been so hard for you to just tell me that? I didn't want to play without you." She sucked in a breath, and he clung to that admission. "But you thought it was better to lie to me instead of trusting me."

Was that true? No. Not completely. "And you would've continued with the Boardroom if you'd known about Gregory and Trevor?"

No reply came, which was answer enough. She wouldn't have. But he still shouldn't have made that decision for her. He closed his eyes as the silence stretched. His pulse was steady, his emotions frozen in a state of suspended wait. His regrets mounted, yet he couldn't change what he'd already done.

"I need you to go," she said on a low, steady note.

He sat up. "What?" His breath stuck in his lungs, thoughts scattering at the implications. Was this it then?

"I want to go home, and I'm not ready to see you. Not yet."

His mind raced, rejecting and accepting the reality at once. She didn't want to see him. "Can I call you?"

"No." No hesitation. No indecision. "I need some space."

His head fell forward pushed by a wave of…grief. That was it. A huge dose of loss and regret balled in his chest to add to the guilt that still choked him. "Will you be okay?" he managed to ask.

Her brittle laughter was far from joyous. "I'll be fine. I always am."

And that wasn't a real answer. Not the one he was seeking. "I've been fine for years," he said, throwing everything out there. "But I wasn't really good until you."

"Carson." A breathy plea carried in her voice. "Please."

Please what? Leave her alone? Tell her more? "Will you call me when you're ready?"

His stomach churned with a sick acceptance the longer she didn't answer. So this was it. He had only himself to blame.

"Okay," he finally said. "I understand."

The walls started to go back up, one side at a time, around the emotions he'd let free. This was why he kept his distance. Why he never got involved. Love didn't last, and it hurt so fucking much when it ended. He'd stopped relying on it long ago and this proved he'd been right to do so.

"I trusted you." The words were spoken so softly, he almost missed them. But he didn't. He heard the ache and pain in them too. Her own loss.

He'd caused that.

"I know." She'd given him that gift over and over again, and he'd abused it. Or was it that he hadn't believed in it enough? Trusted it? "I'm sorry I broke it."

"You did." The accusation was missing from her tone, and that hurt even more. This was a simple statement he couldn't deny. "And now you have to trust me. You owe me that."

Fuck. There went the damn walls. They toppled beneath the truth of her words. He did owe her that—and so much more. "You're right." Again. "And I do trust you, but not because I owe you." No. He believed in the goodness within her and that damn moral code that he both cursed and adored. It hummed within him, shoving out the past to expose what he'd been missing in the present.

"I'll talk to you when I'm ready."

When she was ready, not *if.*

And there was the relief again. It sank through him only to bottom out in the pit of his stomach to churn with the disappointment. She could still walk away completely, and he wouldn't blame her. But he really didn't want her to.

"Okay." He had to give her the space she needed. "I'll stay away." Even if it killed him. He'd figure something out at work too. Wait… "Are you coming back to work?"

A brief pause followed before she said, "I don't know."

Fuck. Gregory would drag him through the shitter, and rightly so. He pinched the bridge of his nose, hunting for options that didn't exist. "They don't think less of you," he said, kicking himself for his inability to shift her perceptions on that. "No one does. No one ever will. Not within the Boardroom."

"And out of it?"

"Not there either." How did he get her to understand that? Could he? "There is nothing wrong with what you want. Nothing. Some would like you to think so, but they're wrong. That's why Trevor created the group."

"Trevor?" She took another deep breath. "*He* created the Boardroom?"

Why had he said that? "Yes. He did," Carson admitted
after a beat. It was out now and not necessarily a secret.
"Trevor created a safe place for people who have a lot to
lose if their sexual desires are exposed. It's contained,
free from exposure and the fucking judgments society
likes to place on sex."

"And that's just one of the things I didn't need to
know about him," she mumbled before a sharp bark of
laughter cut through the line. "And now I'm the hypo-
crite. Wow."

"Are you judging him?" Her silence gave him his
answer once again. "Don't. Because I can assure you,
he's not judging you. Not for anything you did in the
Boardroom."

"But he is for something else?"

"No." Carson winced, glad she couldn't see him. "Unless you do something malicious to harm the company."

She didn't respond right away, which had him concerned all over again. There was so much he couldn't
change. Not the past or Trevor's priorities. And apparently, not her mind.

Darkness was closing in, and he scanned the street in
the off chance of seeing her nearby. There was a couple
hurrying down the sidewalk about a block down, and an
older woman pulling her little rolling cart behind her, the
basket filled with reusable grocery bags. But no Avery.

"I'll go. But can you promise me something?" He had
no right to ask, but he did anyway.

"What?"

"That you won't judge yourself too harshly."

Her scoff cut through him along with her bitter laugh.
"Too late. I've already tried and persecuted myself."

"Don't. Please." Grief swelled within him until he

swallowed back the bile wrath burning his throat. "Judge *me*. Condemn *me* for what I did. But please, don't put that on yourself. You're too smart for that."

She gave a soft humph. "Apparently, smartness doesn't have a say over emotions."

He snorted lightly. "Too true." Too damn true. He heaved a sigh, already regretting his next words. "I'm leaving now." He started the engine, the low purr barely audible. "And I'll stay away. But we're not done." They couldn't be done. There was too much good between them.

"Thank you, Carson." She sniffed, and he thought she was going to say more, but there was only silence. The distinctive click of the call being disconnected had him pulling the phone from his ear to verify it.

His heart contracted with the loss when he confirmed their call had ended. It was done.

He set his phone in the cup holder as a vague numbness settled into him. There was nothing more he could do. Nothing he could say or change. Not right now anyway.

But he refused to accept that this was the end. He couldn't.

Not when he could finally admit that he loved Avery.

Chapter Twenty-Nine

The scent of ground coffee and baked goods hit Avery as she entered the little coffee shop. She glanced around, palms sweaty. Six days later, and she was still nervous about meeting Tam.

Six days since she'd seen anyone related to work. She'd called in sick for the rest of the week, and Gregory hadn't balked at her sudden absence. But she couldn't continue to avoid her job, not if she wanted to keep it.

And she did.

The train ride down to Burlingame had been quiet, the Sunday crowd thin. The predictable rock and sway of the train car had soothed her. People had gotten on and off, focused on their own lives and destination. Once again, she'd been just one of many.

She ordered an iced coffee and found a table in the shade on the outside patio. A rock song played over the sound system, and a tall hedge provided a barrier from the street.

She glanced at her phone, noting the time. Her foot tapped a nervous beat, but she crossed her legs to quell it. Her shorts and V-neck shirt were comfortably casual, not that she was worried about making an impression.

That had clearly already been done.

A mocking snort snuck out. She shook her head, smiling at her hypocrisy. Hours of analysis aided by a few bottles of wine and Karen's wisdom had brought her to this point. One where she could not only see but accept her own judgments. And she wasn't so squeaky clean.

"Hey," Tam said as she stepped through the doorway to the patio. Her smile was bright, expression warm. Her sunglasses were perched on the top of her head, her hair styled to its normal sleek bob. Tam dropped into the chair across from Avery, her smile softening as she took her in. "I've been worried about you." The truth rang from her voice and eyes.

Avery shrugged, unsure how to respond. "I'm fine," she finally said. At least she was getting closer to that point. "Thanks for meeting me."

"Of course." Tam winced, a hint of guilt creeping into her expression. "I really am sorry about last week." She reached out to grasp Avery's forearm in a comforting grip. "I didn't know I was stumbling into a bad topic. I honestly just wanted to be there for you." She squeezed her arm. "I still do."

Her chest contracted just a bit, her heart pinching with Tam's concern. "I know." She did. "None of this is your fault."

"But I feel like it is." She withdrew her hand and took a sip of her coffee. Her sigh was filled with appreciation. "I never thought I'd miss the buzz of a good espresso." She closed her eyes, inhaled before reopening them. "Sorry. I've digressed." She waved off her last comment. "So what can I do for you?"

Avery sat back, smiling. This was why she'd loved Tam almost instantly. Her quirky but direct approach to life reminded her of Karen, and both of them were so different from herself. "Thank you for taking time out of your Sunday. I—"

"Are you kidding me?" Tam cut in. "This is heaven." She slumped back, face lifted to the sun. "Do you hear that?" She turned her head to listen. "There's no crying. None." Her smile was infectious when she looked back to Avery. "Gregory can deal with it for a while."

Avery laughed along with her. An image of her boss attempting to comfort two cranky babies filled her head. He'd be okay. Maybe frazzled a little, but she admired that he pulled his weight in the parenting department.

She took a drink of her coffee, thoughts shifting to why she'd texted Tam for this meeting. "I have some questions for you, if your offer to talk about the Boardroom is still open." She glanced around, reassured that no one was listening into their conversation.

"Of course." Tam sat forward and crossed her arms on the table. "Shoot." She was completely focused on Avery now, maybe too much.

She shifted in her seat, uncrossed and recrossed her legs. Her stomach fluttered with a nervous energy she had no hopes of squelching. She drew in a deep breath and called up the strength that'd gotten her to California and over every hurdle in her life.

Meet it. Face it. And then figure out how to move on. There was no going back.

"I don't know where to start," she finally said, being honest. The corner of her mouth quirked up in an abbreviated shrug. "I—" She clamped her lips tight, head shaking with her grimace. "Sorry. I'm still a little embarrassed by it all."

Tam tilted her head, eyes narrowing. "About what part, specifically?" Her open inquiry instead of a quick dismissal of Avery's feelings encouraged her to go on. The tightness in her chest eased and she sat back, a little more relaxed.

She fiddled with her cup, playing with the condensation that'd accumulated on the outside. "The everyone-knows part." That was the crux of it. People she knew had knowledge of her sexual activities. Her nonnormal ones.

Tam frowned, her lips twisting in thought. "I can understand that."

Avery's brows winged up, surprised at the admission.

Tam shrugged. "I had some of those same anxieties when I first joined the Boardroom." She sat back, bringing her coffee cup with her.

"You did?" She had a hard time imagining this confident, self-assured woman with any anxieties.

"Of course." Tam gave another shrug before taking a drink of her coffee. She licked her lips, lifted a brow. "What? It's not like society has harsh stereotypes about women and sex or anything, right?" Sarcasm dripped from her words and matched her expression.

Avery couldn't stop the laughter that bubbled out. "Right?"

"What?" Tam covered her mouth with her hand, eyes wide in fake surprise. "You mean women can enjoy sex?" She rolled her eyes, hand falling away. "And heaven forbid if we actually seek it out or deviate from the 'norm.'" She added finger quotes to the last word.

The tightness that'd been holding within Avery for days finally started to unwind. Her shoulders fell, the knots in her neck releasing.

Tam shooed her words away with a flick of her wrist. "It's garbage and we know it. But it's still hard to overcome, especially when it's been ingrained in our psyches since we were born."

Avery stared at her, a wave of gratitude stretching out to wrap Tam in an invisible hug. "Thank you for saying that." Karen had listened and done her best to comfort her, but she didn't fully understand the mass of incriminations and shame huddled within her.

Tam shrugged. "It's true." Her scowl said what she thought about it, in case Avery had missed it earlier. "It sucks, but there's no getting around it. We—" she motioned to the two of them "—are supposed to be prudes until we get into our husbands' bedrooms. Then it's okay for us to be wild, passionate sex goddesses. But only there. And all those women who openly engage in sex or dress in a way that draws attention to their assets? They're great to ogle and fuck, but not to marry. What a joke."

Avery blinked, her smile growing from the core of truth opening within her. She knew all of that. She'd repeated those sentiments many times in her own head, but somehow, they rang stronger, clearer, when they came from Tam.

"It's just one of many double standards women face every day." Tam shook off her annoyance and sighed. "And one I forced myself to face when I got tired of berating myself for being who I am."

The simplicity of her statement diminished the complexity of the task. But it rang loud and true within Avery. She'd been berating herself since she'd first walked into the shocking scene in the Boardroom. For liking what she saw. For wanting to see more. For actually doing it and enjoying it. For every damn desire and want that'd sprung up since then.

And she was so damn tired of questioning that part of herself.

"It's not wrong," she said. "Is it?"

"What?" Tam frowned. "Us liking sex? No," she scoffed. "And it's not wrong to engage in it. Or watch it. Or have it with multiple people. Or outside of marriage. Or in an open relationship. Or any damn way you want it. So no, it's never wrong if it's what *you* want."

"And I know that." Avery pointed to her temple. "Up here. But it's really hard to apply that knowledge to here." She pressed on her chest, wincing.

"It is," Tam sympathized. "I get it. I really do." She made another exaggerated roll of her eyes. "I beat myself up for quite a while over the sexual things I wanted."

And that was another startling revelation.

"So how did you stop? Beating yourself up?" Did she still? Avery couldn't imagine it, but it was impossible to know about the internal battles someone else fought. Fronts of confidence easily hid insecurities, just like displays of anger could hide loneliness.

Tam lowered her gaze. She set her cup on the table as her lips curled with a warm smile. Her expression had softened when she looked to Avery. "Gregory."

Avery's brows went up again. She hadn't expected that, even though she probably should've. "How?"

Tam's shrug was small, like the hint of mischief in her eyes. "I'd been in the Boardroom for a while before I had a scene with him." She stared into the distance, her fingers fiddling absently. "I'd joined out of curiosity and a bit of defiance." She huffed softly. "I'm not sure who I was proving something to, but I enjoyed every second in the Boardroom." She refocused on Avery, a shared understanding exchanging silently between them. Yeah,

Avery had too. Tam sat forward. "But I never dreamed that someone from the Boardroom could love me. Not when they knew about my participation there." There was that double standard she'd talked about. She was good enough to play with but not take home.

Avery shook her head, adamantly denying what Tam was saying. "That's so not true." How could anyone think badly about her? "You're an amazing person who embraces life and goes after what you want. Any man who can't accept that is a fool."

Tam flicked a brow up, a smirk holding her lips in an amused smile.

"Crap." Avery sat back, a defeated laugh hitching out. She closed her eyes, head shaking at her own blindness. She'd just defended Tam for exactly what she was beating herself up over. She opened her eyes to send a joking glare at her. "Nicely done."

A smile beamed on Tam's face as she sat up. "Thank you." She would be hell to face in a business situation. "But like I said. It took Gregory loving me before I fully embraced what I was attempting to preach." And Gregory did love Tam, Avery had zero doubt of that.

"And what about after?" she asked. A wave of heat skittered over her chest and started its slow run upward. "Did you still play there? In public, together?"

She'd explored every corner of the Boardroom app once she'd accessed it, but meetings were archived immediately following their completion. There was zero history stored that she could find.

Another of those secret smiles emerged on Tam's face. "Yes. We play. Maybe not as much and always together, but our kinks didn't go away simply because we're a couple."

Of course they hadn't. Avery's hadn't, nor had Carson's after they'd gotten serious. "So how do you handle it when you see someone from the Boardroom outside of it?"

"And that's your real issue," Tam exclaimed, tapping her palm on the table. "Right?"

Her sigh was long and annoyed. She wanted to object out of sheer stubbornness, but why? Tam wasn't stupid, and in the end, that *was* the crux of Avery's issues. If she didn't care, then she would've been back at her desk after picking up the papers for Gregory.

Tam grinned, winking, and Avery had to chuckle. She had no idea how Gregory won any argument with his wife. Maybe they never fought. And maybe those pigs did fly.

A couple passed them as they left the patio, and another quickly swooped in to take their vacated seats. She watched them settle in, her thoughts wandering through all the varying emotions she'd experienced in the last few days. Betrayal. Hurt. Embarrassment. Shame. Disappointment. Anger. Defeat. Resignation. Loss. Confusion. Could there be any more?

"For me," Tam said, bringing Avery back to the conversation, "I finally, really owned what I wanted." Avery frowned, processing that. "You know? Like, in me." Tam touched her chest. "In here. I took ownership of my wants and amazingly, that shoved the shame away." She inhaled, smiling as she exhaled. "It gave me a sense of power and the understanding that the only opinion that truly mattered was my own. And I'd been judging myself way too harshly."

The truth of that resonated within Avery. She was her own worst critic, on everything. And apparently, this sex thing wasn't any different. Carson had tried to get her to see that, but she'd been so stuck within her shame that she hadn't really heard him.

She remembered that power Tam was talking about too. She'd owned her sexuality the night of the office party, and it'd felt wonderful. Where had that gone? Why was she hiding from it now?

"I can promise you one thing," Tam said.

"What's that?"

"Neither Gregory or Trevor think any less of you for being in the Boardroom." She waited for Avery to acknowledge that, which took a long moment before she slowly nodded. "They don't judge. That's not what the group is about. Trevor ousts anyone who makes even one derogatory comment about another person's wants, as long as those wants are legal and consensual."

She had a hard time believing that. "I've never known of a group that was so…accepting." People always had some sort of judgment or negative thing to say.

Tam shrugged. "Actually, most sexual groups are like that. Once you open yourself up to that part of the world, you find a lot of fluidity and far more acceptance than I've found with most religious groups."

Avery cracked a smile. "So God doesn't judge you in a sex club?"

"It's not God who judges. It's people who do that."

"Touché." Her smile widened, a sense of peace flowing through her when she'd wondered if she'd ever feel centered again. "Thank you for talking to me. You've really helped."

Tam sat up, beaming. "I'm glad." Her smile fell a notch. "And I hope you'll go back to work. Gregory's been bemoaning your loss the whole week."

Avery winced at the stab of guilt. "Sorry. I just couldn't go in."

"Oh, I know." Tam waved off her apology. "I just wanted you to know that you're missed and appreciated at Faulkner. It's a good place. I swear."

She didn't question that. Both the people and the job had been a dream since she'd started there. But could she walk back in knowing others were privy to her deepest secret?

But she also knew theirs.

Karen had tried to hammer that into her over the last few days, but she'd resisted the simple understanding. Why? This wasn't all about her. She knew a lot of stuff, and she had only a smidgen to lose compared to someone like Trevor or even Gregory.

"I'm making too much out of this, aren't I?" she asked, feeling stupid. There, that was another emotion she'd wallowed in for a while.

"No," Tam insisted. "You have every right to be pissed. Carson shouldn't have kept things from you. But," she rushed on, "I also don't think he did it to be malicious. He's not like that. None of the people I know in the group are."

Carson had made a mistake and she'd made some too, including jumping to conclusions based on assumptions.

The app hadn't held any great secrets. There'd been no smoking gun or chain of messages mocking her—or anyone. On the contrary, it'd been basic and straightforward. Every profile had an identifiable picture with hers being her office head shot. Her alias was Shotgun, and the only information provided was a relationship status linking her to Driver, Carson's alias.

Everything in it had validated Carson's claims. He hadn't lied about that.

The hurt over his omission was still there, but she was able to see beyond it now. No one was perfect and no relationship lasted without hiccups, compromise and a few solid disagreements.

She inhaled, let it fill her. She'd go back to work tomorrow, head held high. There were so many worse things in the world than her enjoying some slightly kinky sex. She liked to watch it, live. So what?

So. What.

And there, starting as a little nugget of warmth before it spread through her chest and shoved out the last of her doubts and anxiety, was one more emotion.

Forgiveness.

Chapter Thirty

Carson dropped his bags next to the front door, an exhausted sigh dripping from his lungs. He trudged to the kitchen in the semidarkness, grabbed a beer from the fridge, shucked his suit jacket and tie before plopping down on the living room couch. Another sigh fell out on a groan as he sunk into the cushioned comfort.

What a fucking grueling three weeks.

He'd checked out of San Fran the Sunday after the Avery debacle on an extended investigative run through all of the Faulkner offices. The trip had been more than justified, given their IT upgrade plans, but he'd bumped up the timing to give Avery space. His being out of the office had hopefully lessened the strain on her.

She'd returned to work the day after he'd left on his trip. Gregory had told him that much, but he'd heard nothing from Avery.

He opened the bottle, the quick hiss a welcome sound. He took three long gulps of the beer before stopping to enjoy the hit of relief that flowed through him. He closed his eyes and simply absorbed the silence. Nothing. No hum of an airplane or hotel air conditioner. No pressing agenda or meeting to plan for.

Just…emptiness.

His breaths slowed and his muscles slowly unwound until he wasn't sure if he could move. The desire to go to bed was hindered by the fact that he'd have to move to get there. Was it worth the energy?

Time passed on fluctuating ebbs of random thoughts and nothing at all. Full dark had settled in when he forced his eyes open. The streetlights lit the room with a dull glow through his blinds, indicating how long he'd been sitting there. He scrubbed his face in an attempt to wake himself up. The time difference should've been in his favor since he'd traveled from New York, but the days of hop-scotching across the country and Europe had put his internal clock in chaos.

At least he had the weekend to sleep and readjust to this time zone. And all that free time meant there'd be plenty of room to think about Avery. He'd used work to avoid that, and it'd worked for the most part, but the mess had still hovered around him, taunting, picking, reminding him of what he'd lost.

Her lack of contact sent a clear message of where she stood on them. They were done. Just like that. One mistake, and he'd been given the heave-ho. He scoffed into the emptiness, rubbing his brow. Why had he hoped for something different?

The ache in his chest had dulled to a numb consistency that'd blocked his emotions and allowed him to focus on work. He'd been doing that for years, but it was so damn hard now.

Avery had changed everything.

He'd sworn off relationships, commitment and marriage after his parents' divorce. That had been the final capper after witnessing twenty-five years of falseness. His parents had done a decent job raising them, but they'd done a sucky job of demonstrating a relationship built on love and trust. In the end, theirs had been a marriage of necessity compounded by an inability to do anything else. They'd conformed to expectations, found jobs, raised a family and stayed together because they were supposed to.

And that had lasted until they no longer had to.

Carson had sworn he'd never do that.

But now he wondered about what he was missing. The connection that came with being a part of someone else. The bond that formed from shared experiences. The history created that formed the future.

Someone to come home to, laugh with, love.

Be loved by.

A horrible sense of defeat spread through him to drag him down even further. His throat tightened as a wave of prickles scrambled up it to nip at the backs of his eyes. *Fuck.* He rubbed his eyes, squeezing them tight to hold in the emotions scrambling to break free. He couldn't let them loose, yet he was too worn down to hold them back.

No!

He sat up, blinking rapidly to force back the breakdown he couldn't afford to have. It didn't have to be over with Avery. He'd given her time—lots of it. Gregory had also said that she'd returned without a word to him about the Boardroom. Would she stay at Faulkner when he returned to the office on Monday? How would she react—if at all?

If nothing else, they needed to talk about that. No, he had to know that she was really okay. Guessing and wondering was more agonizing than dealing with a final end.

Three sharp knocks on his door jolted him upright. He frowned, confused and annoyed at once. *Who the fuck is that?* He glanced at the time, frown deepening right before three more knocks beat out in quick succession.

Goddamn it. He stalked to the door, prepared to bark at whoever was on the other side. This was a really crappy time for an impromptu visit from anyone.

He ripped the door open, a harsh greeting prepped and ready, only for it to die.

Avery stood there, a hesitant smile on her lips.

He froze, too stunned to do anything.

Her smile wobbled. "Hi, Carson."

The low note of her voice teased him with memories and promises. Her summer sweater hugged her chest, the cap sleeves and scoop neck both demur and sexy in a distinctively Avery way. The deep purple shade was beautiful against her pale skin, and he couldn't stop staring.

She was there. On his doorstep.

Her hair was down, the gentle waves softening her features. She wet her lips, drawing her tongue over the bottom one. Would he get to kiss them again?

"Avery," he finally said once his brain reengaged. His brows drew down. "What are you doing here?" It was after ten o'clock.

She clasped her hands before her, lips pressing together. "I was hoping we could talk."

"Talk?" His brain misfired once again. "How did you know I was home?" And why was he making her stand in the hallway? *Christ.* "Come in." He stepped back, waving her inside.

Her smile was stiff when she stopped just inside the doorway. "I might've gotten your itinerary off Jean under the pretext of Gregory needing to know."

The admission loosened one of the knots in his chest. She'd sought him out. "Okay." His response was fucking lame, but he couldn't think beyond this was good, right? She could've waited until tomorrow if she simply wanted to tell him to go to hell. He led her into the kitchen, flicking on the light as he went. He blinked against the brightness and opened the refrigerator. "Can I offer you something?" He held up a beer. "I have wine, vodka, scotch and gin too."

"I'll take a beer."

His grin was automatic. She'd picked the beer over wine when he'd expected the opposite, like so many things about her.

He twisted off the top and handed the beer over before opening one for himself. They stood on opposite sides of the island, an awkwardness settling in the longer the silence stretched. But he couldn't stop staring at her. His pulse had kicked up a notch and had not gone down since he'd opened the door. And that silly, flighty thing had sprung to life in his chest to flick at the locks he'd barely reinstalled around his heart.

"So," he started before he got carried away dreaming about new starts when this could be an ending. "How are you?"

Her small laugh was a single note of sarcasm that matched her bemused smile. "I've been better, but I'm doing okay. You?"

"Yeah?" He shook his head in amused disbelief. "I've been better too."

Her smile fell. "I've been doing a lot of thinking."

He'd assumed that. He had too. Was there any chance they'd come to the same conclusion? "And?"

"And..." She set her bottle on the counter and came around to his side of the island. Her fingers trailed over the marble like she was marking a return path, but her expression was open.

His breaths shortened as he tracked her movement. He set his bottle down, turning to face her when she stopped a few feet away. She was close enough to touch, but he fisted his hands at his sides, waiting. Nerves spun a twisted tale of hope and rejection in his stomach and threatened to dispel the awful plane food he'd managed to digest.

"And," she said again, "I want you to know how much you hurt me." The truth of exactly how much was etched into the lines around her mouth and the pain in her eyes.

"I know." God, did he know. "I hope *you* know how sorry I am." He lifted his hand, his movement slow enough for her to deflect. His chest tightened and released when he cupped her cheek. The contact hummed over him, igniting the portion of him that'd felt dead since she'd left.

Her eyes closed, head tilting into his touch, and he couldn't resist pulling her in. And she came, two small steps that had her in his arms. *Yes.* The rightness breathed over him as he wrapped her in a hug. This was what he'd missed. What he would miss out on by denying love.

"I was so worried I'd lost you," he murmured into her hair. He rested his cheek on her head and absorbed everything about her. That faint peppermint scent. The curve of her breasts against his chest. The warm wisps of her breath across his neck.

Her arms came around his back to hold him, and he finally breathed. He squeezed his eyes closed yet again, this time to keep the prickling bites of joy from spilling out.

"You almost did," she said.

"I know." He pressed a kiss to her head and leaned back to cup her cheek again, one arm still holding her close. He couldn't let her go. Not now. Not ever. "What changed?"

Tears sparkled in the corners of her eyes, brightening them to a stunning shade of blue. "A lot of things." Her mouth twisted. "Part of it was accepting my share in causing what happened. I—"

"You didn't do anything," he cut in, adamant.

She cupped her hand over his on her cheek. "That's the problem." She squeezed his hand, giving a small wince. "I let you do everything. It was easier to let you lead. That way I didn't have to own my choice, not completely at least."

What did that mean, exactly? How did he respond?

"You were right," she continued. "About the app." She bit her lip, another wince tugging her brows together. "I wasn't ready to know about it earlier. Heck," she scoffed, "I wasn't ready when I found out about it."

"That doesn't change the fact that I should've told you." Withholding information was another form of a secret. "I have no excuse except to say I was being selfish." Incredibly, possessively selfish. He stroked his thumb over her cheek. "I didn't want to share you."

She blinked a few times before leaning in to rest her head on his shoulder. He held her close, still amazed that she allowed him to do so. "I didn't want to be shared," she said softly. "I still don't."

He squeezed her tighter, his throat thick with relief and gratitude. "And I still want you for myself."

They stood like that for a long moment. A sense of peace settled in, the weeks of angst, regrets and numbness finally departing. Her hand rose and fell in a gentle stroke of comfort over the small of his back. He wanted to stand there forever. A part of him was still afraid that if he let go, she'd be gone.

"Can this really work between us?" she asked.

He shoved back, framing her face with his hands in a desperate attempt to get her to believe him. To trust him. "Yes." He left no doubt in his voice. "Yes. We can work. We already do." In so many ways. From their easy conversations to their shared likes to their mutual kinks. "You—" He swallowed, hunted for the right words. But there were only a few that he needed. "I love you, Avery. I don't know how it happened or if I deserve you, but I love you."

The admission hung between them in that wobbly space of "oh, shit" and "fuck yes." His heart expanded to fill him with certainty. It spread to his face, his mouth curling with a joy he couldn't contain.

"I love you so damn much," he repeated, unable to hold it in now that he'd set it free. He let it shine from him in a way that left him totally exposed. His declaration could backfire, but he was done fearing it. Love could suck. It could change. It could hurt.

But it could bring so much good too.

And he wanted all of it with Avery.

Her mouth quivered, but a smile peeked through as her fingers dug into his hips. She bit her lip, stopping the nervous flutter before it broke free into a full grin.

His heart seemed to race and stop at once. It didn't matter if she didn't return the words, not yet. She just needed to give him a chance to prove how much he meant them.

He dipped his head, pausing right before his lips

touched her. She searched him, a warmth pooling in her eyes that communicated so much.

"I missed you," she whispered, her lips brushing his.

His chest contracted around the hope begging to be set free. He brushed his lips to hers in a gentle agreement. He was afraid to speak again. Afraid to ruin what was so close to being really, really good.

She blinked, swallowed. "We still have some things to work through."

"I know." But they'd do it. He swore they could. "I have a lot to make up for."

She ran a hand up his chest, sending off a wave of longing. "We're still figuring this thing out."

"We are."

"There're bound to be bumps."

"There are."

She circled a hand around his neck to draw him closer. "But I think this is good."

"It is." He could barely breathe let alone answer in more than two syllables.

Her lips brushed his, but just a touch. She nudged his nose with her own in a tender connection that reached his toes. He wrapped an arm around her waist, every nerve ending poised to attack when she gave the signal. "I love you, Carson Haggert."

He swooped in then, unable to restrain himself a second longer. He claimed her mouth with all the love and crazy relief pumping through him. The rightness sizzled over his skin and hummed in his heart. He'd locked love out for so damn long, now he couldn't get enough.

Not of her or her touch or the connection flowing so strongly between them.

He pulled back and sucked in a harsh breath. He lifted

her by the hips to set her on the island. She gasped, but drew him in with her legs in the next moment. She wrapped him up tight with her limbs, a hand snaking through his hair as she smiled.

"I love it when you get demanding like that."

She would never stop amazing him. He dove back in, determined to show her what he'd failed to say. How much he treasured her. How much he cared for her. How much she meant to him.

He softened the kiss until each stroke of his tongue became a promise. This was real, and he fully embraced what that implied. There were no guarantees, but this right here with Avery was pretty damn close to perfect.

Epilogue

Avery followed Carson into the boardroom, her hand clasped in his. A skyline of lights twinkled in the distance through the large windows. Nearby was an array of other buildings, some with windows still lit, others mostly dark.

A smile twisted over her lips as she took in the room. A couple made out at the end of the long table, their embrace heated if her soft moans were an indication. The woman was stripped to her matching bra and panty set, while the man remained fully dressed in his dark suit.

The image was similar to their other visits to the Boardroom, yet each one was uniquely different. Maybe it was the varying locations or the people involved or the energy of each scene, but although the compositions remained similar, the events themselves weren't.

Carson positioned her in front of him and tucked them into the back corner of the room. They were closer to the couple this time. Instead of being separated by the table, they were at the same end. The proximity brought a series of goose bumps over her bare arms, her nipples tightening in response.

She didn't recognize the couple, but the room was very familiar. The cherry credenza at the other end, the long wood table, the black office chairs, the whiteboard and abstract art. They'd returned to the location of her first introduction to the Boardroom, even if it'd been accidental. There was something naughty about that. Both exciting and wrong at once.

Would anyone know tomorrow when they sat at the table? Would that heavy sent of sex and lust linger to give them a hint? Would the table bear any marks? Or a chair?

She doubted it, but *she* would know. She'd remember how the woman arched her back, head falling to expose her throat. And how she followed the motion, her own head dropping to rest on Carson's shoulder.

"What do you want?" Carson whispered into her ear. He ran his hands over her abdomen, his touch firm, sure. So like him.

She lifted a hand to grasp the back of his head, holding him close. "Whatever you give me." Her voice was quiet, yet husky with desire. She trusted him again, with this and her heart.

Their first trip back to the Boardroom after the app incident had been another learning experience for both of them. She'd discovered that she liked not knowing what to expect as opposed to reading the details beforehand. The app showed everything. The players, the scene expectations, limits, safe words and kinks. All of which were essential to a safe and successful scene, but it spoiled something for her.

She didn't have to know the information if Carson was with her. He took care of the details. He ensured she was safe while giving her more than she could imagine on her own. She wasn't wearing blinders or denying her wants. No, if anything, she'd admitted more.

She liked having Carson in charge. Trusting him set

her free to simply feel. No worries. No concerns. No more fear. Even the threat of exposure was minimized with Carson at her side. He gave her strength, which allowed her to pull from her own.

The Boardroom had brought them together, and now it brought them even closer.

"Have I told you how beautiful you are?" He nipped her earlobe, the sting sharp yet hot.

"Yes." He told her all the time, but he showed her even more frequently. With his tender touches and the heat in his gaze. And when he brought her coffee at work or made her breakfast or held her hand as they walked or…

The door opened, and Avery stilled. Her heart jumped, pulse thumping hard. Had they been caught? By whom?

A stocky man with dark hair and a beard shadow stepped into the room, his presence capturing the attention of everyone. He shut the door, a smirk curling the edge of his mouth.

"You can see we waited," Carson said, a dryness to his tone.

The new guy loosened his tie, tugging it off to spread it across the table. The streak of red lay like a declaration against the wood. He undid his belt buckle, slid his belt off before curling it into loose loops and setting it beside the tie.

Avery could only stare, enthralled by the power reeking from him and the authority of his movements.

Carson stroked his hand down her side as he scraped his teeth up her neck. "He's going to fuck her," he whispered. "Hard and deep."

She swallowed, the image already seared into her

mind. Her pussy clenched, that crazy wanting need vibrating from her core.

"They both are," Carson said. He cupped her breasts, one in each hand as the new guy rolled up his cuffs and undid the top three buttons on his shirt.

Her breath caught, desire racing through her on the rapid beat of her pulse.

"At the same time." Carson pinched her nipples through the silky material of her dress, the dual sensation driving home the implication of his words.

Her eyes widened and her legs dipped with the sudden flash of heat that raced south from her nipples. She'd fantasized about that the first night in this boardroom. She'd mentioned it to Carson one night when they'd been cuddling in bed, their limbs heavy from sex. She had no doubt that he'd planned this for her.

In any other situation, she would've been embarrassed, but not here. Not with Carson.

These scenes were about feeling without guilt or shame. It'd taken her a while to reach that point, but she had and she wasn't going back. Carson had opened a door into a secret part of her soul that had exposed a passion she reveled in now.

This was her. Carson was hers, and she had nothing to be ashamed of. Not at work. Not in front of others. Not in her own head.

Avery sucked in a breath and rocked her hips against Carson's erection. It slid along that line up her back in a declaration of his lust. Their relationship had evolved into so much more than this, but she'd never regret how it had started or where it'd brought them.

This was a part of them, but not even close to all of what they had together.

"Go to them," Carson ordered.

The new guy came up behind the other woman. He wrapped an arm around her waist before jerking the other guy in with a hand at his nape. He claimed the guy's mouth in a hard kiss that was at once brutal and stunning.

Oh...hell. That was so damn hot. The men's kiss contained a hard possessiveness that wrapped around Avery and drew her in. It was raw and intense, yet there was a woman between them. She sucked on the neck of the first guy and writhed between the two hard bodies.

Avery's head spun on the wave of eroticism. She never would've had the nerve to suggest a scene like this, yet she didn't want it to stop. No, she couldn't wait to see where it went.

Just like her relationship with Carson. This was her happy-ever-after and she wasn't going to judge it. Not now, not ever.

This was them and the only opinions that mattered were theirs.

* * * * *

To purchase and read more books by Lynda Aicher please visit Lynda's website at lyndaaicher.com.

Turn the page for an excerpt from
DONE DEAL by Lynda Aicher, now available at all
participating e-retailers.

Now Available from Carina Press and Lynda Aicher
In the Boardroom, exhilarating pleasures happen
after hours.

Read on for an excerpt from
DONE DEAL,
the first Memo in Lynda Aicher's
BOARDROOM series

Danielle Stables inhaled, eyes closing. She held the breath for a beat before releasing it on a long, slow exhale. She had this.

The thin straps of her dress slid from her shoulders with nothing more than a light brush and a nimble shrug and roll. The loose baby doll style was meant for comfort more than appeal, and really didn't matter since no one would see it. Her nipples puckered when the cooler air hit them. A shiver overtook her as goose bumps chased down her arms.

She stepped out of the material and laid it over the back of a chair next to her trench coat. The darkness provided a protective barrier from the outside world, which was spread out on the other side of the floor-to-ceiling windows in the small conference room. The view was stunning. She barely saw it, yet she was very aware of the wrongness. Being almost naked in a public setting screamed of deviance.

Energy wound through her in a slow crawl from her toes, up her calves, thighs, past her pussy to her chest and finally her mind. There was such power in secrets. Everyone had them, but few wielded them successfully.

Most tried to hide them. Stash them away in shame or guilt or fear.

But not her.

No, she embraced every damn one of hers.

The soft ends of her hair tickled her shoulders when she released it from its loose bun. She swiveled her head and let the strands slither between her shoulder blades. She parted her mouth, swept her tongue out to moisten her bottom lip.

A small bundle of nerves fluttered in her stomach. They twisted around a knot of acceptance that'd been lodged there forever. Long before she'd joined the Boardroom. Years before she'd married and divorced. Eons before she'd risen to the VP level at a prominent Silicon Valley company.

This was simply a beat in time. A night of freedom and release. Of mutual desires shared to the extreme.

And there was a strength in owning that.

She rolled her shoulders back, smoothed a hand over her abdomen and let everything go. The stress from the day. The residual nerves. The tension that lined her neck and clenched through her shoulders. The expectations and disappointments.

She closed her eyes as she dipped her fingers beneath her panties to stroke a single finger over her clit. She sucked in a sharp breath and let the desire spread through her groin. It was just a little tease. A primer for the night ahead.

The hallway was empty when she exited the conference room. The shadowed darkness and line of closed office doors added to the clandestine aura that tingled over her skin. She strolled the short distance to the boardroom, hips rolling. The decadence of parading through an office building in nothing but her lace panties and heels sunk into her mindset to hum beside the lust.

A low moan snaked through the air to call her forward. A sultry gasp. A mumbled word she couldn't understand. Those notes of freedom welcomed her into their fold.

She stopped in the boardroom doorway, a hand braced on the doorjamb, pulse rising in expectation. She found him in less than a second. A blink, really. On the other side of the long table, leaning against the windows. Arms crossed, shirt gone, the button on his dress slacks undone.

Her heart hitched, then stalled on her long inhalation.

She'd skimmed right over the other two couples in the room. They were already deep in the throes of foreplay, clothing mostly discarded, mouths locked together in heated kisses, hands roaming over bared skin.

The hedonistic indulgence rippled through the semi-darkness to cloak the room in sin and acceptance. There was something dark and edgy that called to her whenever she entered a Boardroom scene. Lush. Bold. Defiant.

Hers to own.

Don't miss
DONE DEAL by Lynda Aicher,
available now wherever
Carina Press ebooks are sold.

www.CarinaPress.com